"This is all wr

"Her life will never be the same." Brooke looked at him.

Audy's blue gaze met hers. "She's a little thing, Brooke. She can't miss what she doesn't remember." He cleared his throat. "But I agree with you. This is all wrong."

Since he'd shown up at Young's Salon, she'd seen a different side of Audy Briscoe. Vulnerable and uncertain, but he was trying... It gave her hope that, maybe, the two of them could find a way to make this work.

"Kent and Dara should have left Joy to you," Audy added. "We both know I'm just going to get in your way and make a mess of things."

She shook her head. "But they didn't, Audy. Joy is our responsibility. Joy isn't a dog or a horse— she's a little girl." She smiled down at the baby.

"We are all she has. We can't let her down."

Dear Reader,

Howdy from Texas, y'all. I am so excited to share my very first Harlequin Heartwarming novel with you. Right from the start, I knew Garrison would be a magical place. I could picture its downtown square and all the little storefronts with big picture windows—perfect for watching and keeping tabs on who's who and what's what.

The women of the Garrison Ladies Guild are the best at this, and they are a hoot. They might be into everyone's business, but how else can they make sure everything turns out just right? From matchmaking to saving the oldest tree in Texas, they get things done. Their latest challenge: Audy and Brooke.

Audy Briscoe is a bigger-than-life cowboy with Paul Newman good looks and a love of all things adrenaline-inducing. Brooke Young is as no-nonsense and responsible as they come. Of course, the two don't see eye to eye on a thing—so how are they supposed to raise their best friends' baby together? It's not easy, let me tell you, but their story is all about hope, second chances, community and the power of love. I hope you love your first visit to Garrison and that you'll come back real soon.

Thank you so much for reading!

Sasha Summers

HEARTWARMING

The Rebel Cowboy's Baby

—

Sasha Summers

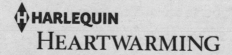

HARLEQUIN®
HEARTWARMING™

Recycling programs
for this product may
not exist in your area.

ISBN-13: 978-1-335-42641-3

The Rebel Cowboy's Baby

Copyright © 2021 by Sasha Best

All rights reserved. No part of this book may be used or reproduced in any manner whatsoever without written permission except in the case of brief quotations embodied in critical articles and reviews.

This is a work of fiction. Names, characters, places and incidents are either the product of the author's imagination or are used fictitiously. Any resemblance to actual persons, living or dead, businesses, companies, events or locales is entirely coincidental.

This edition published by arrangement with Harlequin Books S.A.

For questions and comments about the quality of this book, please contact us at CustomerService@Harlequin.com.

Harlequin Enterprises ULC
22 Adelaide St. West, 40th Floor
Toronto, Ontario M5H 4E3, Canada
www.Harlequin.com

Printed in U.S.A.

Sasha Summers grew up surrounded by books. Her passions have always been storytelling, romance and travel—passions she's used to write more than twenty romance novels and novellas. Now a bestselling and award-winning author, Sasha continues to fall a little in love with each hero she writes. From easy-on-the-eyes cowboys, sexy alpha-male werewolves, to heroes of truly mythic proportions, she believes that everyone should have their happily-ever-after—in fiction and real life.

Sasha lives in the suburbs of the Texas Hill Country with her amazing family. She looks forward to hearing from fans and hopes you'll visit her online: on Facebook at sashasummersauthor, on Twitter, @sashawrites, or email her at sashasummersauthor@gmail.com.

Books by Sasha Summers

Harlequin Special Edition

Texas Cowboys & K-9s

The Rancher's Forever Family
Their Rancher Protector

Harlequin Western Romance

The Boones of Texas

A Cowboy's Christmas Reunion
Twins for the Rebel Cowboy
Courted by the Cowboy
A Cowboy to Call Daddy
A Son for the Cowboy
Cowboy Lullaby

Visit the Author Profile page
at Harlequin.com for more titles.

Dedicated to the readers who love cowboys, falling in love, and small towns full of characters and fun!

Acknowledgments

This book would not have come to be without Johanna Raisanen. Not only does she make every one of my stories better, but I know she is invested in me and my career. Go Team Sashanna! To my amazing writing tribe, Jolene, Teri, Allison, Storm, Patricia, Frances, Kelly, Makenna, Molly and Julia—you guys are the best! Thank you for always being willing to talk story—or everyday real-life stuff. Thank you, Kathleen Scheibling, for believing in my stories to let me keep writing them. You ladies fill my heart with heaps of love and unwavering gratitude. From the bottom of my heart, thank you.

CHAPTER ONE

"DON'T LOOK. IT will only encourage him." Brooke kept her eyes on the road in front of her. She could all but feel the eyes of the passengers in the truck next to them staring at her—waiting. He can just keep on waiting. She hadn't had enough coffee to deal with Audy Briscoe yet. He required at least three cups. She'd only had time to have one.

Brooke glanced at her watch. Her little sister, Tess, was almost ten minutes late now. At the rate the late drop-off line was moving, she'd miss her first period altogether. "I can't wait until you get your driver's license." Then she wouldn't be stuck in the drop-off lane of Garrison High School, needing coffee, while doggedly ignoring the man in the truck next to her.

"Like you're going to let me drive." Tess laughed. "Why drive when I can walk, though, right?" Tess did a spot-on impersonation of Brooke.

"I might have said that a time or two, huh?" Brook glanced at her little sister, smiling.

"Um, maybe, yeah." Tess paused. "Still, I am sorry about this morning. I know you have your early appointment this morning and you need more coffee."

Her little sister knew her so well. Brooke reached over and took her hand. "It's not a big deal, kiddo." She winked. In the grand scheme of things, going without coffee to get Tess to school was a mere inconvenience. A little one at that. Definitely not something worthy of starting the day off tense or crotchety. She took a deep beath, teasing, "It's not like I haven't slept through my alarm once or twice—or ten times."

"I guess. But I know you have other things to do—" Tess broke off. "Oh, nooo... Beau waved, Brooke. *He waved.* How can I ignore that? I mean, *I can't,* can I?"

"No." Beau was Audy's younger brother. Poor kid had to be mortified by his older brother's behavior. *At least, I hope he is.* "That would be rude." Brooke was pretty sure having Hank Williams's "Your Cheatin'

Heart" blasting from your pickup truck was rude, however. And that's just what Audy was doing. The base was so loud, her seats were vibrating. Audy didn't seem to grasp the current reality of their location: the drop-off line at the high school versus a rodeo or honky-tonk. Then again, he'd always been really good at living in his own little world.

"Oh…oh, wait, *and* Audy. Now Audy is waving, too. Brooke? Even his giant dog is looking at us." The panic in Tess's voice was endearing.

And wrong.

It wasn't a secret that she and Audy didn't get along. Everyone knew that Brooke could *not* stand Audy Briscoe. But that was because she and Audy had a long history, one her little sister had nothing to do with. Tess shouldn't get caught up in the middle. "It's okay, Tess. You can wave. Be neighborly." Brooke smiled at her.

Tess waved. "That dog is huge. They must be really crammed in there. I wonder why Beau is riding with his big brother? He normally drives his own truck." She chattered on. "It's so pretty, Brooke. His truck, I mean. He got it this year after he got that scholarship to University of Texas. Pretty cool, right? He's only a junior. He leaves next summer for Austin. I bet that'll be a big change from Garrison."

It would be a change. Not everyone who left Garrison stayed gone. *I know that all too well.* But she was exactly where she needed to be, doing what she needed to be doing. And right now, that was waiting. They were next in line—the front door of the school was in sight. All Brooke had to do was sign the tardy clipboard that Vice Principal Gutierrez was holding. She took her foot off the brake and edged forward—but Audy's large black truck cut in front of her and slammed on the brakes.

Brooke stomped on the brake, threw her right arm out to protect Tess and winced as her 1952 Chevrolet Bel Air slid. Her car, Betsy, was old, solid metal—a tank, basically. Not the sort of vehicle that could stop on a dime. But Betsy managed not to crash into Audy's truck. *Barely.* "That man… *That man.*" Her hands tightened on the steering wheel as a whole string of less-than-flattering descriptors flashed through her brain.

But Tess was visibly rattled. "He didn't even use his blinker."

Vice Principal Gutierrez walked around the driver's side of Audy's truck, scowling, holding the clipboard toward the driver's window.

"Do you think he's in trouble?" Tess asked. "Mr. Gutierrez can be really scary when he gets mad. He looked mad. I bet he's giving Audy a talking-to. He should, anyway."

"Sadly, I think Vice Principal Gutierrez lost his ability to discipline Audy once he graduated." Not that Audy had listened or cared even when he was in school. If anything, his behavior had earned him more bragging rights. He'd loved getting in trouble—Audy Briscoe had loved getting attention. He still did.

"Well, Mr. Gutierrez should talk to him anyway. That was so *not* cool." Tess crossed her arms over her chest. "Like, seriously. We could have hit his truck and, according to my driver's ed teacher, it would have been our fault since we'd rear-ended him."

Brooke smiled. Even in the midst of her outrage, her little sister was all practicality. "It's okay, Tess, but you're right he is *not* cool." She hurried to add, "Audy, I mean. Beau seems pretty cool." She had absolutely no reason to pick on Beau Briscoe. By all accounts, the youngest Briscoe was a sweet kid. Good grades. Polite. Helpful around the community. *And* Tess had a little crush on the boy.

"Beau's not at all a jerk," Tess confirmed, gushing. "He's…he's…nice."

Brooke gave Tess a quick look. Her sister was red cheeked, leaning to peer out her window—watching as Beau climbed down and out of Audy's truck. *Okay, maybe not so little.*

"Don't let this ruin your day," Brooke said, relieved when Audy's big black truck finally drove off. She pulled up, put the car in Park and turned. "Morning, Mr. Gutierrez. It's my fault. I slept through my alarm." Brooke shrugged.

"No problem." Mr. Gutierrez smiled. "It happens. Take this to your first-period teacher, Tess. Go straight to class now, so you don't miss anything."

Brooke handed the pass to her little sister. "See you after."

Tess nodded and slid from the car, slamming the door. "Bye." She hurried down the walkway and inside the high school.

"I spoke to Mr. Briscoe about that little

stunt." Mr. Gutierrez shook his head. "I keep thinking that boy will grow up."

"Oh, I gave up on that years ago." She smiled, signing the clipboard then handing it back. "But I appreciate the effort."

He grinned. "Have a good day, Miss Young."

"You, too." She waved, waited for him to step back onto the curb and drove around the curved driveway to the stop sign—where Audy Briscoe had pulled over and was leaning against the side of his truck, arms crossed, cowboy hat tipped forward, looking like he didn't have a care in the world. His massive dog leaned out the window, tongue lolling out and ears perked up.

What now?

She had a stop sign, she didn't exactly have a choice in the matter. But she seriously considered ignoring the sign and pulling through the intersection just to avoid the now-advancing cowboy with the all-too-cocky grin on his undeniably handsome face.

Handsome might be an understatement. Audy Briscoe had Paul Newman good looks. Crystal-blue eyes, dark brown hair, dimples in both cheeks, a dimple in his chin and the

I-work-out physique that drew all sorts of ad-miration.

"Morning, Brooke," Audy said, tipping his hat and stepping forward. He bent, resting his hands on the window frame of her car. "Mr. Gutierrez got me thinkin' I might owe you an apology."

"Oh?" She barely glanced his way. "Well… go on."

He chuckled. "I didn't mean to upset you."

"That's what you're apologizing for?" Her knuckles were white from the death grip she had on the steering wheel. "You didn't *upset* me."

He shrugged. "I didn't think so. Your sis-ter waved us on, so—"

"Tess?" Brooke's gaze darted up at him. "My little sister was waving good morning, nothing more. Being neighborly, is all."

"I *was* trying to catch *your* eye." He ran a hand along his stubbled jaw.

"I hadn't noticed." She stared out the front windshield. "I'm sure you need to get wher-ever it is you're in such a hurry to get to, so I'll say good morning." She waved. "That was a good-morning wave."

Audy chuckled. "Duly noted." He stepped

back, tipping his hat again. "You have a good day, now, Brooke."

She didn't spare him another look. She rolled forward, turned left onto School Street and headed down to Old Towne Books & Coffee. The only thing that was going to get her morning back on track was some coffee—and a lot of it. She had just enough time before her early-morning trim and color arrived at the salon. Brooke parked Betsy, exchanged morning pleasantries with the town librarian out for her morning run and headed inside the bookshelf-lined coffee shop.

"Morning, Brooke." Hazel Dertz smiled warmly from her place behind the counter. "What can I get you? We have some new dark roast that's heaven and Ryan made good fresh cinnamon almond scones, too."

"Good?" Ryan asked, hugging his wife from behind. "I thought you said they were delicious."

"I did." Hazel tilted her cheek up for her husband's kiss. "Let me start again. Ryan made some delicious cinnamon almond scones. You should definitely get one."

"Much better." Ryan kissed her cheek and let her go.

"Sold." Brooke suppressed a grin. Hazel and Ryan were newlyweds and it showed. One of them was always making an excuse to give the other a hug, touch or quick kiss. Even without having adequate caffeine in her system to function, it was impossible to deny just how adorable they were. "Coffee. Hmm… Which has more caffeine? The dark roast or a regular with an espresso shot? I need the one with the most. Maybe two."

"Uh-oh." Hazel's nose wrinkled. "Rough morning?"

"You could say that." Brooke smiled. "More unpleasant than anything."

"Want to talk about it?" Hazel asked, putting a scone into a white paper bag.

"Yeah, Brooke," the deep voice at her back made her jump. "Want to talk about it?"

She knew that voice. She knew the voice and heard the not-so-subtle hint of amusement coloring his words. "If I didn't know better, I'd say you were following me." She turned. "Audy."

"Guilty." Audy chuckled. "And I needed some coffee."

Brooke suspected he'd come for coffee and overheard just enough to think he was the topic of conversation. She stood, arms crossed over her chest, and waited. *What are you up to?*

"I realized I hadn't apologized." He hooked his thumbs in the belt loops of his painted-on dark blue jeans.

She blinked. He'd followed her to apologize? *You are definitely up to something.*

"But now I'm curious, too. You had a rough morning?" He paused, those clear blue eyes sweeping her face. "I know it can't be me, since you said I didn't upset you and all."

Brooke wasn't going to play this game. Not now, not ever. "No, I don't want to talk about it. Go ahead and apologize now so I won't worry about you popping up later."

Audy took a deep breath. "I'm sorry for—"

"That's all," Brooke interrupted. "That's enough." Over the years, Audy had apologized to her many times. He had unapologetic apologies down to a science. He'd say I'm sorry *but*... If there was a *but* attached to it, it wasn't a real apology. "You're sorry. That's all I need."

Audy was laughing.

"Brooke," Hazel said. "Coffee, double shot of espresso and a scone."

Brooke turned back to the counter to find Hazel and Ryan watching the exchange. Hazel was wide-eyed, Ryan looked like he was trying not to laugh. "Thank you," she said, sliding money across the counter. "Have a great day," she said, injecting as much sunshine into her voice as possible. She grabbed her coffee and her scone and hurried outside, to Betsy and escape. She had her coffee, her space and a full schedule of appointments over at her salon. Knowing Miss Ruth, her first appointment, there'd be no lull in the woman's chatter for Brooke to fill. She could drink her coffee, listen to all the ins and outs and gossip of her small town, and forget all about this morning. *Good plan.* The day was looking up already.

Audy Briscoe had to admit Brooke Young was a fine-looking woman. He didn't want to, of course. She was as prickly as a prickly pear cactus. Never, in all the years they'd known one another, had she given him the time of day. If anything, he was a nuisance to her. A feeling she didn't bother trying to hide. Maybe that's why he enjoyed getting under her skin. If he couldn't charm her senseless, he'd get her riled up. As long as she knew that he knew she wasn't as immune to him as she liked to pretend.

The only time he and Brooke called a truce was when Kent and Dara were around.

Kent was his best friend. Dara was Brooke's. Somehow, someway, the two of them had fallen in love, gotten married and started a family. Through all of that, he and Brooke had remained civil to one another in their presence. Once Kent and Dara had moved to Houston, they didn't see them as often—meaning Brooke didn't have to bother with civility when their paths did cross.

Why she treated him like he'd done something to personally offend her, he didn't know. "There's just no pleasing some people," he said, scratching his part Great Dane, part Great Pyrenees, Harvey, behind the ear. "And she is one of those people."

Harvey made a somewhat agreeable canine sound before turning to rest his chin on the open passenger windowsill.

"Glad you agree." Audy patted the dog on the back, stepping on the accelerator as they cruised down the long country road leading to Briscoe Ranch.

His phone rang, but he ignored it. It was probably his big brother, Forrest, wondering why he was taking so long. Or his other brother Webb texting him to complain about Forrest. His sister, Mabel, was off working in Wyoming—so she wouldn't be calling. Or it was Uncle Felix, finally remembering whatever it was he needed from the store that he couldn't quite remember when Audy had left to take Beau to school this morning.

Right now, it was Harvey and him, the wide-open road, peace and quiet.

Brooke wasn't the only one who'd had a rough morning. First Forrest, then Beau, then Mr. Gutierrez, and then, finally, Brooke Young. Every single one of them seemed to feel he needed a talking-to about something he was doing wrong. The poor example he set, his music, his driving, his waving…

But he always listened to his music that loud, he liked it that way. He didn't have a single ticket on his driving record—he'd taken defensive driving more times than he could count to make sure each of them was erased. The waving?

It's possible Brooke's sister didn't understand I was wanting to slide in front of them…

But there was no need for Beau to have slammed the truck door so hard he all but knocked it off its hinges. That boy was too much like Forrest. Too uptight. Too worried about what everyone else thought. Too caught up in schedules and action plans and goals and all the little things that sucked away all the spontaneity and excitement in life.

"At seventeen, I was too busy making memories to sweat the small stuff." He sighed, draping his right arm along the back of the truck's bench seat.

Harvey glanced back over his shoulder at Audy, his long plume of a tail thumping against the seat.

"I know." Audy nodded. "My little brother needs to learn how to live a little. Live in the moment. Maybe I can give him some pointers on that?" He patted Harvey's back again. "Forrest would love that." He chuckled.

Harvey yawned.

Audy's phone started ringing again, but he turned off the ringer, blasted his music and turned onto the gravel drive that led to the main house. He slowed, not wanting the rocks to ding and chip the paint on his truck. His truck was his baby. A fully restored 1986

Chevrolet K-20 Silverado Fleetside, with all the bells and whistles. Forrest said it was the only thing in the whole world Audy took pride in. Audy was pretty sure his big brother had meant that as an insult. Instead, Audy agreed.

Poor Forrest. Audy couldn't remember a time when his big brother wasn't acting like some uptight eighty-year-old. What did he have against having some fun? Living a little? Then again, Uncle Felix wasn't much of a disciplinarian. It wasn't his fault, though. He'd been a confirmed bachelor, no cares in the world, until he'd moved out here to raise the lot of them. Audy shuddered at the thought.

Poor Forrest? More like poor Uncle Felix. He'd gone from single and carefree to guardian of six kids. *Six.* He shuddered again.

You only get one life, so make the most of it.

Audy wasn't sure where he'd seen the quote, but it'd spoken to him. He'd taken a good, long look at the world around him and decided he was going to do just that: make the most of every day. Audy's risk-taking, thrill-seeking to-do list was never-ending. There was always some new thing—something that pushed the boundaries of safety and acceptability and got his adrenaline pumping. He was always ready for a challenge. Always.

The only thing he wasn't ready for? Winding up in a situation that would saddle him with the sort of burdens and responsibility his family was always on him about. He'd grow up and do something with himself… But not yet. He had more living to do first.

With that in mind, he turned onto the barn road instead of heading back to the main house. If he got his horse, Dusty, saddled and gone before Forrest got here, he wouldn't have to listen to another one of his big brother's lectures. It might not start out that way—but it always turned into one. Forrest didn't seem to know how to speak to Audy without coming across like an arrogant know-it-all.

He was parking the truck when his phone started ringing again.

"Persistent, aren't they?" Audy said to Harvey.

Harvey yawned.

Audy pulled the phone from his pocket. Not his uncle or his brother. Not a number he recognized. Maybe something rodeo related? Maybe RJ had found out something about the snot-nose youngster pretending to be a bull rider, Sterling Dunn. No one tried to make a fool of Audy Briscoe, especially not some upstart wanting to build a name for himself. He'd been waiting for a chance to ride against the punk and, when it came, he was going— no matter how mad it'd make Forrest. Forrest didn't get the whole bull-riding thing, which made sense since Forrest didn't get much about Audy.

"Yello?" he answered.

"I'm looking for Mr. Audy Briscoe?" The man's voice was brusque. "This is Giles Vincent. I'm an attorney."

An attorney? *This couldn't be good.* "What would you be looking for Audy Briscoe for?" He rested his elbow on the bed of his truck. "Is he in trouble for something?" He racked his brain for any possible mishaps.

"No. Nothing like that." Mr. Lawyer-man paused. "Am I speaking with Audy Briscoe?"

"As long as you're not looking for me to buy anything, sell anything, or anything along the likes, then, yes, you are speaking to Audy Briscoe." He winked at Harvey.

Harvey rested his head on his paws, not looking the least bit amused.

"To confirm, this is Audy Briscoe? This

has to do with a legal matter pertaining to Joy Adams, daughter of Dara and Kent Adams." Lawyer-man waited. "Her co-guardianship."

He frowned. "I signed that paper saying I'd do it, didn't I?" Audy frowned. Hadn't he? That was right after their daughter was born. He'd told Kent they were making a mistake, but he and Dara had laughed off all his protests and handed him a pen. "But, hold on, now. This is about paperwork, right?" The silence that followed was so loaded, Audy felt a prickle of unease race down his spine. "Why are you calling me, Mr...."

"Mr. Vincent." The man drew in a deep breath. "I work here in Houston. I was one of Kent's colleagues. Good man. Good friend."

Audy nodded. The best. Kent might be doing the white-picket-fence thing, but he didn't hold it against his best friend. Kent had the best sense of humor—always quick with a comeback or a joke. He'd managed something no one else had: Kent—and Dara—made the whole grown-up thing look decent enough. "He is," he said.

"There is no easy way to say this, Mr. Briscoe, so I'll get right to it. Kent and Dara Adams were in a fatal automobile accident this morning—after dropping Joy at day care."

Audy could scarcely breathe. The world came to a screeching halt, and he wasn't sure where the roaring in his ears was coming from—only that it was getting louder. "What?" He'd heard wrong. Or...or... Audy was gripping the side of his truck then, a surge of fury rising up in him. "Is this some sort of joke? Kent is a practical joker but this isn't funny—"

"No, it is not funny." Mr. Vincent sighed.

"Then tell Kent to knock it off and I'll call him later—"

"Mr. Briscoe." The man cut in, cool and calm and far too serious. "I realize this is somewhat of a shock. I, too, am struggling to process this sudden loss. All I can do is carry out their wishes...now that they're gone."

Gone. Audy focused on a tiny scratch in the paint of the truck bed. The scratch was fine. Hair-fine. So fine it was almost invisible. *Kent. Dara...* The man kept talking about Houston, the thunderstorm that morning and Kent swerving to avoid a fallen tree limb— he'd hydroplaned into oncoming traffic and hit head-on. The more the man talked, the bigger the scratch seemed to grow.

Why is he still talking? Audy didn't want to picture what the man was saying. He didn't want to think about Kent behind the wheel of the eyesore of a family SUV he'd bought when he'd found out Dara was expecting. Audy had teased him mercilessly—still teased him when he had the chance. It was what they did. Joked. Teased. Pushed buttons. He didn't want to picture the two of them scared or panicked or…

"When do you think you can be here?" the man asked.

"There?" Audy cleared his throat and tore his gaze from the scratch. All around him, life was going on. He could hear the horses in the barn, the low rumble of conversation from the men getting ready for the day, and the distant lowing of their Red Angus cattle out to graze. The morning Texas sun, higher now, was already beating down on him—promising triple-digit heat by noon. Audy ran a hand over his face, trying to make sense of…everything. *What is happening?* How could this happen? Kent and Dara were good people, good parents. Things like this didn't happen to people like them. It wasn't right. Nothing about this was right. "Where?"

"Here. To Houston. To pick up Joy." The way Mr. Vincent delivered the statement, it was almost like he hadn't just uttered the most alien and horrible, life-changing words ever.

Ever.

"Um…" *He* was supposed to pick up Joy? His throat seemed to shrink, pulling in on itself until it was a chore to breathe let alone get words out.

"I realize this is sudden, but Joy will be placed into child protective services until you arrive. We both know Kent and Dara's top priority was Joy. So, the sooner we get her settled, the better. Don't you agree?" The man stopped talking.

Something clicked in Audy's brain. Of all the words Lawyer-man had said, one stood out. It was the sort of information that eased up just a little on the tightness of his throat and the panic hammering away inside his chest. "Co-guardian." He sighed. *Yes.* He wasn't the only one who had signed the papers that day. He wasn't the only one who'd looked at Kent and Dara like they'd lost their minds… *Thankfully*.

"I called you first," Lawyer-man continued. "I will call Miss Young once we hang up. Unless, of course, you'd rather?"

He shook his head. Chances were, she wouldn't even take his call. "No, sir." Besides, there was no way he was going to break Brooke Young's heart. Brooke and Dara had been best friends since…well, forever. She'd been horrified that he'd been picked as Joy's godfather and co-guardian—something that had tickled him pink at the time. Now? He'd never, in his whole life, been so relieved. He wasn't alone in this, she'd signed those papers, too.

"Fine. Perhaps the two of you could arrange to make the trip together?"

"Yeah." Audy didn't want to take a long car ride with Brooke but it made the most sense to ride together. Truth be told, he wasn't equipped to handle this. Not the accident or the passing of his friends or being a guardian to any living thing. But Brooke? She was. If he were smart, he'd stay out of the way and let Brooke handle this. "I'll head over to her place now—should give you just enough time to call her and...let her know."

Mr. Giles Vincent gave Audy the address of where to meet him and hung up.

"Well, Harvey." Audy stared up at the blue sky overhead. "Looks like it's going to be one humdinger of a day." It could be worse—he could be alone in this. He wasn't. Like it or not, he and Brooke were in this together. He was pretty sure that was a good thing. Wasn't it?

CHAPTER TWO

BROOKE BEGAN ASSEMBLING foil sheets on the mobile cart, nodding as Mrs. Ruth Monahan—Miss Ruth to her friends—said, "You won't believe what I heard—" Which is what the older woman said whenever she had an extra juicy something to tell.

"Just touching up the roots?" Brooke asked, needing an answer before Miss Ruth launched into one of her stories. No matter how many times she'd gently tried to get Miss Ruth to start toning down the fire-engine red that was only found in a bottle, Miss Ruth always said no. The senior citizen would say she might look old, but she didn't feel old. And, until she felt old, she didn't want to see a single gray strand on her head.

"Yes, yes, just the roots." Miss Ruth nodded, her bright red curls bouncing. "Same as always." Her gaze met Brooke's in the large

illuminated mirror at Brooke's workstation—
all but bursting with gossip.

"All right." Brooke smiled. "Do tell, Miss
Ruth. I can't wait to hear." While she didn't
necessarily approve of Miss Ruth's fondness
for being right in the middle of things that had
nothing to do with her, Miss Ruth always had
interesting tales to tell.

"It's that Briscoe boy, again." Miss Ruth
shook her head. "I've been in this town forever and a day and I can tell you that there's
never been a Briscoe up to this much no
good."

Brooke didn't have to ask which Briscoe. It
would be Audy. *It was always Audy.* If there
was a person that embodied the phrase "Trouble is my middle name," it was Audy Eugene
Briscoe. She was still bent out of shape over
this morning's run-in.

"You don't say," Brooke murmured, using
the end of her comb to section off strands of
red hair. Was she really going to have to listen
to an hour-plus recounting of yet another one
of Audy Briscoe's antics? She had plenty of
stories of her own. He'd been a braid-pulling
terror on the elementary school playground,
a point-and-laugh sort of bully in middle

school, a conceited hot-or-not-list-making scholarship-stealing jerk in high school and a no-good bull-riding heartbreaker ever since. She didn't have time for that sort of careless and reckless existence, she never had.

That is why she and Audy Briscoe didn't see eye to eye. *And never will.*

"Sometimes I think that boy has a death wish." Miss Ruth clucked her tongue, knowing not to move while Brooke was doing her hair. "You'd think he'd take more care—after his brother's passing and all."

Brooke nodded, in full agreement. Garrison, Texas, wasn't a big town. It took pride in being a county seat, the county courthouse standing proudly in the middle of the downtown square. But it wasn't the tidy storefronts or the myriad of festivals that set Garrison apart. For Brooke, it was how people looked out for one another. Some folk were closer than others, of course, but the faces and names of everyone who lived in her small town were familiar. There were a lot of Briscoes—six siblings, five surviving—but Gene and Audy were the ones everyone knew best. Gene had been the golden one, he'd been a good boy and he'd grown into a good man. He was respected and liked by all who knew him. When they'd heard he'd been killed overseas while serving in the army not a year after enlisting, the whole town grieved for him.

Audy? Well, everyone knew Audy for entirely different reasons. Ninety percent of those things weren't appropriate to discuss in polite society.

"Now, I was not there to witness this first-hand, of course. One thing's for certain, I'm long past the days of staying out into the wee hours of the night causing mischief. Not that I ever did such things, mind you." She paused, winking. "It was Earl Ellis that gave me an earful about the whole thing when I went to pick up my new fertilizer spreader for my garden."

Brooke grinned, folding the foil around the short curl she'd coated with color. She could easily imagine Miss Ruth being a trouble-maker in her heyday.

"Such foolhardy nonsense won't stay innocent fun for long. I just hope those boys wise up before something happens to one of them." The older woman sighed. "Once again, he and that RJ Malloy were up to no good—"

Of course they were. Even when they'd

been little, Audy and RJ were causing trouble. Big trouble. Half the time they didn't get caught—the other times, they got away with it.

"—running back and forth across the bullpens last night." Miss Ruth sighed again.

That gave Brooke pause. "On the fairground?" She frowned. "But aren't they—"

"Full of bulls for this weekend's rodeo? Yes, ma'am, they certainly are. That was the whole point. I guess they were trying to see who could make it back and forth more times." She lowered her voice. "But then Tyson Ellis showed up… You know Earl's son, Tyson? Isn't he doing a good job as the assistant city manager? And being in charge of the rodeos that come through? Such a good man, don't you think? Ya'll dated for a spell, didn't you?"

She nodded. "I do and we did. He's a good man." Her phone started vibrating in her pocket, but she ignored it. If it was a client, they'd leave a message.

"Just not the one for you, eh? You know, when I was your age people weren't so picky. I saw someone I liked, he liked me—that was that." She blinked. "Where was I?"

"Tyson Ellis showed up." Brooke finished

the last foil wrap and began brushing color along the scalp, completely unperturbed by Miss Ruth's slight deviation in the conversation. She'd been single in a small town for a long time and her singleness was a frequent topic of concern. No one seemed to believe her assertions that she was perfectly content as she was and in no hurry to settle down. Most people, especially Miss Ruth and her lady friends, didn't understand that she preferred being the one making all the decisions in her life.

"Right." Miss Ruth chuckled. "Tyson turns up, hears the bulls making a ruckus and turns on the floodlights—worried it might be dogs or coyotes or something. Boom, lights so bright, RJ and Audy are shielding their eyes and, guess what? Here come the bulls. Earl said Tyson said he'd never seen two grown men move so fast in all his life. RJ about tripped over his own feet and Audy barreled over the top of the gate and landed, headfirst, on the other side."

Brooke started rinsing out the bowl, shaking her head. It was one thing to do such foolish things in high school. But now? It was sad…and embarrassing.

"That's when Audy realized his boot was caught on the gate latch and that the gate is swinging open, dragging him along, and letting the riled-up bulls out." Miss Ruth was wiping tears from her cheeks. "Good thing *Tyson* was sober enough to have fast reflexes. He got Audy clear and the gate closed before things took a nasty turn."

Audy had always been lucky that way. Somehow, someway, he always came out unscathed. Not that she wished him any ill will. "Is Tyson pressing charges?" She couldn't help hoping Audy Briscoe would have to answer for his behavior one day—preferably before one of his stunts got him killed.

"You know better than that." Miss Ruth was still chuckling. "Tyson's too good a friend to go causing trouble for the other two."

Tyson wouldn't be the one causing the trouble, Audy and RJ had done that on their own. But Brooke decided to keep that to herself. Instead, she got Miss Ruth set up under the dryer with a glass of iced tea and the latest entertainment magazine.

Her phone started ringing again and, since Miss Ruth was preoccupied and everything was washed and put away, she pulled the phone from her pocket. The number was unknown—but it was the same number that had called earlier.

"Hello?" she answered, prepared to hang up if it was another telemarketer.

"Is this Brooke Young?" The male voice was all business and not in the least bit familiar.

"Speaking." She pushed her long braid from her shoulder. "If you're selling something—"

"No. Miss Young, it's nothing like that." He cleared his throat. "My name is Giles Vincent. I'm a lawyer. I have an important matter to discuss with you. I'm sorry to say it's rather…bad news."

She didn't know any Giles Vincent, so—

"You were friends with Dara and Kent Adams, is that correct?" the man asked.

Brooke sank onto the stool next to her hair-washing station. "I am friends with them, yes. Dara is my best friend." He'd said *were*. It could have been unintentional, of course… But he'd said it. And the word seemed to hang there, echoing, louder and more important than all the rest. She shivered.

"I'm afraid there was an accident this morning, Miss Young. I am sorry to have to tell you that neither Kent nor Dara survived." The man cleared his throat.

What? She and Dara had had an hour-long FaceTime chat only two days ago. Dara was fine. She was laughing, a lot—she was always laughing. She's fine. *This has to be some sort of mistake*.

"You are the designated co-guardian for their daughter, Joy. As you can imagine, my top priority is to get Joy settled and with people who love her as soon as possible."

Joy. Her shock gave way to something more urgent and colder.

"I understand that this must be somewhat of a shock, Miss Young," he said, clearing his throat again. "But we were hoping you could come right away."

Joy. Brooke's toes were frozen. And the icy-coldness was rising. Slowly. Numbing her feet, her calves, her legs... Little needle pricks of ice all along her skin to deep inside her bones. Her stomach felt bottomless, aching and hollow. *Snap out of it, Brooke*. For Joy. Dara would be mortified if her little girl was scared or alone or...or... *Dara*. "I'm sorry." But her voice was weak, her lungs gasping. With a deep breath, she tried again.

"Yes. Yes, of course. I'll be there as quickly as possible."

"I spoke with Mr. Briscoe already. He agreed that it might be best to consider carpooling—since we will need you both present to sign some paperwork."

Brooke rested her elbow on the counter, covering her face with her free hand. "Of course."

"Good." Mr. Vincent sounded relieved. "I'll see you both this afternoon."

Brooke sat there, the phone pressed to her ear, long after he'd hung up. She needed a minute to collect herself. If she was the least bit emotional, Miss Ruth would get suspicious. Right now, she couldn't answer questions—she could barely think.

"Everything okay?" Myrna Ingells, one of the beauticians who had a station in Young's Beauty Salon, glanced at her. "You look a little pale."

Brooke sucked in a deep breath. "Are you free to finish Miss Ruth's hair? Something has come up and I need to leave."

Myrna's eyes went round as saucers. "Brooke… Of course." She blinked. "Are you sure everything is okay?"

Brooke shook her head. "I…I don't know."

"What else do you need?" Myrna asked.

Brooke's brain was spinning. "I need to cancel my appointments for today…and tomorrow." There was no way this was a quick fix.

"I'll check with Inez and Portia. If they have room, we will try to cover—if you'd like?" Myrna was clearly concerned.

Brooke nodded. "Yes, thank you. I know it's an inconvenience—"

"Brooke, you've been running this place since you were twenty years old and I've never known you to take a sick day or ask for help, so I get the feeling this is important." Myrna patted her on the shoulder. "You go on and we'll take it from here."

Brooke nodded, so thankful for Myrna. The woman was fourteen years her senior, calm and efficient, and maternal at just the right times. Like now. She was already tasking Portia and Inez with a list and reaching for the phone.

"Miss Ruth." Brooke reached for her purse, ignoring the roar of the diesel engine announcing the arrival of Audy Briscoe and his large black truck. One thing at a time.

"Something unexpected has come up." The words got stuck in her throat. "I have to go."

"Land sakes, Brooke, whatever is the matter?" Miss Ruth was frowning.

"There's been...an emergency." She glanced out the storefront window of her shop to find Audy getting out of his truck. *No.* No, he could not come inside. "I have to go. I'm so sorry." She was walking to the door. "You're in good hands with Myrna." She knew the four women inside were watching her, that they'd continue to watch her through the large picture window that took up most of the front wall. They had a front row seat for whatever scene might unfold outside. *There will be no scene.*

But then she was outside, staring at Audy, and her feet were leaden—each step heavier than the last. Her pace slowed and her heart lodged itself in her throat, making her breathing labored and the ground beneath her feet unsteady. Once she got in his truck, it was real. Once they were on the way to Houston, there was no turning back. There was nothing she wanted more than just that—to turn back time.

Audy nodded at her. "Brooke." Her name

was thick and gruff and just enough to break her. He reached for her.

"No," she whispered, and it was all she could manage. "People will talk—"

"People always talk, Brooke." He pulled her into his arms. "Right now, I don't care." The gruffness was thicker, more urgent—rawer.

For a minute, she crumpled into him. She was drowning in a sea of hurt and shock and grief—buoyed by Audy's fierce hold. Even though they were oil and water, they'd had Dara and Kent in common. From engagement parties to weddings to baby showers and more, now was not the time to focus on all the little things about Audy that normally got under her skin. They both lost someone today...

Dara was her best friend—she always had been. When Dara fell for Kent, Brooke promised herself she'd never put Dara in an awkward position. There was no way she was going to lose Dara just because Kent had seriously questionable taste in friends. And, to give Audy credit, he *had* always seemed to be on his best behavior when they were all together. So maybe he felt the same way she did about Kent and Dara. Theirs were the most important of friendships.

And now they're gone.

She held on to Audy—willing herself to be strong. She had to be. For Dara. And for Joy.

AUDY WAS PRETTY sure he'd made a mistake. A big mistake. The sort of mistake he'd regret any minute now.

It was only a hug. If there was ever a time in his life when he'd needed a hug, it was now. From Brooke's washed-out face and wide-as-saucer eyes, he was pretty sure she needed a hug, too. Like it or not, he'd done what had seemed like the most natural thing in the world: pulled her into his arms. And, for a split second, it had *felt* like the most natural thing in the world. He knew she was hurting like him, knew she'd loved Dara and Kent, too. And Brooke Young, soft against him, was warm and solid and, most important, comforting. The thing was, once he was holding on to her—he wasn't sure who was holding who up.

"We should go," she whispered against his shoulder, her arms falling away from his waist.

He let go of her and stepped back—grateful he was steady on his feet. He swallowed against the hard lump all but blocking his windpipe. "Ready?"

Her nod was stiff and, by all appearances, she seemed braced and ready to take on whatever came her way.

"Good." He cleared his throat but the lump stuck. "I'm not."

There was a flash of emotion on her face—one that echoed the panic and uncertainty he was struggling with.

What was he supposed to say? Or do? He'd never been one to offer a shoulder or work through someone's problems with them. He was the one someone called when they wanted a night out. Audy Briscoe knew how to show someone a good time. There was no way to good-time his way out of this one. But instead of standing there, smack-dab in the middle of the salon's picture window—on display for each and every inhabitant likely gawking at the two of them—they should get out of the sun and hit the road. It was a four-hour drive to Houston. And that was if traffic cooperated.

He opened the passenger door for Brooke

and closed it once she'd climbed into his truck. He headed around the hood of his truck, tipping his hat at the four women all but pressed up against the glass window, and climbed into the driver's seat, slamming the door a little harder than necessary.

"You need anything?" he asked, starting the truck. But a quick look her way revealed she was on her phone.

"Hi, Kelly, this is Brooke," she said, staring out the passenger window. "I'm so sorry to ask this, but would it be okay if Tess came home with Alice today?" There was a pause. "There's been a…an emergency and I'm heading to Houston. Hopefully, I'll be back tonight."

Hopefully?

He was still processing where they were going. He wasn't ready to consider what would happen once they got there. His stomach seemed to flip itself over and that knot, still caught in his throat, grew larger, making him swallow. Not that it helped. Not in the least.

Brooke's sigh was pure relief. "If you're sure that's not a problem—" A much longer pause this time. "Well, I can't thank you enough. I'll call the school to let them know, too."

"Kelly Schneider?" Audy asked.

"Yes." Brooke nodded, scrolling across her phone screen. "Tess and her daughter, Alice, are good friends." She held the phone up to her ear again. "Yes, I need to change how Tess Young is going home today."

Audy's phone was synced with his truck. When his brother's name popped up on the navigation screen on his dashboard, he sighed and clicked Reject. He hadn't just taken off— he'd left a note. It had been short and to the point, but it was still a note.

Brooke finished making phone calls.

Audy ignored another call, this one from Webb.

After that, they drove on in silence. Not by choice so much as it didn't feel right to play music or force conversation at the moment. Besides, conversation would likely center around where they were headed and whatever was going to happen when they got there. Maybe the four-hour trip would give him the time he needed to prepare himself. His stomach did the whole inside-out-and-upside-down thing as he tried not to think about what was waiting for them in Houston.

His phone rang again.

"Does your family know what's happened?" Brooke asked.

He glanced her way to find her staring at him. "I left a note."

Her brows rose and her lips pressed flat.

He sighed, the weight of her gaze kicking up the temperature in the truck a good ten degrees. *Fine*. He accepted the call. "Hey."

"Hey?" Forrest barked. "I've got one of the ranch trucks loaded up with barbed wire and ready to go and you're not here. You were supposed to be helping restring the fence line in the south pasture, Audy. You remember? I've had to pull men from the barn repair to fill in."

"Did you get my note?" Audy asked, his irritation barely in check.

"You mean the note that read, 'Something came up, keep an eye on Harvey'?" Forrest barked again. "That note?"

From the corner of his eye, Audy saw Brooke cover her face with her hands and shake her head.

"I was in a hurry." Audy ran a hand along the back of his neck.

"I can see that." Forrest took a deep breath. "I do my best not to rely on you, Audy. I know the ranch isn't at the top of your priority list… But it is your home and you need to earn your keep around here. We all do. So, when I ask for your help, I need it."

"I wouldn't have taken off if it wasn't an emergency, Forrest." He pushed back, wishing he'd followed his instincts and ignored the call.

"Oh? A rodeo emergency? A truck emergency? A female emergency?" His big brother paused. "Or does it have something to do with last night? And what happened at the stockyards?"

"None of the above." Audy sighed, knowing his brother deserved a real explanation. "Kent…" He swallowed, that knot bigger than ever. He shook his head, cleared his throat and tried again—only this time nothing came out. He jumped when Brooke's hand covered his. She wasn't looking at him, she was staring straight out the windshield—but he saw how hard the muscle in her jaw was working.

Seeing her struggle, knowing she was hurting just as much as he was, helped some.

Sitting here, he was sure something inside was broken and bleeding. The way he was feeling reminded him of the time he'd been trampled by a bull. World spinning. Ground shaking. Nauseated and hurting so he could barely think straight... But broken ribs and a cracked clavicle couldn't compare to this pain.

He caught Brooke's hand in his.

"Kent was in an accident this morning." His words were brittle and gruff, but he got them out.

There was a long silence before Forrest asked, "Is he okay?"

"No." Audy cleared his throat. "He didn't make it. Dara... Dara, too." He cleared his throat again.

Another long silence. "Audy. Where are you? I'll get Webb to cover things here and drive—"

"Brooke is with me." He cut in. "We're headed to Houston. We...we've got to get things squared away with Joy."

There was a slight break before Forrest said, "Whatever we can do—you let me know." He cleared his throat. "I mean it, now. Kent was…well, he was family."

Audy nodded, words failing him again.

"Call me when you know what's happening, will you?" Forrest asked.

"Can do." He forced the words out and hung up. As soon as he hung up, Brooke let go of his hand and went back to staring out the window.

The closer they got to Houston, the more anxiety stacked up on his chest. It'd been one thing deciding Brooke could take care of everything when it was just him, Harvey and his truck—it was something else entirely now that they were side by side. The chance that he'd be of any use was just about nonexistent but he didn't want to go into this Giles Vincent guy's office without the two of them talking through a few things first.

"So…" he started, the sentence he'd been working through vanishing the instant her eyes met his. "I know I should know about what…this means, but…" He shrugged, his gaze bouncing off hers before he turned his attention back to the road.

"Mr. Vincent emailed me the paperwork

when we left," Brooke said, holding up her phone.

"Oh?" It shouldn't matter that she'd been reviewing this information for the last few hours and hadn't bothered to share it with him. But it did. "Since you've had a while to read through it, maybe you could catch me up to speed?"

"You and I are co-guardians for Joy." She turned her phone over on her lap. "It's pretty straightforward."

"So…what does that mean?" he asked, trying not to panic.

"What do you mean, what does that mean?" Brooke's irritation was back and stronger than ever. "Your uncle Felix is—was your guardian. I'm Tess's legal guardian. I'd say we are both uniquely qualified in knowing exactly what this means."

He did. But he was hoping, somehow, someway, that *guardian* might mean something different in this situation. It had to. How could he and Brooke possibly co-guardian a baby? A baby he'd met…once? Twice? Considering she just sort of sat there and drooled on herself, he wasn't sure that counted. "I guess I thought it was a figurative sort of thing," he mumbled.

"It was. Until they…this happened." Brooke broke off. "Dara's grandmother is too old to raise Joy. Dara's mother died when she was in college and her father is in an Alzheimer's unit. Kent's family situation's no better."

He knew that, too. Kent had bounced around in the foster system until he'd been placed with the Whitman family there in Garrison. But the Whitmans had moved to Oregon to be close to their son and, since Kent had never been adopted, there was no real claim or connection between Kent's little girl and the older couple. If he and Brooke decided not to take Joy, he imagined the lawyer would reach out to them… *What other options are there?*

"I'm having a hard time wrapping my head around this." He confessed. He was having an even harder time with the idea that *he* was the only option for this baby girl.

"It hasn't exactly clicked with me, either. But…but, what I can do—we can do—is think about what Dara and Kent wanted." Brooke took a deep breath, pinching the bridge of her nose and closing her eyes. "Right now, the two of them would be worried sick about Joy. That's it. That's all. Joy." Her jaw muscle clenched tight.

Right.

"So, then, what's the plan?" he asked, trying not to let his tension seep into his voice.

"Plan?" Brooke shot him a confused look. "Audy, this is the plan. We are picking up Joy and bringing her back to Garrison. To raise her."

The lump in his throat was back. So was the overwhelming sense of doom he'd been grappling with for the better part of the morning. Him? Raise a baby? If it wasn't so terrifying, it'd be laughable. "I'm the least qualified person on the planet to raise a child." He waved a hand. "Don't bother trying to save my feelings, either—we both know it's true."

She didn't say a thing.

He glanced at her. *Harsh.*

"You said not to bother." She glanced at him. "Are you looking for a way out of this, then?"

If he said yes, he was pretty sure the vein sticking out of Brooke's forehead would pop. Best course of action? Keep his mouth shut. Besides, he didn't know what he was doing yet.

"You agreed to this, Audy. We both did." She swallowed. "We never expected this to happen, how could we? But now... Now it's up to us to honor our promises. Both of us. We owe it to Kent and Dara and Joy to follow through. This little girl has no one in the world except us."

Which was both terrifying and heartbreaking.

"So, we handle the paperwork and...we take Joy home. With us." She took a deep breath, her posture stiffening and her jaw clenched tight. "Whether you like it or not, Audy, that *is* the plan. It's the only plan."

Like it? What was there to like? At the time Kent had suggested the whole guardianship thing, it had felt like a big joke—a joke he hadn't thought of once since then. But now? If Kent had meant this as a joke, he was definitely getting the last laugh. No. He wasn't. Kent was gone. Dara was gone. The whole world was falling apart and now he and Brooke were supposed to step in and make it better... Maybe it was a joke, after all. *A big, bad joke.*

CHAPTER THREE

BROOKE'S PLANS TO take detailed notes about their meeting with Mr. Vincent had been derailed by the arrival of Joy. Joy was adorable. There had been no tears or panic. She'd been placed in Brooke's lap, all smiles, a single blond ringlet atop her tiny head, big brown eyes and little hands that wanted nothing more than to grab Brooke's pen. After several minutes of staring around her, Joy had tucked her thumb into her mouth, curled into Brooke's chest and fallen asleep. Instead of shifting Joy to one arm and going back to her notes, Brooke had drawn the baby close and rocked her. She didn't know that her whole world had changed, but Brooke did. And, in comforting Joy, she was comforting herself. And right now, she needed comfort far more than she needed notes.

Giles Vincent kept on talking, reading over pages and posing questions, but every few minutes, Brooke's attention would wander to little Joy. She was all snuggles, bows and pink ruffled-bottom bloomers.

As soon as Dara had found out she was expecting a girl, she'd begun to collect the pinkest, frilliest and most feminine wardrobe for her daughter. Kent, having grown up with next to nothing, indulged Dara. Staring down at the sleeping baby, Brooke thought Joy looked like a perfect china doll. A Cupid's bow mouth and long, thick lashes resting against rosy, round cheeks.

You're beautiful. Not that it was a surprise. Dara and Kent were both attractive people. *Had been attractive people.* The thought had her hold on baby Joy tightening just a bit. With her other hand, she smoothed the wisp of a curl that crowned Joy's head. The curl immediately bounced back, sticking straight up like a silky gold antenna right on the top.

She glanced at Audy. And frowned… He'd officially assumed deer-in-the-headlights status the minute Joy had arrived. He had yet to do more than stare at Joy, break out in a visible sweat, then go back to staring at the crystal paperweight on the edge of Giles Vincent's massive wooden desk.

"I'll give you a copy of everything, of course. And you have my number. I'm certain questions will arise—since this has all been rather sudden," Giles Vincent said, scanning over the papers spread out across the top of his impressive desk. "From here, you might have an interview or two with a social worker and a couple of home visits."

"Home visits?" Audy asked.

Brooke glanced his way, hoping his question meant he'd been listening. Today was a nightmare—there was no denying it. But they were in this together... *Like it or not.* Wasn't that what she'd said?

"It's a formality." Mr. Vincent added his signature to the pages she and Audy had already signed, then put the cap on his ridiculously fancy-looking pen. "To make sure that the environment, or environments in this case, are suitable for Joy and her needs." He placed the pen on the table and collected the pages, one by one, into a neat packet. "If there are concerns, then the courts might decide to get involved and reassess what is best for Joy. I'd expect one, maybe two visits—nothing to worry about."

Meaning she and Audy had to make this work so they didn't lose Joy.

"Shouldn't that have been done before we signed the paperwork?" Audy asked, watching the deliberate and methodical way Mr. Vincent flipped through all the pages again.

Mr. Vincent glanced up at him. "I suppose that does make more sense."

Audy's brows rose and he nodded.

Mr. Vincent glanced back and forth between them. "Have you two considered what sort of living arrangements will suit you all the most?" He placed the stack of pages inside a manila folder.

Audy's wide-eyed gaze was answer enough.

"My sister and I live in town in a four-bedroom house right off the main street and a few blocks from where I work." She swallowed. "It makes sense for Joy to live there—close to doctors and schools and such."

Audy was looking at her, she could tell. If he disagreed, he didn't say a thing.

"These home visits. Is there something to be aware of? Something they look for? Red flags and that sort of thing?" She didn't want Joy's security to be jeopardized over a simple mistake one of them made. She had every intention of making her home Joy-proof but she had no say-so in how Audy handled things. That's what worried her most in all of this. Audy.

"Considering the parents named both of you as Joy's guardians, there shouldn't be many hurdles. The court tends to honor the parents' wishes—especially ones that are signed and dated and filed with their lawyer. Me." He sat back in his leather chair, resting his elbows on the arms and steepling his fingers. "In general, they want to assess the cleanliness and safety of the home itself as well as the bonding and investment of the appointed guardians." Mr. Vincent's gaze moved back and forth between the two of them. "Everything from bonding with the child to the order and noise in a home to the ease of access to resources and medical facilities, that sort of thing. Basically, the visits are to confirm that the two of you are acting in Joy's best interest at all times."

"That's all?" Audy's sarcasm was unmistakable.

"That goes without saying." Brooke was quick to jump in. "Of course."

Mr. Vincent glanced at his wristwatch. "I apologize for keeping you so long."

It was almost six.

"Here are the keys to their condo." Mr. Vincent slid the keys across the desk. "I'm sure you haven't had time to consider what you'd like to do with their property, but now is a good time to sell. If you decide to sell, feel free to call me. I can help with that, as well."

Audy took the keys.

"For now, you'll want to gather Joy's things." Mr. Vincent's gaze slid to Joy. "I know that Kent and Dara would be at ease now that you two have Joy."

The sting in her eyes was so unexpected that Brooke began blinking furiously. She'd kept it together so far, she was not going to burst into tears in this very nice, very professional man's slightly intimidating office.

"Let me have my secretary make a copy of these papers for each of you and we'll be done here." Mr. Vincent stood, took the manila folder and left his office.

Brooke continued to blink but the stinging wouldn't subside. She sniffed and stared at the blond curl on the top of Joy's head.

"You okay?" Audy whispered.

She nodded.

"I don't know about you, but I'm ready to get out of here." Audy sighed. "The sooner we get back on the road—"

"I think it might make more sense if we stay at their place tonight, Audy." Brooke cut him off, needing to gain control of herself. As long as she had purpose, she'd be fine. "Tomorrow, after we've packed up all of Joy's things, we can head back." Considering he was the one driving her, she probably shouldn't be issuing orders. Besides... *We're in this together.* She paused, swallowing hard. "If that's all right with you?"

"Um...sure." Audy was staring at her—wary. "Makes sense."

Mr. Vincent came back and handed over the two white legal envelopes that contained copies of all the documents. Audy collected the car seat that the day care center had left when they'd delivered Joy, and the two of them—three of them—headed into the elevator and downstairs.

Brooke stared down at Joy, still sleeping, in her arms. Her heart twisted sharply. "This is all wrong, Audy," she whispered. "Her little life will never be the same." She looked at Audy.

Audy's crystal-blue gaze met hers. "She's a little thing, Brooke. She can't miss what she doesn't remember." He cleared his throat. "But I agree with you. This is all wrong."

It wasn't the first time she'd seen Audy run a hand over his face, it was a habit of his. It was the sort of gesture that lacked any hint of his usual confidence. Since he'd shown up at the salon this morning, she'd seen a different side of Audy Briscoe. Vulnerable and uncertain, but trying… It gave her hope that, maybe, the two of them could find a way to make this work.

"Kent and Dara should have left Joy to you," Audy added. "We both know I'm just going to get in your way and make a mess of things."

It would have made life easier, but… She shook her head. "But they didn't, Audy. Joy is our responsibility. I have a feeling there will be plenty of messes and getting in each other's way from here on out, but we will make it work. Joy isn't a dog or a horse—she's a little girl." She smiled down at the baby. "We are all she has. We can't let her down."

AUDY WAS READY to bolt.

All afternoon, he'd felt like his stomach had been punted around inside his abdomen. Every time someone said *responsibility* or *duty* or *long-term*, his stomach took a hit. And he'd heard those words a lot today—too many times for his liking.

Now he was hauling a car seat across the parking lot for Joy. How it worked, he had no idea. But, according to the day care worker who had dropped it off, it was against the law to transport a baby in a vehicle unless they were in one of these things. Thankfully, the day care worker had also printed off a sheet with the instructions for installation— so hopefully even he couldn't mess this up.

"Huh," he said, reading over the pictures and buckling the seat in. "That was easy."

"You're sure you did it right?" Brooke asked, gently rocking Joy.

He ignored the dig and stepped aside, helping Brooke—who was still holding Joy—into the truck before heading around to his side. He climbed up and froze. "She's awake?" he murmured, still not moving.

"Yes." Brooke nodded, snapping Joy into the car seat. "And ready to get home."

"Uh-huh." Audy slid into the truck, wishing the car seat didn't need to be in the middle of the bench seat. As it was, Joy was right beside him. Her rear-facing seat gave her a perfect view of the back of his seat, Brooke and him... Right now, she seemed a little too interested in him. He swallowed, trying not to make eye contact with her. "Let's go."

He started the truck, the roar of the engine so loud and sudden that he risked a look Joy's way.

Joy's eyes went round and then she...giggled.

Audy had to admit she was a cute little thing—even wearing all that frilly pink stuff.

"Good thing she's not scared of loud noises," Brooke said, giving Joy a goofy grin. "'Cause Audy drives a big, loud, angry-sounding truck."

"Angry?" Audy shrugged. Big and loud, yes. But angry?

Joy turned his way as soon as she'd heard his voice. Once again, those big brown eyes were glued on his face. She wasn't smiling or giggling. She was staring. Hard.

"What's she doing?" Audy asked, scared to make any sudden movements.

"She's looking at you, Audy." Brooke sighed. "I'm sure she's feeling about you the way you're feeling about her."

Audy made a dismissive sound. "I seriously doubt that." He shook his head, put the truck in Drive and headed onto the freeway. For the next twenty minutes, he kept his eyes on the road—all the while fully aware of Joy's every move.

The way the baby kept looking at him was unnerving.

Her little squeaks and giggles didn't help.

Neither did the sweet tone Brooke was using—unlike anything he'd ever heard from her before—when she was talking to Joy. *Baby talk, I guess.* He wasn't sure how he felt about it yet. But Joy seemed to like it, so who was he to complain?

When they pulled into the driveway of Kent and Dara's small condo, Joy was jabbering away—as if she was carrying on a real conversation instead of a string of incoherent noises.

Brooke seemed equally delighted, saying things like, "Really?" and "You don't say."

"I don't know what you two are carrying on about," he said. "But we're here."

"Good. I bet someone could use a dry diaper." Brooke began unbuckling Joy's seat, in no rush.

But the word *diaper* had Audy considering retreat once again. *Diapers are not part of my life.* He'd no interest in anything that wore them... Now he was supposed to change them? *No way, no how.* "I'll get the door." He all but jumped from the truck and hurried to unlock and open the front door.

Brooke followed, a chattering Joy in her arms. "Relax," Brooke said. "She's not going to explode."

"Ha ha." He wasn't laughing.

But Brooke was. "Audy Briscoe, don't tell me you're scared of a little baby's diaper? You're all about taking risks." She stopped, watching as he closed the door, then headed into the condo's open kitchen and living room combo. He flipped on the lights and stopped, staring around. It was surreal, standing there—without Kent offering him a beer or Dara laughing over something Kent had said. It was quiet. And still. An empty room.

"Ma ma ma," Joy called out, peering around.

Audy winced. Up until now, Joy's sounds

had been just that—sounds. Was she looking for Dara? Or was it just more gibberish?

"Let's go get a clean diaper." Brooke's singsong baby voice wavered but she didn't linger. "Then we'll see what to do next." She glanced his way. "I've got this, Audy."

Audy held up both hands in mock surrender. He needed a minute. He needed a whole lot more than a minute, but he'd take what he could get. Outside. Inside, he felt claustrophobic—he always had. Problems seemed bigger, overwhelming even, when there was a roof pushing things down on top of him. He was already feeling that way... trapped. Right now, he needed fresh air, blue skies and room to move. He crossed the living room and opened the back door. A wave of heat rolled over him. The birdsong was audible—if muffled by the roar of nearby traffic. Overhead, beyond the power lines and around the apartment complex, the white clouds moved slowly across the wide blue sky.

Times like this, he appreciated the size and scope of the ranch.

I'm a long way from home.

He sighed, running a hand along the back of his neck.

Did Brooke really think they could do this? *Maybe she can.* But he wasn't cut out for this sort of thing. Diapers and baby talk and putting Joy's well-being first, or however Mr. Vincent had put it. He had a career to think of. Bull riding was the only thing he was good at. He was young and fit—that wouldn't last forever. This was *his* time for rodeo. He was making a name for himself, winning big purses and climbing up in ranks. He'd worked too hard to just…stop. The bottom line was, this wasn't for him. *This* wasn't who he was.

He had a hard time believing Kent ever intended to leave him on that paperwork. *Why would he?*

Kent *knew* Audy. He knew Audy wasn't a role model. *More like an anti role model.*

That was all Brooke. You couldn't get more responsible than Brooke Young.

Brooke—who no one had a bad thing to say about. To hear people talk, she was close to sainthood. How, after her mother's illness, she'd learned to do hair so she could support the family. Brooke, who'd given up on college to keep the salon open and running while taking care of her mother and stepping in to raise her little sister. And when Mrs. Young died four years ago, it was Brooke who became Tess's guardian, without hesitation.

Brooke knew how to do this. *She's done this before, she can do it again.*

But the minute that thought cycled through his head, he heard his brother's voice. *You can always choose to do the right thing, Audy. It's up to you. At some point, you've got to stop doing what you want and start doing what's right. In the end, you'll be glad you did.*

Audy wasn't convinced his brother had taken this sort of situation into consideration. He'd been talking about the drinking and mischief and the everyday bad choices Audy tended to make—not Audy stepping up to raise a child he had no business raising. Forrest would be the first one to agree he was a liability to Joy's future—not a blessing.

There was one way to find out. He had texted Forrest to let him know they'd arrived in Houston, but he owed his brother a phone call anyway. He'd call, lay everything out there and get the confirmation he needed. *I can't do this.* For reasons beyond understanding, he needed to hear Forrest say as much. And he would. When it came to listing off Audy's shortcomings, Forrest never held back.

"Audy?" Forrest answered on the second ring. "Any news? What about the baby?"

Audy ran a hand over his face. "That's what we're working through." All the words he wanted to say got stuck in his throat.

Forrest asked, "Kent didn't have any family, did he?"

"No. Neither did Dara." He stared overhead, watching an airplane track across the blue. "Luckily, Kent and Dara left a will—and designated guardians. I'm not so sure Kent was serious when he picked them, though." Not that Kent or Dara ever expected this to happen when they signed the papers. "You know how Kent was... He loved a good joke." The airplane was gone, so Audy started pacing the length of the small yard. "But, well, this isn't a joke."

There was a long pause. "Are these guardians having second thoughts?" Forrest asked.

Audy sighed. "You could say that."

Another long pause. "I guess that's understandable, considering. Raising a child is no small thing."

Exactly. Audy kept on pacing. "Some people just aren't cut out for that sort of thing."

"I agree." Forrest's answer was quick.

Thank you. Audy knew it.

"But if Kent picked these people, he must have believed otherwise." Forrest kept on, sounding confident. "He and Dara picking them is a testament to the faith they had in these people."

What? How would you know? "What if Kent was wrong, Forrest?" Audy kept on pacing. "What if he made a mistake?" He looked up to find Brooke on the back porch, Joy in her arms.

"You're really worried about this, aren't you?" Forrest cleared his throat. "There are ways to challenge these things, in court. If you're that worried about their daughter, maybe you should."

"I'm worried, all right." Audy saw no point in trying to cover up the truth of the conversation. She had to know what he was feeling. Surely?

Brooke's hazel eyes searched his. With the slightest shake of her head, she carried Joy back inside.

He didn't know what that look meant, but it

didn't help with his already twisted-up stomach or the mounting pressure in his chest. "I should go," Audy said.

"If you need me to call Mr. Sandoval, let me know. He does family law stuff now and then. Maybe he could help? Or give you some advice?"

"Thanks, Forrest." He shook his head. This had backfired—something terrible. His brother thought he was fighting to protect Joy from someone else. Would his brother do the same if he knew Audy was talking about himself? Or would his big brother be more disappointed in him than ever? He was pretty sure he knew the answer. "We're staying put tonight but I'll be home tomorrow."

After he hung up, he gave up pacing and headed inside—braced and ready for what was sure to be an unpleasant conversation with Brooke.

Brooke sat on the couch with Joy in her lap, reading a book with the picture of a cow on the cover. She read through the whole book using her singsong baby voice. Joy clapped and patted the book and smiled up at Brooke.

Audy stood and stared, the dread mounting and pooling in his chest.

She smoothed a hand over Joy's single shiny curl, in no hurry to speak. But when she did, it was clear she was struggling. "Audy Briscoe, I'm going to ask you this one time." Her hazel eyes met his. "Are you planning on backing out on this? On me?" Her voice cracked. "On Kent and Dara? And Joy?"

Audy was frozen, struggling with the best way to answer her.

"Because if you are, we need to talk to Mr. Vincent about what that means, legally." She smiled at Joy, who was holding the book. "I don't give a lick about you or your doubts. All I care about is making sure Joy is safe and cared for. I can do that with or without you."

"I know it." He agreed. "I'm not cut out—"

"Don't feed me excuses that ease your conscience." She drew in a deep breath, her tone light but her words sharp. "Your word might not mean a thing, but mine does. I won't dishonor Kent and Dara's wishes or lose Joy because you're a coward."

It wasn't the first time he'd had insults hurled at him, and it likely wouldn't be the last. But that didn't mean Brooke's words didn't hurt and kick up the embers of his temper. "If you're trying to goad me—"

"Oh, Audy." She shook her head, lifting Joy up and into her arms. "That's the thing. This is bigger than you. Or you and me. This is even bigger than your ego." She shook her head. "I guess that's answer enough. In the morning, we'll call Mr. Vincent so we can have everything squared away before we go home. Once that's done, I think it's best if you and I don't speak for a while."

She was giving him an out. Without saying a word directly to her, he was getting what he wanted. This was good. This would be better for them all. So why didn't he feel better? Why did he feel more twisted up inside than ever?

CHAPTER FOUR

BROOKE STARED UP at the ceiling, a pale beam of light rolling across the dark surface before fading. Headlights from outside. The little gated neighborhood of townhomes and apartments was busy. Too busy. Lots of coming and going, car doors slamming, and the occasional thump of a radio base turned up so loud she was confident the person playing the music would suffer hearing issues in the long run.

She turned onto her side, the crossbar of the sleeper sofa pressing against her hip bone. No matter how she shifted or lay, it was there. Hard and rigid and inescapable—a physical representation of her current situation and reminder of just how out-of-whack everything was right now.

"Everything," she murmured, her gaze sweeping over the assortment of photos along Kent's home office desk and occupying the windowsill. Pictures of him and Dara, laughing. Wedding pictures. Pregnancy pictures. And Joy.

Joy from day one to now. The two of them had been so in love with their daughter—they were those obnoxious parents who seemed to think every tiny sound or expression or movement was worthy of sharing via text. Whenever a text from Dara rolled in, Brooke fully expected a picture or video of Joy. To make absolutely certain they didn't miss a thing, Dara had a professional photo every month for Joy. She had a special Baby's First Year frame, with twelve windows to show Joy's growth over the first twelve months of her young life. But only ten of the slots were occupied. "Ten months old." Something razor-sharp and cold rose up inside her chest, making it hard to breathe.

This is wrong. She wiped at the sudden tears leaving hot tracks down her cheeks. *This is all wrong.*

How was it only ten months ago that Brooke had taken a couple of days off to come help Dara with Joy once they'd been released from the hospital. She'd been entranced with the baby girl, but her adoration couldn't compare with how in love Dara and Kent had been. To them, baby Joy was the sun and moon and…well, she had been everything to them.

Brooke sat up, dried her tears with the corner of her sheet and kicked off her blankets, restless and hot and needing something to do to occupy herself. *Clean. I'll clean.* When her brain wouldn't shut off and she couldn't sleep, she'd organize her pantry, scrub the bathtub, or—if things got dire—she'd break out an old toothbrush and attack the grout on the kitchen floor. *Not that I'd know where Dara's grout-cleaning toothbrush would be.* She stood, tugged down the top of the cotton pajamas she'd borrowed from Dara's chest of drawers, and opened the guest room door.

On tiptoe, she crept past Joy's nursery. Brooke didn't want to wake the baby—she'd cried and fussed and called out, "Ma ma ma," for almost an hour before she'd fallen asleep. That hour was torture for them all. Brooke was tempted to give in and cry along with Joy but she hadn't. And Audy? He'd gone pale, locked his jaw and retreated downstairs after the first ten minutes. *Definitely don't want to wake her up.* As silently as possible, she went down the stairs to the entryway. She headed back to the kitchen but paused in the living room. The television was on and Audy sat, his chin in his hand, watching what appeared to be a video recording.

Brooke lingered, the images on the screen holding her attention.

Audy and Kent. Cowboy hats and smiles. Audy was skinny—more boy than man. Kent was all ears and a prominent Adam's apple.

"Didn't mean to wake you." Audy's voice was deep and thick and so sudden it startled Brooke.

She shook her head, her hand pressed to her chest. "You didn't."

"Didn't mean to scare you, either." The corner of his mouth kicked up, but it was a half-hearted attempt at a smile.

Even from where she stood, Brooke could see the grief and loss on Audy's face. It tugged at her heart and forced her into the room and onto the couch at his side. "No... I was just caught up." She pointed at the screen.

"The good ol' days." Audy ran a hand along the back of his neck. "Team roping. Back when I was still all-around." He nodded as a burst of action played out on-screen—so fast that if she'd blinked, she'd have missed it. "We were good. Good enough to go pro." Audy was the header, Kent brought up the rear—working together like a finely oiled machine.

"Dara used to worry about that." Brooke drew her legs up, curling into the corner of her end of the couch. "That she'd taken Kent's dream away—that he'd resent her for it, someday."

Audy scrubbed both hands over his face before taking a deep breath. "She was his dream. This was what he wanted. All that—" he nodded at the screen again "—Kent did that for me."

Brooke glanced at the television then back at Audy. "He was a good friend." She had to stop then, swallowing against the tightness closing her throat.

"The best." Audy nodded. "You might not know this about me but I'm not all that easy to get along with."

Brooke covered her mouth to stifle the laughter bubbling up and slipping out.

"Never mind." He chuckled. "I forgot who I was talking to."

For a second, their eyes met. Brooke couldn't

remember the last time she'd looked at Audy and felt anything other than frustration—or downright exasperation. But, right now, it didn't matter that her feelings for Audy Briscoe usually resembled those she bore for a deep splinter she couldn't remove. No matter how hard she tried, she couldn't shake him or the constant irritation his presence caused. But the only thing she was feeling right now was understanding. They were both brokenhearted over the loss of people who held a special place in their hearts—and their lives.

"Kent put up with…well, a lot." Audy shook his head, his gaze holding hers. "You know how I was in high school—"

"Was?" she interrupted. "That implies past tense." But she smiled. "And, yes, I do know."

His gaze sharpened, zeroing in on her with an intensity that seemed to thin the air in the room. "*He* never held it against me. All my tomfoolery, that's what he and Uncle Felix called it. He took it in stride and said there was a reason I was always taking risks and acting out but until I figured out what that was, there was no changing it. Me, I mean. No changing me."

There was a little voice in the back of her

mind warning Brooke to keep her guard up. He was hurting, yes, but all this? What was he saying? Was he still trying to justify his decision to waive his co-guardianship? And using Kent's words as the justification.

"He stood by me—sometimes when he probably shouldn't have." Audy's smile was tight, a flash of raw grief twisting his handsome features. He cleared his throat then, sitting forward to prop his elbows on his knees and bury his head in his hands. "And, unlike my own brother, Kent got *me*—who I was—and he always believed in me."

Like it or not, she couldn't ignore his vulnerability. It was so…so unlike him. At least, it was unlike the Audy Briscoe she knew. "He loved you." Brooke's words were soft, offering up what comfort she could. It wasn't enough, she knew that, but she wasn't good at this sort of thing.

Audy nodded but stayed as he was.

Brooke didn't push.

The television was muted but the vivid images of Audy and Kent, young and laughing and carefree, were inescapable. They were mesmerizing to watch. It felt like yesterday and a lifetime ago, all at once. As she watched, the images slowly chipped away at her self-control. Normally, she had to be the levelheaded one. Since she'd turned eighteen, she'd had a business to run, bills to pay, a mother to care for and a little sister who relied on her to be rock steady and predictable. She was responsible—the practical grown-up. Letting herself get caught up in memories and overrun with emotions was the opposite of practical. So, she didn't. She kept a firm hold on her emotions, for Tess—and herself.

"There will be no calling the lawyer," Audy murmured, his voice thick. "Kent never asked me for a thing while he was alive… I'm not going to turn my back on him or his wishes now that he's gone."

Brooke froze. She wanted to believe him. But…it was two in the morning, and they were both running on fumes, teetering on the verge of tears and processing the loss of their best friends. Now might not be the best time for him to make this decision—especially since he'd been looking for a way out only hours ago. "Audy…"

"I mean it." He sat up, rolling his head slowly, but avoiding her gaze.

"Are you sure?" She cleared her throat,

knowing this wouldn't be an easy conversation. She'd heard him on the phone. He didn't believe he could do this and if he didn't believe it, why should she? But saying that would likely only get his back up and lead to an argument. *I'm too tired for that.* She paused, choosing her words with care. "It will be better for all of us if we get things settled now—before we head back to Garrison." As much as she loved her hometown, she knew bringing home a baby would put her and Audy in the line of fire for every citizen of Garrison with advice or an opinion to offer. *So, basically, the entire town was likely to sound off.* Going home as Joy's sole guardian versus this questionable joint guardianship would save both of them a whole heap of drama. Especially when he did change his mind—again. "You know how people are."

He looked at her then, the muscle in his jaw clenching before he said, "I... Today's been... It's been just about the worst day ever, Brooke." His eyes narrowed slightly. "I'd appreciate it if you'd give me a break on this one."

Give him a break?

"I panicked." He shrugged. "I... It won't

happen again." He stood, running the back of his hand along his neck. "I made a commitment and, no matter what you think, I'm not breaking it."

She took a deep, steadying breath. "Audy, don't you think we should talk about this?"

"No." Hands on hips, he faced her. Everything from the thrust of his chin and the angle of his head to the challenge in his posture screamed defiance.

"Fine." She stood.

"Fine."

Her sigh was pure exasperation. "Good."

He nodded, those eyes of his pinned on her face. "Good."

If he was hoping to get a rise out of her, he would be disappointed. He was being a stubborn fool, putting them both in a no-win situation, but if he was too pigheaded to see that, she wasn't going to waste her time trying to explain it to him. "Great." She shook her head. "I'm going to bed."

"You do that." He didn't exactly snap, but there was a definite edge to his tone. An edge that sounded a little too condescending for her liking.

"Well, as long as I have your permission…"

She shook her head and walked out of the room, back up the stairs and into the small home office. In the gloom, she eyed the horrible fold-out bed in dismay. She loved Dara with all her heart—Kent, too. But there was no way they had thought this out. How had they imagined this would work? That, out of nowhere, Audy would become a completely different man. And, suddenly, she and Audy would get along? *What a joke.*

But, when they'd written the will and she and Audy had signed the paperwork, none of them could have imagined they'd end up here. It was all so horrible and…unexpected. As unexpected as the full-body sob that rolled over her, beyond her control. She covered her mouth with her hands, smothering the sound of loss and pain and shock she could no longer fight. It dragged her under, floundering and struggling to find balance beneath the crushing realities of the day. Dara and Kent. Gone. There would be no more proud-mom texts detailing her daughter's brilliance over things like burping and smiling and other firsts—with photos. There would be no more hours-long FaceTime chats that were of no importance but meant everything. No more of

Dara's mostly inedible "creative" meals and desserts that Kent always managed to choke down while Brooke watched in awe. No more of Dara's laughter or Kent's bad jokes or… Her heart seemed to give, torn wide, the pain sharp and unrelenting. She pressed her eyes shut and leaned against the door. *This isn't helping.*

She took a deep breath. Then another one. *It will be okay.* She could do this. She would do this. Baby Joy might not have her mother and father, but Brooke would make sure Joy grew up surrounded by love. That wasn't the part that worried her. Raising Joy, watching her grow up—that was a gift. Unexpected, but a gift nonetheless.

No, all of her stress could be traced back to one thing—well, one person: Audy Briscoe. She didn't know which was worse—Audy breaking his promise to Kent or Audy keeping his promise. If he broke it, this was over and she wouldn't have to worry about incorporating him into her everyday life. But if he didn't… If this surprising bout of honor stuck and he decided to stick around, Brooke suspected she'd be raising Joy—and Audy Briscoe, too.

She shook her head. "I love you, Dara, but I didn't agree to anything when it came to that man."

Besides, Audy Briscoe is a lost cause.

AUDY HAD NEVER wanted to throw a CD out the window then run over it—a couple of times—before driving off in a cloud of dust as much as he did right this minute. The more they listened to the same chipper nursery rhyme songs, the more appealing the idea became. But Brooke was insistent that they do what they could to keep Joy calm. From music CDs to the toys in her crib to Joy's baby book and a stack of neatly typed check-off schedule forms he had found in a drawer by the back door, they'd taken it all. He wasn't sure whether he was impressed or amused by the detailed What Joy Did Today empty graph with notes on what she'd eaten, how she'd slept, or whether she'd done anything unusual or new. Not only had he found the empty ones, he'd found a slim binder with filled-out forms inside—completed by Dara and the day care—stored in date order. And the baby book? He wasn't sure how Dara managed to be a successful marketing designer and keep it up-to-date. From the looks of it, Dara added to it daily. But, as Brooke had pointed out, all those details might be useful to them in their day-in-and-day-out existence.

That's Dara, Brooke had said, tucking the forms into the binder. *She's a stickler for keeping everything organized.*

Organized? Well, that was one way of putting it. Uptight seemed more like it. Or, as Uncle Felix liked to say, persnickety. *Like Forrest.* Not that Audy was going to say so out loud. He'd only nodded and watched as Brooke put the binder into one of the bags where she'd collected must-have items to take back with them.

He'd never thought of a nursery rhyme CD as a must-have item, but once Brooke had put it on, Joy's fussing stopped and her little pink-ruffled sock-covered feet began to bounce along with the music. That was the only reason he hadn't thrown the CD out the window. About forty minutes into the trip, and before the magical CD had been discovered, things had gotten a little too much for Audy.

Audy hadn't been prepared for Joy getting sad, but he learned real fast that it was a no-go zone for him. Kent had called Joy his "little angel" and Audy got it—she was the sweetest thing he'd ever seen. Seeing her do this flippy thing with her lower lip had sent Audy into a panic. An honest-to-goodness panic. Heart hammering, lungs emptying a what-do-I-do-now-because-something-has-to-be-done-to-make-her-stop-that-now sort of panic. But it got worse.

Her lower lip flipped out *and* her huge brown eyes got all shiny with tears... Tears. Audy didn't do tears. He avoided them altogether. But tears from this honest-to-goodness angelic little doll? No. It couldn't happen. Not here. Not now. Not ever. At least not when he was around. It was enough to have sweat beading on Audy's forehead. Looking away didn't help—he knew she was there, he could feel those big brown eyes staring up at him as she curled into the side of her car seat and pressed her face against the fabric, almost like she was hiding.

Then she sniffed. Then hiccuped. Audy made the terrible mistake of looking down at her... The tip of her little nose turned red and he couldn't take it. He'd never felt so helpless and desperate all at once.

When Joy had started calling, "Ma ma," he was having a hard time breathing. It hurt, something fierce, not to explain things to Joy. *Not that it'd give her any comfort.*

Luckily, that was when Brooke unearthed the CD. If she hadn't? Audy wasn't sure. It likely wouldn't have been pretty. He might not be a baby person, but Joy was about the cutest thing he'd ever set eyes on and he felt certain he'd act like a fool to keep her from being sad. And, come on, that lip-flip thing? *Nope. Nuh-uh.* He could not handle that. Which meant he was stuck with the CD. Over and over.

If he hadn't known the words to "There Was an Old Lady" before this trip—and he hadn't, of course—he knew every single one of them by heart now. Chances were, the song would haunt his dreams that night. The same perky-sounding woman singing into his ear. Playing on repeat. Audy shuddered at the thought. "Twinkle, Twinkle Little Star" and "Bingo" were close seconds, but the only song that made Joy happy and had her little feet bouncing along with the music was "There Was an Old Lady."

Now that Joy's little eyes had drifted shut

and Brooke turned down the music, he could think a little more clearly. Though, he wasn't sure that was any better.

Thoughts of Garrison, his family, co-parenting with Brooke—not to mention Joy herself… No, he didn't want to think right now. From the look on Brooke's face, she was pondering the same worries he was. *Looks like we both need to get out of our head.*

"It never says why she swallowed the fly," he said, without really thinking through what he was saying. "Does it?"

Brooke's astonishment was funny. Sort of. It would have been funnier if her eyes weren't red-rimmed and bloodshot. "What?"

He didn't blame her for being shocked. It wasn't exactly the sort of thing he'd ever imagined saying but…now that it was out there and he had her attention, he kept on going. "The song. It says why she swallowed the spider, bird, cat and dog but…after that, the whole thing goes off the rails." He shook his head, giving her a disbelieving look. "A goat? To catch a dog. What does it mean by *catch*? It's a goat. It doesn't have any hands, so it can't *catch* the dog. It can't catch any-thing."

Brooke was full-on staring at him now, her mouth open.

"And if she swallowed the goat to *eat* the dog, that wouldn't work. A goat will eat just about anything but I've never, in all my days, seen a goat eat a canine. And I've seen my fair share of strange things, let me tell you. As far as I know, a goat is an herbivore. That part and then that last bit?" He shook his head. "About the horse. You're telling me swallowing the *horse* killed her? She's fine swallowing a whole barnyard of livestock—doesn't even bat an eye—but, no, it's the *horse* that finally did her in."

Brooke blinked, her mouth opening and closing and opening again.

"It's far-fetched, is all I'm saying." He shrugged. "She probably had internal hemorrhaging long before she went and swallowed some poor old horse. Not that it's physically possible for anyone to swallow a horse. Not whole, that's for sure. But it'd be pretty hard to swallow any of the other things, really—once you get past the bird. Even then, it depends on what type of bird we're talking about. A finch? Maybe. A blue jay? Unlikely." He paused, then swiveled his thumb in Joy's direction. "Come to think of it, why is this okay for her to hear? All this one thing eating another thing—all inside some poor old woman's body. That'd give a little one nightmares, wouldn't it? Some poor old woman that, for no known reason—none the song ever explains, anyway—ate a dadgummed fly. Plus some."

Brooke made a sound, startled and high-pitched and along the lines of a giggle. She cleared her throat. "Audy…" She stopped.

"Go on. I'm all ears on this. Animals eating animals seems downright inappropriate for baby music. I'm not sure it's good for her, is all I'm trying to say." He tapped along with the music, then stopped and pointed at the radio console. "Oh, and another thing. Which song came first, 'Twinkle, Twinkle Little Star' or the 'Alphabet Song'?" He waited but she'd gone back to silently staring at him, so he went on. "It's the same music. You hear it? Listen." He stopped for a second, then nodded. "Exact. Music. Sure, they changed the lyrics, but the music? Same. Isn't that like… plagiarism or something?"

Another giggle. This time, there was no denying it *was* a giggle.

"What?" After twenty-four hours of tension so thick he'd nearly choked on it, he was all too content to savor Brooke Young's smile. Her laughter, too.

She shook her head, still laughing.

"No, no, now, come on." He was smiling now, he had to. "After listening to the same songs for the last three-plus hours, questions are going to come up. That's all I'm saying." He glanced at Joy sleeping soundly. "She's asleep, so you can say what you're thinking. And don't tell me you weren't thinking the same things—"

"I wasn't." She was a little breathless. "Honest. That… Everything you just said? No. That was an entirely…unique take on—"

"A song kids shouldn't be listening to?" He finished for her.

She grinned. "I never thought I'd hear Audy Briscoe get all worked up over what was suitable music for a baby."

"And why is that?" he countered, glad for the conversation—even one that was mostly nonsense.

"Mr. Break-Into-The-Stockyards-And-Rile-Up-The-Bulls Briscoe? Oh, I don't know. Maybe because I'm more familiar with the

tractor-racing-then-ditch-crashing Audy?"
She sighed.

How did she know about the stockyards?
As far as he knew, that wasn't common
knowledge. Not yet, anyway. It wasn't like
a person could keep a secret in Garrison,
though. Too many eyes and ears and people
with too much time on their hands for that.
"Well, just because I've been known to sow
some wild oats every now and again doesn't
mean I'm okay with a little thing like Joy
being entertained by this sort of thing." He
pointed at the radio. "It's not right, Brooke.
There's nothing wrong with some classic
George Jones or Charley Pride or Patsy Cline.
No dog-eating goats in any of *their* songs."

Brooke smiled again. "No, just drinking
and cheating and heartbreaks."

"You're saying those things are worse than
a little old woman eating a bunch of animals
and dropping dead?" He shook his head.

Her chuckle was soft. "We're almost home
anyway. I doubt you'll have to listen to it for
much longer."

Home. What did that mean now? Part of
him wanted to ask—there was a whole slew
of unanswered questions they'd need to hash

out. But that conversation would wipe away her smile and make things stiff and tension-heavy in no time.

Being an adult isn't all fun and games. It's hard choices and hard conversations. Forrest's voice, all condescending impatience, played through his brain.

Fine. Twenty-seven makes me an adult. I can be a grown-up. No point putting it off, anyway. In thirty minutes, they'd be pulling into town and, he suspected, there'd likely be a welcome party of curious townsfolk eagerly waiting for their arrival.

"How are we doing this?" he asked, diving in. "With Joy, I mean?"

"What?" she asked, tucking a long strand of caramel-colored hair behind her ear.

"You told the lawyer-man you wanted Joy in town and I think you're right about it being the best for her and all." He swallowed, all too aware of the odd expression on her face. "I understand and agree but I want to know where I fit into this…" He nodded at Joy. "On a daily basis, I mean."

"Well…" She shrugged. "I don't know, Audy. How do you envision it? I've got the salon to run. You've got work at the ranch. And your *rodeos*."

He heard the disdain in her voice but let it go. "I figure we should sort this stuff out before we get to your place. You know, come up with some half-with-you and half-with-me sort of time-share thing?"

"Time-share?" she repeated, her eyes narrowing.

"You know what I mean." Why was she being so prickly about this. He'd told her he wasn't backing out and he'd meant it. "We're doing this together. Being co-guardians." He pointed at himself. "With you." He pointed at her. "For her." He pointed at Joy now, swallowing hard. He'd made a promise and he'd keep his word—but that didn't mean he'd made peace with it. Not yet, anyway. "I figure we should sort out how we're doing this."

Brooke blinked.

"Right?" he asked, wishing he was better at reading her. Brooke Young mad? He knew that look. Brooke Young frustrated? He knew that one, too. Those were the two emotions he most often inspired in her—the rest were a mystery. Sort of like Brooke.

He knew her, sort of. He knew what she let

him know—which was what everyone knew. She'd given up college and a life beyond Garrison to take care of her mother, raise her sister and run the family business. That was it. Sure, he'd seen snippets of carefree Brooke when she was with Dara, but she'd shut that down once he took notice.

That was one other thing he did know about Brooke. She didn't like him. She didn't like him and she didn't bother hiding it. He'd never understood why. He'd never treated her any differently than anyone else he'd gone to school with—but, even then, she'd seemed to have an ax to grind with him.

"I guess we should back up." He stared out the front windshield, more and more familiar landmarks passing as they drew closer to Garrison. "I know I'm not one of your favorite people, Brooke. I guess I don't have to be for us to do this. But I'm thinking it'd be easier all around if we could be friends." He glanced at Joy. "For her and for us. What do you say?"

The noise Brooke made now wasn't a giggle. In fact, there was nothing comical about it. Her sigh was all impatience and frustration—Brooke sighed like that a lot when he was around. He was all too familiar with the sound. Brooke wasn't the only one who acted like he was a nuisance—poking at her last nerve. Forrest did, too. *Maybe I should fix the two of them up. Then they could bond over what a total disappointment I am.* He frowned, his hands tightening on the steering wheel.

"I guess we can try." Brooke sounded doubtful.

Hardly the best way for them to start. "And the schedule?" he asked, his gaze darting her way. "What did you have in mind?"

It was Brooke's turn to swallow hard and squirm under his gaze.

The longer he waited for her answer, the redder her cheeks became. And then he knew. "You were still counting on my backing out, weren't you?"

There it was, the flash of defiance on her face as she crossed her arms over her chest. "Yes."

The certainty of her answer was a slap to the face. A jagged knot formed in his throat, making it hard to go on. Did he have his doubts? *Yes.* Was he worried he'd mess this up? *Oh, yeah.* But was he going to try—as hard as he could—to do right by Joy and the promise he'd made Kent and Dara? *Without a doubt.* And he wasn't going to let Brooke's sighs or Forrest's impatience or Joy's lip-flip stop him. Well, Brooke and Forrest, at least. He was having a hard time imagining a time when the sight of Joy's little lip-flip thing didn't gut him on the spot. *I'll figure it out.* One thing at a time. "I'm sorry to disappoint you, Brooke."

"Audy…I don't see how this will work. We live very different lives, you know that," she said, those eyes of hers searching his. "We are different people."

"I do know that." *And if I ever forgot, you'd be sure to remind me.* "But you said you wanted to make sure Joy was settled and there would be no reason the courts would take her away from us. Lawyer-man said they'd want to see us bonded and invested in Joy's life. To do that, I have to be part of her daily life." He paused. The words that bubbled up were childish but they came out anyway. "Unless you've changed *your* mind?"

There was that flash and outrage he knew like the back of his hand. "You'd like that, wouldn't you, Audy Briscoe? If I throw up my hands and walk away, you get off scot-free, don't you? Is that what this is about? If you think my dislike for you can compare to the love I have for Dara, you're more self-centered than I imagined." She was fuming now. "I'm not going to let Joy get taken by strangers just because you're incapable of owning up to any sort of responsibility."

If her quick assumption that he'd been planning to bail on her had stung, this was more like a kick in the chest. By a bull. Did she really think so low of him? What had he *ever* done to her to make her think he was that sort of man? So, he liked to have a good time now and then and up until now, he'd flinched at the idea of children… But surely that wasn't reason enough for her to form this low of an opinion of him? He wasn't heartless. Joy was a cute little thing. Cute and helpless and all that was left of Kent and Dara. The thought of Joy left with strangers that never knew her parents turned his insides cold. He might not be able to handle her tears or her lip-flip but, surprisingly, he didn't want anyone else doing it, either. *Neither did Kent. Nor Dara.*

That steadied him. They knew him and yet this was what they wanted. *He* was who they wanted. And even though the idea of Brooke Young on a daily basis made his jaw clench so tight he worried about cracking his teeth, he'd work through it—because Joy needed him to.

After his folks were gone, Uncle Felix had taken them in—he'd stepped up and done what needed doing. Now it was Audy's turn to do the same. Brooke had made up her mind about him and it was all bad. She, like Forrest, would never give him the benefit of the doubt. Maybe that's why he put on his best grin and turned, all charm. "You're getting the pleasure of my company from here on out—daily. I know a lot of ladies who'd be happy to change places with you." Her lips pressed tightly together and disapproval rolled off her in waves, but he wasn't going to let on that her low opinion got to him. He wasn't about to give her the satisfaction.

Instead, he winked.

CHAPTER FIVE

BROOKE HAD NEVER been so happy to see the slightly sagging front porch of her childhood home. Even better, seeing her younger sister, Tess, sitting on the steps, reading a book. In a patch of sun at her feet sprawled her giant orange-and-white cat, Marzipan. He never strayed far from Tess. It was all so normal. Her sister. The cat. The old tire swing hanging from the pecan tree in the front yard, swaying in the light afternoon breeze. The old family home had never looked so good. She didn't care about the chipping paint, the slightly sagging porch and the missing wooden step. Being here calmed her, instantly. The sense of belonging and comfort, security and permanence. Since yesterday's phone call, things had flipped upside down. Nothing had made sense. Nothing. What sort of world existed without Dara and Kent? It had been beyond imagining. *But now, it was time for reality.*

Tess looked up as the truck slowed, set her book aside and stood.

Brooke had rehearsed this in her mind. What she'd say. How she'd say it—maintaining her in-control older-sister vibe while informing her little sister that things had taken a somewhat unexpected, and permanent, turn

But the minute she stepped out of the truck, Tess was launching herself at her. And Brooke caught her—like she'd done since Tess was a baby.

"Brookie, are you okay?" Tess's voice was muffled against her neck. "I'm so sorry. So, so sorry. I'm in shock." She sniffled, her thin arms wrapped around her—with no signs of easing. "I can't believe it."

"I know." Brooke closed her eyes and held on to her sister. Tears burned, threatening to slip between her eyelids, but she tried to hold back.

"I got your texts and I just… I mean, I'm still… I…" Tess's hold loosened and she stared up at Brooke with huge owl-like eyes, tears flowing freely down her cheeks. "I mean, it's Dara."

"I know." Maybe it was the pain and despair on her little sister's face or it was the way that Tess was clinging to Brooke's hand or that Tess was saying all the things Brooke couldn't say because saying them would make her cry—but something inside seemed to shift and open the floodgates she'd been fighting since she'd answered her phone yesterday morning. The tears started. All she could do was cry. And cry. With no sign of stopping. "I'm sorry," Brooke said, frantically wiping at the tears streaming down her cheeks. "I've been okay—"

"Why are you apologizing?" Tess asked, crying anew. "Because you're crying? Brooke, it's, like, totally normal." She sniffed, giving her sister a look. "If you didn't cry, it'd be way weird and I'd totally freak out. Besides, you have to or it'll build up inside and make you sick. You're supposed to cry when someone you love dies." She was hugging her again. "And you loved Dara."

"I did. I do." Tess didn't understand. It was Brooke's job to be the strong one, always. Crying wasn't something she did—not normally. But there wasn't a single thing about the last twenty-four hours that she'd call normal. And since there was no stopping the sudden outpouring of emotions, she gave in, embracing her little sister's wisdom and ignoring everything else.

Until Joy started crying.

"Oh, right, poor little thing." Tess instantly let go and hurried to the truck. "Hi, Joy. You remember me, of course. Your most favorite… cousin in the whole wide world," Tess cooed. "Are you ready to get out of that nasty-wasty car seat?"

Brooke followed her little sister, watching as Joy's tears instantly vanished and a beautiful smile took their place. Tess had babysat for Joy when Dara and Kent had come to visit, but there was no way Joy could remember that. At that point, she'd been a teeny-tiny thing, sleeping almost the entire weekend that Tess had carried her around like her own doll. But, as far-fetched as it seemed for Joy to remember any of that, there was no denying the baby girl's response to Tess.

Joy made a series of pitched noises and gibberish with a big grin on her face.

"I bet." Tess climbed up and into the truck, unbuckling the car seat and reaching for the baby. "Let's get down. You can meet Marzipan and we will get you a snack and make your room pretty and have all sorts of fun."

Tess didn't seem aware of the hand Audy placed under her elbow to help her down from the truck…or the incredibly endearing smile on his face as he watched Tess with Joy.

Oh, that smile. She hated how it—he—could make her feel. There were times she wished she didn't dislike the man as much as she did. *Too bad he makes it so easy.* She tore her gaze away, his snarky, *I know a lot of ladies who'd be happy to change places with you*, and cocky wink had been enough to get her blood boiling all over again. They were…stuck together.

Stuck was exactly the right word. *Stuck with Audy Briscoe.* While she had yet to come to fully consider all that that implied, she wasn't feeling very optimistic. How were the two of them going to work together? *Assuming he does stick around.* He wouldn't. His cocky declaration was pure defiant push-back at her honest take on how things would wind up.

Lucky for her, Joy chose that moment to giggle, stopping any further mental rants about her predicament. The baby's laugh was the sort of gleeful sound that warmed the heart—free and easy and full of sheer delight. Before she knew it, Brooke was smiling right along with Joy and Tess, caught up in the baby's wide-eyed sweetness.

"I think she likes my shirt," Tess said, using a baby voice.

Joy giggled again, one hand patting the stitched flowers decorating the front of Tess's shirt. "Ba ba ba," she said, her chubby little fingers running through the pom-pom in the center of a flower.

"I think she likes you." Brooke's smile only grew at the way Joy stared up at Tess before resting her head against her shoulder.

"Who doesn't?" Tess teased, patting Joy on the back. "I'd like to think I'm totally likable."

"What do they say about kids and dogs?" Audy joined in. "They're the best judge of character?"

That was the moment Tess realized that Audy was standing there, watching—and smiling that way-too-appealing smile. Brooke sighed.

"Hey… Hi, Mr. Briscoe," Tess mumbled, her cheeks going pink.

Audy burst out laughing. "Mr. Briscoe?" He shook his head. "Now, hold on there. I appreciate the respect and all, but let's stick with Audy."

Tess's cheeks went from pink to scarlet. "'Kay."

Audy nodded, pushing his cowboy hat back on his forehead. "Guess I'll get things unloaded, then we can work out a schedule." He barely glanced Brooke's way before heading around and leaning over the truck bed.

"A schedule?" Tess whispered, her eyes wider and rounder than ever.

As far as Tess knew, Audy was no longer in the picture. That's what Brooke had texted her—before Audy had told her otherwise. Brooke sighed. "I'll explain in a bit." This time, she hoped she'd be able to stick to the script she'd come up with. Tess was a gentle soul, she always had been. Instead of flipping out over the addition of Joy to the household, she'd welcomed the baby with open arms. Brooke had expected as much. But Audy? She didn't want Audy to be a fixture in her little sister's life.

Tess was a teenager and Audy was…well, he was a lot. Once the shock of how ridiculously good-looking he was wore off—assuming it wore off, that is—there were still the layers of charm and charisma to work through. But that was all there was to the man, hot air and good looks.

And there was also Tess's crush on Beau to consider. No. Just because Audy was around didn't mean Tess needed to spend time with Beau. Her little sister needed to focus on her grades, not getting moon-eyed over some boy. Their parents had met in high school. For Brooke, that was all the motivation she needed to keep Tess away from Beau. No one should end up as miserable and alone as their mother had. *No one.* Definitely not Tess. Her little sister would be the first Young woman in four generations to leave Garrison and have a bright future far away from their small town.

"Where is this going?" Audy asked, the plastic-wrapped pieces of Joy's crib tucked under one arm like the whole thing weighed next to nothing. But the taut ripple of muscles in his arm said otherwise.

She shook her head. *I am not looking or thinking about his arm or his muscles.* "This way." With a wave of her hand, she led him across the well-worn pavers that made up the uneven path from the sidewalk to the front steps. "Watch your step. There's a board missing," she pointed out, hurrying up the stairs and across the wide porch to the front door.

"That'll need fixing," he said, hopping over the lack of step with ease. "Before the home visit."

"I'll take care of it," she snapped. She hadn't meant to snap, not really.

"All righty, then." His brows shot up and the corner of his mouth curved just enough to set Brooke's nerves on edge. Again.

She held the old screen door wide, waited for him to pass, then followed. She led him past the formal living room that had remained untouched since her mother's passing and took a left down the hall. When she came to the spare bedroom, she opened the door—and smiled. "Looks like my sister got a head start in here." The walls were bare, all the knickknacks and smaller pieces of furniture had been removed. Only the wooden-framed four-poster bed remained, and even that had the sheets stripped and the quilt folded up on the foot of the mattress.

"She's a junior?" Audy asked. "Like Beau? Your little sister?"

"Tess?" Brooke nodded.

"Tess…" His whole face changed. Like he'd just found the final piece of a puzzle or made a surprise discovery. "*She's*… Right. Of course. Her name is Tess."

Brooke stopped, her concern mounting as a cheerful smile creased his undeniably easy-to-look-at face. "Yes… Why?"

"Hmm?" His gaze flitted her way and his smile dimmed just a bit. "Oh, no reason. Just wanted to get her name right, is all."

Brooke didn't believe that for one second.

"Where are we setting this up?" He stood, sizing up the space. "If we get the bed out of here, it'd fit perfectly on that wall." His gaze swiveled her way.

She was still trying to figure out what had been going through Audy's brain to make him smile like that. She didn't like not knowing… especially if it had something to do with Tess. And, clearly, it did.

"Brooke?" he asked. Those sky blue eyes pinned her.

"Yes," she managed, clearing her throat against the sudden tightness pressing in. "Against the wall makes sense. That way she will have plenty of room to play."

"I guess I'll need to look into getting her

a room set up at the ranch. Don't want her sleeping on the floor or anything." He was teasing but it wasn't funny.

It was almost impossible to imagine Joy on Briscoe Ranch. More specifically, Audy taking care of Joy... Unless he was planning on enlisting help? But who, was the question. She didn't relish the idea of him handing off Joy to someone she might not approve of. Like his friend RJ. "I feel like we should establish some ground rules we need to go over, so we're on the same page."

"I can't wait to hear this." One brow cocked.

"No...no drinking or rodeo or entertaining... No lady friends." She put her hands on her hips and waited. There was plenty of gossip surrounding Audy and not all of it was about whatever mayhem he'd been causing. No, there was a fair amount of talk about who he'd been seen out and about with. His little comment about plenty of ladies willing to take her place? It was true. "Not when you have Joy, that is."

Those blue blue eyes didn't waver but the corner of his mouth kicked up a little. "I can't have Miss Ruth over? Now and again, she'll stop by with some oatmeal raisin cookies, my favorite, and we play some Skip Bo—"

"No, Audy." She focused on moving the bed, not how amused he looked. "That's not what I mean." Brooke reached for the corner of the mattress and gave it a tug but it didn't budge. She tried again and this time it moved so suddenly, she almost fell over.

"Oops," Audy chuckled, holding the corner of the mattress up. "So, what you mean is—no dates."

She caught herself before falling onto the mattress and turned, nodding her thanks. "No. I mean, yes, no dates." Together, they carried the mattress out into the hallway and propped it against the wall.

"What about you?" Audy asked, following her back into the bedroom.

"What about me?" She stooped, peering under the bed and running her hand along the screws holding the frame together. "I need a screwdriver." She headed back down the hall and into the kitchen—where Tess was dancing with a smiling Joy in her arms. "You two good?"

"Two girls, living it up." Tess nodded, spinning and making Joy giggle.

"I mean the same rules apply to you?" Audy asked as he followed her. "Fair is fair."

Brooke pulled open the kitchen drawer that held every bit of overflow in the room. From twist ties to clothespins, batteries to rolls of tape, and an assortment of useful tools. "There it is." She grabbed the screwdriver and turned to find Audy waiting. She sighed. "How about we get this bed taken care of."

"As soon as you answer the question, we'll finish. Or are you trying to dodge my question? Seems to me we should *both* follow these ground rules of yours." He paused. "So, we both agree—no bringing dates back to the house when we have Joy."

"Wait, Brooke? Are you finally going to start dating again?" Tess stopped dancing to stare at her, openmouthed.

Audy was staring at her now, too. No, more like studying her. *What does that look mean? Was he laughing at her? In shock? Not in the least bit surprised? Not that she cared. Her life was in order and she had a very clear set of priorities. Dating wasn't one of them. Now, with Joy, chances were that wouldn't change anytime soon. She was okay with that. More than okay with that.

Audy still didn't get it. "Right now, my focus is on incorporating Joy into our lives,

Tess. Making sure she feels at home. Which is something you might want to think about, too, Audy." She crossed her arms over her chest and asked, "But, since you're so worried about dating, we might as well get a schedule in place so you can make sure to rearrange your social calendar accordingly." The sooner that was done, the sooner Audy could go and Brooke would have room to breathe again.

IT WASN'T THE first time Audy found himself admiring Brooke Young. There was no way—no way—she didn't have suitors lined up around the block. And he wouldn't believe anyone who tried to tell him otherwise… Except, maybe, Brooke's own sister, that is.

Brooke sat, with her long braid over her shoulder, at the kitchen table with her calendar square between them.

Her eyes were clear, light hazel and fringed with dark lashes. She shied away from makeup—something he'd noticed. The rose on her cheeks was natural, not powder. And there was no need to add color to her lips, either. They were full and red and…

"How does this look?" Brooke asked,

glancing up from the calendar and tucking a loose strand behind her ear.

He cleared his throat and leaned forward to see what she'd come up with. She was using a pink highlighter for her days and a blue highlighter for his. "It looks like a spiderweb." He shook his head.

"Does that mean it won't work for you?" She pinched the bridge of her nose. "It's two days on and two days off, like you suggested."

"No, now, I didn't say it wouldn't work." It had been his idea… But that had been before he'd taken a look at what that actually meant. Now those little pink and blue marks seemed downright ominous and far too permanent. "It's fine," he lied.

Fine? It wasn't fine. He didn't know a thing about babies. But now, in two days, he was supposed to take over the feeding and cleaning and…whatever else little Joy needed to be happy. He frowned. What if she wasn't happy? Here, she had Tess—who made little Joy light up like a Christmas tree. Out at his place, she'd have…who? He better think of something, and fast, or he'd have two days of dealing with that little lip-flip thing.

There was no way he could handle that for two whole days.

"Audy?" Brooke asked, her voice low.

"Hmm?" He tore his gaze away from the pink-and-blue map of his future. "Sorry, did you say something?"

"I did." Brooke sat back in the kitchen chair. "Everything all right?"

Was she serious? But something stopped him from admitting he was freaking out over the whole plan-the-next-month-of-their-lives thing that was happening. Not to mention the whole taking-care-of-baby-Joy thing. "Taking it all in." He did his best to muster a smile.

"Is that it? You look a little pale." She stood. "Would you like some lemonade?"

"Sounds good." He cleared his throat against the tightness, fully aware of the assessing way she was looking at him.

Brooke took her time pouring them each a tall glass of lemonade, glancing out the back door at Tess and Joy sitting on the wooden porch swing, then carried the glasses back to the table. She waited until he took a sip to ask, "Have you ever changed a diaper or had to treat diaper rash?"

He inhaled a good bit of the sip he'd taken,

hacking and coughing until she pounded on his back. Diaper rash? He'd never heard of it, let alone *treated* it. "No," he managed tightly.

"I'm guessing you've never made a bottle, either?" she asked, standing at his side.

"You'd guess correctly." There was no missing the snap to his words. "What are you getting at, Brooke?"

She sat, pinching the bridge of her nose again and staring at the brightly marked calendar. "Have you ever held a baby?"

He'd held Joy once—maybe twice. "Yes."

She glared at him. "Other than when Dara or Kent made you hold Joy?"

"Your point is that I'm unqualified for this?" He sighed. "I said as much back in Houston, didn't I?" He took a sip of lemonade, watching the fluid shift of emotions on her face. "But—"

"I think we should hold off on this." She tapped the calendar with the end of the highlighter. "Until you've learned how to do those things, and bought the things she'll need, I think it makes more sense for Joy to stay here."

He frowned. "Not that I'm trying to pick a fight here, but how am I supposed to learn how to do any of those things if she's here and I'm there?"

Brooke propped her elbow on the table and rested her chin, looking beyond tired. "Maybe…" She swallowed. "Maybe some mornings you can come over and help with the morning routine and other days you can come over in the evenings and help give her a bath and put her to bed." Her gaze darted his way. "What do you think?"

He was thinking that, for all her crusty exterior and judgy looks and condescension in her voice, Brooke Young was a decent person. She didn't like him, so it wasn't a huge leap to assume she didn't want him around. And yet, here she was, offering to teach him everything he needed to know to care for Joy. "I think I owe you my thanks, Brooke. Sincerely. And I heartily accept your proposal." He nodded. "For the time being, that is."

"Two weeks." She tapped the calendar and used the pink highlighter to circle the day, exactly two weeks from today, on the calendar. "That should be more than enough time."

Two weeks? It didn't seem long enough to him, but he'd take it. He nodded.

"Good." She stood, returning the calendar

to its hook on the wall. "If you're free, you can stay and have dinner and help out tonight?"

Meaning plans for a long horseback ride, a cold beer and some time to himself wasn't going to happen. "Sounds good." He stood, carrying his empty glass to the counter. "Need help with anything?"

She handed him the screwdriver.

"Got it." He took the tool, his gaze catching on Tess and Joy. "Your sister... Is she seeing anyone?" The mounting concern on Brooke's face had him rushing to add, "My brother Beau has mentioned Tess."

Brooke's eyes widened. "Oh?" She turned, her expression softening as she took in the scene.

Tess had Joy in her lap, one foot keeping the swing moving in an easy rhythm. From here, he couldn't see what Tess was pointing at, only that Joy was listening and watching every word the young girl was saying.

But Brooke's reaction ate at him. "You didn't think I...I was asking about your little sister..." He couldn't finish that sentence.

Brooke's cheeks were flaming.

"Right." Audy shook his head. "Right. I

keep forgetting how low your opinion is of me." He spun on his heel and headed for the bedroom.

It didn't take long for him to break down the old wooden four-poster bed. Once he'd carried all the pieces onto the back porch, he put together Joy's crib and wiped it down with the disinfecting wipes they'd brought back with them.

He stepped back, pleased with his work, and ran a hand along the back of his neck. A crib. He was putting together a baby bed. Him. Audy Good-Time Briscoe. Daredevil. A party in a Stetson. The go-to for fun cowboy. He was putting together a baby bed. And now that he was staring at it, his heart was thumping against his rib cage, so loud his pulse echoed in his head.

I'm glad you think I can do this, Kent. Audy shook his head, eyeing the bags he and Brooke had unloaded before they'd sat down with the calendar—when Brooke had, once more, made him feel lower than dirt. He'd never had anyone look at him with such… such resentment before. Was *resentment* even the right word? That was part of it, though why she'd resent him had origins just as mysterious as her total dislike for him. Brooke would be happy if he walked out and never looked back.

It wasn't the first time the urge to run overtook him, but it seemed stronger this time. It wasn't just because Brooke had no faith in him or that Joy made him nervous or that he had no idea what the contents of half of these bags were for…it was the weight of responsibility he now felt for someone and something beyond his control. That was it.

If he was going to hold up his end of this bargain, he was going to have to rethink who he was. How could he go out dancing and carrying on when he had a child, a sweet angel of a little girl, looking to him for guidance? The very notion was ridiculous.

From the corner of one of the bags, Audy spied Joy's epic-sized baby book. He pulled it out, sat on the wood floor and propped himself against the wall, and ran his hand over the pink embossed cover. His calloused fingers snagged a thread on the lace binding. *Seems right.* With a shake of his head, he carefully detached the thread without further pulling or fraying the delicate fabric.

He didn't linger over the first few pages—

one look at the proud new parents cradling their brand-new baby had him flipping ahead. He remembered that day. He and Brooke had sat on opposite sides of the waiting room, eager for news of Dara and the baby. Funny how, then, he'd just accepted her hostility as who she was. It was easier that way, not caring about why she was hostile but enjoying the rise he could get from her when he was in the right mood.

He kept flipping until he saw Dara's even handwriting. He'd laughed at the extreme thoroughness of Dara's notes but now he was thankful. He skipped the first few months but started reading when Joy turned eight months. It wasn't exactly scintillating reading, but it was educational.

Babies didn't do much.

Sure, they were cute and they could make a whole lot of noise but that was about it. If he could get a handle on Joy's routine, maybe he'd feel less out-of-control.

From the looks of it, Dara was big on routines. Same times, every day. Breakfast—which she listed. Normal diaper or cause for concern. He frowned. What was concerning about a diaper...? Then he realized she was referring to what was in the diaper and not the diaper itself, and shuddered. *Moving on.*

From nine to five it read, See Day Care Sheet. He set the baby book aside and rummaged through the bags until he'd found the binder with the day care sheets all neatly organized in date order. Back and forth, baby book and day care sheets, he scanned over page after page.

"Mr.—Audy..." Tess's voice wavered, loaded with nerves.

He looked up, giving the girl a winning smile. "What can I do for you, Tess?"

She blushed fiercely, her gaze shifting to the floor at her feet. "Oh, nothing... You don't have to do anything." She glanced his way. "Brooke said she thinks Joy is hungry..."

"Right." *Let the lessons begin.* He closed both books, stood and stacked them on top of the chest of drawers he'd left in the room. "You have much experience with babies, Tess?" he asked. "'Cause, I confess, I feel like I'm about to go toe-to-toe with a rattlesnake. A cute one, sure, but unpredictable and potentially dangerous."

Tess giggled. "Joy is the sweetest baby I have ever met." She shrugged. "I babysit a lot. If there's a baby in Garrison, I've probably watched it a time or two."

"So, what you're saying is…you are a baby expert?" If he could get Tess to school him on all things baby, he'd have less time with Brooke. And, right about now, he didn't think he had the patience to face a hungry baby and Brooke's ever-present irritation.

"I did have to take a class at the community center." She nodded. "They taught me all the basic stuff and emergency training, too. Even baby CPR."

Just the thought of giving Joy CPR had his palms sweaty and his stomach in his throat. There was nothing in Dara's notetaking about the need to give Joy CPR. He sure didn't want to find himself in that situation. "Classes?" He might just have to look into that.

"Yes, sir." She smiled. "But you don't have to worry Mr.—Audy, I'll help out with Joy. You'll see, once you get the hang of it, it's pretty easy."

He shook his head. "If you say so."

"I do." Her confidence was surprisingly reassuring.

"Well, all right, then. I appreciate the vote

of confidence, Tess. I truly do." He rubbed his hands together. "Let's get this baby fed."

She giggled again, sounding every bit the teenager, before heading back down the hall to the kitchen. "I believe in you," Tess said, shooting him a smile over her shoulder.

That smile had Audy's thoughts instantly shifting to his little brother Beau.

Beau was all school and athletics and it had paid off with a full scholarship to the University of Texas after he graduated the following year. The only things Beau showed interest in besides his schoolwork and athletics were his new truck and Clement, his horse, and Tess Young. While his little brother engaged regularly with his truck and Clement, he'd never made a move on the girl he was so clearly sweet on.

But was Tess interested in his brother?

The last thing he wanted to do was encourage Beau to pursue someone uninterested.

"There they are." Brooke had Joy on her hip, rocking back and forth on her feet, all smiles. "Dinner is just about ready."

Audy glanced at the clock. "Six o'clock." He nodded as he visualized the schedule on page after page of Joy's baby book. Same time, every day. "Dinnertime."

Brooke shot him a questioning look.

He smiled, oddly pleased that he'd taken the time to read as much as he had. There was no way he was ready to dive into this whole baby thing on his own, but he had the feeling Dara had left a pretty solid how-to manual for baby Joy. If he could take some of the classes Tess was talking about, he wouldn't have to rely on Brooke for much at all—which was the way he'd prefer it. As long as Joy kept the lip-flip thing to a minimum, he'd be okay— even if Brooke and those clear hazel eyes of hers told him otherwise. Contrary to what she believed, this wasn't about him proving her wrong...

But that was definitely a perk.

CHAPTER SIX

GARRISON FAMILY GROCERY was surprisingly busy—meaning there was no way she'd be able to sneak in and out undetected. Especially not with Joy and Audy in tow. She tried not to think about the neatly organized stack of diapers lining the bottom of Joy's closet back in Houston. She didn't know how he'd missed them, but he had. Now, with only the few diapers remaining in Joy's diaper bag, their stock was running dangerously low. So, here they were, a few hours home, putting Joy's car seat into the grocery cart and setting a brisk pace as they ventured inside.

It had been too much to hope that Audy would offer to watch Joy for the thirty minutes it'd take Brooke to get the shopping trip done. Just her suggestion had turned him a shade of green that'd reminded her of pea soup. Tess had taken pity on him and offered to babysit, but Tess had a pre-calculus test tomorrow—her weakest subject—so she needed to study. Besides, Brooke didn't want to set a precedent of Tess covering for Audy. Tess was a teenager. Audy was Joy's legal co-guardian.

Brooke made a silly face at Joy, earning a delighted giggle from the baby, and kept her head down. She ignored the looks they were getting and headed straight for the baby aisle in their local grocery store.

"They were in a red-and-white bag," Audy offered, hands on his hips, as he stared blankly at the wall of diaper packages.

Brooke didn't acknowledge him. *Red-and-white bag.* The fact that he hadn't at least taken note of the diaper brand shouldn't bother her… but it did. "Cuddlers. Cuddlers, size two."

"Diapers come in sizes?" Audy leaned closer to the packages, eyes narrowed. "Well, lookee there."

She managed not to laugh, but no luck holding back her smile. Audy seemed sincerely surprised and more than a little overwhelmed by this new information. There was something alarmingly adorable about Mr. Too-Confident-For-My-Own-Good looking so lost and befuddled.

But as soon as Audy's attention wandered and he realized there was a handful of very curious Garrison residents watching the three of them, his I'm-charming-and-I-know-it smile was back in place.

Because he has an audience.

"You got that?" he asked.

"Yes." She pulled two packages of diapers off the shelf and put them in their cart.

"Making sure," he murmured.

She glanced his way—and rolled her eyes. He wasn't watching her, he was all smiles for Judy Eldridge. "Thanks."

The snap in her voice grabbed his attention.

At least he had the decency to look a little embarrassed.

"Ma ma ma," Joy announced, at the top of her lungs. She smiled, clapped her hands and bounced her sock-covered feet before adding, "Bi bub u…" and then another gleeful shriek.

Brooke laughed.

Audy didn't. He eyed Joy warily, taking two steps away from the grocery cart. "We ready?" he asked.

"Wipes." Brooke pointed.

"Is there a size difference for them, too?"

He tipped his hat back on his head, looked at her and waited.

"No." She smiled. "But the brand in her bag was for sensitive skin." She scanned the neatly lined-up boxes of baby wipes. "The last thing we want to do is give her diaper rash."

"No, no, let's not do that," Audy agreed, stepping closer to the shelf and reading each label carefully.

Brooke couldn't stop smiling now. Apparently, the fear of diaper rash was stronger than the need to charm the growing number of women now inhabiting the baby aisle.

"Those?" Audy asked, staring up.

"Yes." Brooke stepped forward, standing on her tippy-toes to reach the single package—on the top shelf. She stretched but... "I can't reach them." She turned to find Audy, arms crossed over his chest, wearing an all-too-smug smile.

"You don't say?" he asked. He stepped closer, reached up and retrieved the bag. "Here you go."

It was only because all eyes were on them that she didn't snatch the package from his hands. She was tempted, mighty tempted, but she decided to go another route. "Why, thank you, Audy," she gushed, smiling broadly. "Aren't you a gentleman?"

Audy's smile froze and a deep crease formed between his brows. If he'd been wary before, he looked downright terrified now.

Brooke wasn't having to work at smiling anymore.

"It is the two of you," Miss Ruth, who'd just steered her cart around the end of the aisle, said loudly. "I heard you two were here and had to come see this with my own eyes." She looked back and forth between them. "Of course, we've all heard about...Kent and Dara now. I am sorry."

Brooke found herself pulled into Miss Ruth's rough embrace.

"I was just beside myself when word reached us." Miss Ruth released her. "I just knew that's what'd taken the two of you off like that. Together, no less." She patted Audy on the cheek. "Is this...is this their little one?" She leaned over Joy. "I can see that it is."

Brooke nodded.

"I guess it'll take them some time to get family notified and travel arranged to get this little angel." Miss Ruth cooed. "It's good of you two to take her in until then."

"Ba ba ba," Joy said, grabbing her toes and nodding her head.

It was Joy's animated babbling that drew the other women closer. Dorris Kaye, with her perfect white pin curls and bright floral dress, shook a bottle of Tylenol over her head like a rattle. Miss Ruth's red lipstick made her smile a little clown-like but Joy didn't seem to mind. Judy Eldridge and her mother, Barbara, oohed and aahed, and Joy giggled and chattered and seemed quite content to be the center of attention.

Brooke glanced Audy's way... And did a double take. He was studying Joy. Not in outright fear or panic, which had been the trend up until now, but curiosity and, maybe, interest.

"Audy?" The male voice rang out over the chorus of women cooing over baby Joy.

She didn't recognize the voice, but Audy did. His jaw tightened and his posture stiffened before he turned. She did her best to sneak a peek around Miss Ruth's fluffed and sprayed hair, but that wasn't going to happen so she moved around the grocery cart under the guise of checking its contents... It was a flimsy excuse since the cart only contained two packages of diapers and one bag of wipes but it was all she had to work with.

Forrest Briscoe's expression was a mix of confusion and anger. "You're back?" he asked, his jaw going rigid—just like Audy's.

There's no missing they're brothers.

"I was going to call you," Audy said, running a hand along the back of his neck.

"It would've been nice." Forrest sighed. "I'm guessing you got everything worked out, then?" His gaze darted beyond Audy and landed on her. "Hold on." He brushed past Audy and headed straight for her. "Brooke, I'm so sorry. When Audy told me…" He shook his head. "I know how close you and Dara were. I can only imagine the hurt you're feeling."

An unexpected lump lodged itself in her throat, forcing her to nod in reply.

It was Joy's sneeze, and the half a dozen women that said "Bless you" that had Forrest staring at the grocery cart. For a second, he went into full statue-mode—as if he was scrambling to make sense of what he saw. "Is this their little girl?" he asked.

"Joy," Brooke murmured.

"She looks an awful lot like Dara." Forrest's brow furrowed. "Audy said something about concerns over the guardians—"

"Forrest," Audy interrupted, shooting a pointed glance at the women.

Four members of the Garrison Ladies Guild. The Garrison Ladies Guild did all sorts of wonderful things for the community. From maintaining the gardens around the courthouse and in the park around The First Tree, to selling jam and jellies at the spring fair, making quilts for the Quilt and Wildflower Weekend and the Founder's Day celebrations, to providing cookies and hot chocolate to every participant in the Garrison Christmas Parade. But the Garrison Ladies Guild was also known for one other reason—gossip. If a mother wanted to fix up her son or daughter, these women were the ones who'd know who was available and have the scoop on any past transgressions of said potential suitor. They filed away information and were likely listening in on everything Audy and his brother were saying.

"Right." Forrest's lips pressed flat.

"You're welcome to come back to the house with us? I'll make some coffee." Brooke glanced back and forth between the two of them.

Forrest had turned the full force of his

laser-focused stare upon Audy. "That'd be real nice, Brooke. I'll finish up here and meet you over there." He turned. "That okay?"

That was the first time Brooke saw Beau Briscoe standing at the end of the aisle.

Oh, no. She blinked. She suspected things had the potential to get super awkward between Audy and Forrest. She could be wrong but it didn't appear that Audy had filled Forrest in on the fact that he was Joy's co-guardian and that the Briscoe family home would be receiving some big-time babyproofing within the next week. Definitely awkward. Add to that her sister's reaction to Beau Briscoe walking in their front door? *It's going to be a long evening.*

"Sure." But Beau didn't look too happy about it.

"Ten minutes?" Brooke suggested.

Forrest and Beau didn't linger but it took a good five minutes to extricate Joy, and their cart, from the doting women. After that, she grabbed a few more things, then steered the cart to the register.

"What's the pie for?" Audy asked, eyeing the delicious-smelling pastry she'd picked up.

"Company is coming," she explained, putting the rest of the items on the counter.

"Company, as in Forrest and Beau?" He frowned. "They're just my brothers."

"I was raised by a Southern woman, Audy Briscoe. You keep an orderly house, a tidy yard, look out for your neighbors and always have something to feed company when they stop by—even unannounced." Her mother had lived by those words, and Brooke's grandmother before that. Brooke had never stopped long enough to consider doing things differently—mostly because she didn't have time. Time was always in short supply, any normal day scheduled down to the minute. It was just the way things were—and had been since she'd turned eighteen. It worked for her so there was no point in changing it now. Kind of like having something on hand for company. It was just the way things were. "If you don't want pie, I'll split your piece between your brothers."

"I didn't say that." He shrugged. "It's just… it's a treat, is all." He started bagging up their items. "Mighty generous."

Brooke waited. "And?" Any minute, he'd drop the punch line.

Those crystal-blue eyes locked on her face. "No. I mean it. Thank you."

"Oh." Something about the way he was looking at her was unnerving. "You… You're welcome."

"Besides, if Forrest's mouth is full of apple pie, he'll have a hard time yelling at me for not telling him we're co-guardians of Joy." The corner of Audy's mouth kicked up, but there was no sign of his usual bravura. If anything, he seemed to be looking to her for reassurance.

But how could she reassure him when she was still convinced he was going to throw up his hands and walk away, leaving her and Joy on their own.

AUDY GLANCED AT the clock on the wall again. When Brooke had initially invited his brothers over, he'd been irritated. But the more time that passed, the more it went from irritated to angry. He didn't like being handled and he'd been handled a whole lot the last couple of days. The accident. Joy. Staying at Kent and Dara's. Being prodded into going to the grocery store… If she'd let him stay behind to fix the step as he'd suggested, none of this would be happening. He'd tell Forrest on his own terms, someplace where he didn't feel out of sorts, without an audience—without Brooke and those judgy hazel eyes of hers.

"The dessert plates are in there, Audy." Brooke nodded at the far cupboard, holding Joy in her lap for a bottle. "There should be enough for all of us."

"All of who?" Tess asked, coming into the kitchen. Her hair was pulled up into a messy twist with a pencil through it. "Hey, Joy. Did you have fun at the store?"

"Half of the Ladies Guild was there." Brooke peered down at Joy. "She had them all eating out of the palm of her hand."

"Because she is the prettiest, sweetest and happiest little angel-baby ever." Tess's enthusiasm had Joy pushing her bottle away and reaching for Tess. "You want me?" she asked.

"Go ahead." Brooke stood, let Tess take her spot and placed Joy in Tess's arms.

Watching them with Joy made it look easy. Almost like Joy wasn't breakable and droppable and capable of doing that lip-flip thing that triggered his flight mode.

"Are they coming over?" Tess asked, eyeing the pie. "They took one look at you and they can't stay away." She wrinkled her nose at Joy, then made a silly face. "Isn't that right?"

Joy let go of the bottle long enough to smile up at Tess.

Audy was pretty sure any faces he made at Joy would make her start caterwauling. He was pretty sure she could sense his fear.

"No." Brooke opened a drawer. "Forrest and Beau are stopping by."

The change in the room was instantaneous. Brooke was counting forks out of the drawer at snail-speed while Tess looked like an animal caught in a trap—fully prepared to gnaw off her leg if need be. But he had no idea why Brooke was avoiding her little sister's gaze or what had Tess in a full-blown panic—none whatsoever.

"What?" Tess whispered. "Here? Here *here*?" The last "here" was more squeak than anything. "Brooke." She shifted Joy to one arm and reached up to run a hand over her hair, squeaking again when her fingers encountered the pencil. "But…I… I mean…" She sort of sputtered to a stop, her eyes as round as the dessert plates he was carrying to the table.

Audy wasn't sure what to do, only that he felt the need to do something. "Is…is there a problem? Something I can do?" He looked back and forth between the sisters.

"No!" The word erupted from Tess, startling everyone in the room—including Joy. "Sorry," she murmured, bouncing Joy and saying in singsong, "I'll just…stay in my room." Tess swallowed. "I have so…so much studying to do." Her cheeks were growing pinker by the minute but she kept on singing her words for Joy's sake. "Like, way more than…than I thought, I mean." She cleared her throat.

"I doubt they'll be here all that long," he offered, puzzled over her reaction. "They're only coming so I can share the news about Joy. Chances are, that'll put a bee in Forrest's hat and he and Beau will skedaddle before you know it."

"Oh, well… That's family…stuff." Tess's gaze darted to the front door. "Let's finish your bottle, Joy… I can even skip pie—"

The knock on the door had Tess sitting bolt upright. "They're here?" she whispered.

"I'd imagine so." Audy's answer was cautious, his gaze bouncing to Brooke for clarification.

But it seemed Brooke was avoiding his gaze, too. For some reason, those forks she was collecting were downright riveting. "Audy, do you mind getting the door?"

He did mind. He also minded that she'd invited his brothers over. Yes, he needed to give Forrest the lowdown on what was happening. But he wasn't thrilled about doing it here or having her present—judging him. *Because she's always judging.* And it got to him far more than he wanted to admit. Maybe that was why he pulled the door open with a little more force than necessary.

Forrest's and Beau's eyebrows shot up in surprise.

"Did we come at a bad time?" Forrest asked.

Beau didn't say anything but his discomfort was clear.

"No." Audy waved them in. "Come on in. Brooke has pie."

"Pie?" Beau asked.

"What are we celebrating?" Forrest asked, closing the front door and bringing up the rear.

"Company?" Audy shrugged.

"You three act like you've never had pie just to have pie." Brooke stood, regarding the three of them closely.

"Uncle Felix isn't the pie-just-to-have-pie sort of fella." Forrest's gaze wandered, taking in the high chair in the corner and the baby supplies stacked up on the counter before coming to a stop. "So... You're sure this isn't a bad time?"

Audy followed his gaze...to Tess. Tess was beet red and frozen.

"I'm..." Tess took a deep breath, held Joy close, kept her gaze glued to the floor and said, "I'll take Joy so you-all can talk." She kept going, her voice returning to normal. "I've got to study for my test tomorrow."

"Pre-cal?" Beau cleared his throat and added, "Mr. Hillard?"

Tess looked up, momentarily speechless. "Um...yeah."

It was Beau's turn to get a little red in the cheeks. "I've got him second period."

Audy was having a hard time not smiling. Now that he saw the two of them together, he knew exactly why Tess was acting so skittish. Brooke's little sister was sweet on his little brother. A good thing, too, since Tess was pretty much the only girl Beau had ever mentioned. And, as awkward and bumbling as the two of them were, there was something sweet about the way they were sizing each other up, turning various shades of pink and red, and generally making fools of themselves.

"You have a test, too?" Forrest asked, irritated.

"Yeah." Beau shrugged. "But I'm good—"

"You two can study together?" Audy suggested. "Same class, same test—why not?"

That got Brooke's attention. "In the front room."

Beau wouldn't have cared where they got to study. From where Audy stood, his little brother had yet to take his eyes off Tess.

"Okay." Tess shifted from one foot to the other.

"Here." If Audy had been thinking straight, he never would have offered to take Joy. Not in a hundred years. For one thing, he was standing up and he could drop her. For another thing, he could take her and she could cry and then he'd have to deal with that lip-flip. And lastly, he could feel Brooke's eyes boring into him. *Judging.*

"Okay." Tess eased Joy into his arms, bottle

and all. "Thanks." She smoothed her hands over her oversize black T-shirt that in large white letters read, "I'm not short, I'm fun-sized." "I'll go get my notes and textbook." She spun on her rainbow-striped feet and hurried from the kitchen.

Audy started swaying, like he'd seen Tess and Brooke do, but refused to look at the baby in his arms. *One thing at a time.* He felt like a fool, but so far, Joy hadn't started crying. *Don't panic.* Especially not with his brother and Brooke watching.

"Beau?" Forrest's sigh was all put-upon irritation but Beau didn't answer.

Audy caught sight of Beau, openly staring in the direction Tess had gone, and almost chuckled. *Little brother has got it something fierce for Tess Young.*

When Beau didn't move, Forrest frowned. "Beau?" he repeated, louder this time, missing the meaning behind their younger brother's flushed face and statue-like stance. "Your backpack is in the truck, isn't it?"

"Yes, sir?" Beau snapped to.

"Go on and get your backpack." Forrest waved him to the door, all the while shaking his head. "I never know what's going on in that boy's head."

For a minute, Audy thought his big brother was teasing. But no, one look at Forrest said otherwise. *I'd say it was written all over Beau's face.* Not that Forrest had ever been the sort to be "in touch" with his feelings. He was too uptight for that.

Somehow, Audy's and Brooke's gazes collided. She looked exactly the way he felt— incredulous. Was his big brother really that clueless? He shrugged, she shrugged and they both smiled. For all of about one minute.

Brooke's smile slipped away. "You like whipped cream on your apple pie?" she asked, already cutting slices.

"I'll take it however you're serving it." Forrest sat at the kitchen table. "Now, catch me up on things. Joy is here, so I'm thinking something's changed?"

Brooke slid two plates with pie onto the table. "Let me." She scooped up Joy before Audy could answer.

Audy studied the cinnamon-sugar-crusted pie and picked up his fork. "No, nothing's really changed." He used the tines to flake away at the crust. "I still have my doubts about their

choice of guardians. One of them, anyway."
He didn't look at Brooke. "That one would
be me."

Forrest set his fork down, leaned back in
his chair and swallowed hard. "What, now?"

"You heard me. Kent and Dara picked
Brooke…and me." He ran a hand over his
face.

Forrest stared at him for a long time, not
moving. Long enough for Tess to carry her
books through the kitchen to the front room.
Then the front door opened and closed upon
Beau's return. The soft mumble of the teens'
conversation carried on a solid five minutes before Forrest spoke. "So, all that talk
about Kent making a joke and having second
thoughts was about you?" He leaned forward
and scooped up a big bite of pie.

Audy had made a lot of mistakes in his life
but calling his big brother that day was at the
top of his list. His big brother didn't let things
go, not ever, and if Audy didn't set the record
straight, his words would be thrown back at
him for years to come.

Forrest swallowed his pie. "And the bit
about how some people aren't supposed to be
parents?" His gaze met Audy's. "What were

you looking for, Audy? Were you hoping I'd say what you needed to hear to walk away, guilt-free?" He laid the fork on the plate. "Don't you think knowing that we were talking about *you* would have made a difference on what I was going to say?"

Audy frowned, doing his best not to bark. "Yes. Definitely. And since I know what you think of me, I was pretty sure I knew what you'd say. In five seconds flat, you'd have agreed Kent made a mistake. It might be hard to believe but, after the day I'd had, I wasn't quite up for another one of your long-winded lectures about all my failings."

Forrest's face turned a deep red.

"I shouldn't have called at all. Only excuse? My head was a mess. Part of me was looking for a way out, the other was looking for…direction." He met his brother's gaze. "The thing is, my path seems pretty clear now. Kent always believed in me, even when I didn't give him reason to—to let him down now is just about the worst thing I could do. I'll find a way to make it work, you'll see. No matter what you or Brooke might think of me, I won't dishonor Kent, his wishes, his memory or his faith in me."

Once again, Forrest took his time before he said, "No offense, Audy, but it takes more to raise a baby than good intentions. Right now, you're raw and hurting and not thinking all that rationally. But when things settle and you're done changing diapers instead of riding bulls, I hope you two have a contingency plan in place." He stood, carrying his plate to the sink. "Did you at least talk to the lawyer? See what would happen if you decided—"

"I have decided." Audy saw red. "I didn't ask you here to get your approval or your permission. I don't want or need either. If you're done eating the pie and telling me how I'm going to change my mind, you might as well leave."

"You're too pigheaded for your own good, Audy." Forrest's eyes narrowed a bit. "For *her* own good." He glanced at baby Joy. "What happens when RJ calls, wanting you to run off for a rodeo in Amarillo? What then?"

"Forrest, Audy isn't in this alone." Brooke's voice caught them both off guard. From the look on her face, she was a little surprised, too. "It'll take patience and time and planning but we will work it out."

The last thing Audy had expected was backup from Brooke.

Forrest's gaze darted from Brooke to Audy then back again.

"Audy is right, we will work this out. It would be nice, for both of us, to know that we can count on your support." Brooke shifted Joy to her hip.

"We're family. Like it or not, we look out for one another." Forrest moved next to Brooke, smiling at Joy. "Guess that makes this little thing family, too."

But Joy's reaction was hardly welcoming. Her whole little body stiffened and she turned away, burying her face against Brooke's chest, before a building cry emerged.

I get it, Joy. It was more than a little satisfying that Joy was bawling over Forrest but, when he'd held her—not a tear in sight. That was something. It was a good place to start.

CHAPTER SEVEN

"ARE YOU SURE?" Brooke hadn't finished her first cup of morning coffee—it was too early for this. It wasn't like she'd expected it to be smooth sailing from the get-go, she was a realist. This was a huge change and it'd take time to sort things out. But sorting things, to her, had been balancing her work with Audy's, a feeding schedule, a sleep schedule and generally getting to know baby Joy. She'd never once thought it would mean sending her little sister off to school with Beau Briscoe the first morning back.

"It's not like he's not already headed that way," Audy offered, looking far too amused.

"I'm a good driver, Miss Young. No tickets." Beau glanced at Tess. "And seat belts. I mean, I... Anyone who rides with me has to wear their seat belt." By the time he'd finished his halting little speech, his cheeks were a splotchy red.

"I'm sure you're a very good driver." There wasn't a single concrete reason for Tess not to ride to school with Beau. It was a feeling… A feeling that got stronger when her little sister and Beau Briscoe made eye contact. The doe-eyed look and uneven breathing and flushed cheeks. That. *That is the reason Tess should walk to school.* "I just don't think it's a good idea."

"Well, that's just the most ridiculous thing I've ever heard." Audy scratched his head.

"You see, as adults, this is the kind of conversation we have alone. Then we are presenting a united front." She forced smile.

"Explain to me why it's a bad idea?" Audy gave her a hard stare. "'Cause this just doesn't make a lick of sense to me. Beau is here. Tess is here. They're both going to the same place. Why make the poor girl walk?"

"I guess I feel like our families are going to be overlapping enough as it is. You and I will be spending more time together because of Joy. But… Maybe it's not such a good idea for the two of them to be spending too much time together when they have their own lives to keep on leading." She realized she'd gone too far then. "But you can ride with Beau this morning."

Silence. Nothing. But all eyes were on her.

Eventually, Beau said, "I don't want to cause any trouble." He glanced between Brooke and Audy.

"Me, neither." Tess shifted the strap of her backpack on her shoulder. "I'm fine walking. Really."

"Good grief." Audy rolled his eyes. "Whatever."

"No. It's fine." Brooke pushed. "Thank you, Beau. You two have a good day." She felt like a fool as the two of them gave her awkward waves and headed out the front door.

Audy waited for the front door to close before he rounded on her. "Their own lives? Too much time together? I'm pretty sure that adding last night the two of them haven't said more than five words together the whole time they've been going to school. And that would be, oh, let me see…at least the last, what, ten years?" Audy's brow rose. When she didn't answer, he went on. "What was that all about? Getting a little riled up for no reason. What do you have against my little brother?" He nodded at the front door. "Beau is a good boy.

He's nothing like me, if that's what you're thinking."

"Why do I need to worry about anything?" Brooke decided avoidance was the only option at this point.

"Who said worry? I didn't say worry. Come on, now, Brooke, I know better. I saw the way you reacted to Forrest last night. You see my little brother's sweet on your little sister. And I'm pretty sure your little sister is sweet on my little brother."

"Your point?" Brooke asked.

"No point really. More an observation. And I don't quite understand why this is getting to you. So much so that your sister is walking to school instead of taking the ride my brother offered her." Audy was staring at her with his eyes narrowed and his hands on his hips.

"Maybe I just want my sister to keep focused on her schoolwork. And not on boys." She glared his way. "Even if Beau is a good boy, I think they're too...young to get involved."

"Too young?" Audy chuckled. "I'm pretty sure I kissed my first girl long before I had my driver's license."

"How nice for you. It sounds super special."

"All I'm saying is those two are plenty old enough." Audy held up both hands in defeat. "I get the feeling this is one of those things we're going to have to agree to disagree on."

"Agreed." Brooke turned and tried to look busy tidying up the kitchen—the kitchen that was already clean. "Why don't we talk about how it's going to work today."

"Talk about it? Or instead tell me how we're doing this? Not that I'm complaining. Considering I have no idea what's what, I'll follow your lead."

"I have to admit, I'm a little shocked you just said that." Brooke turned and gave him a full head-to-toe once-over. "I'm not sure whether I should be pleased or nervous?"

"I guess you have to wait and see." Audy chuckled.

Considering it was morning and they were starting a new routine, things went pretty well. Audy put the diaper on inside out and backward twice before he figured out how it actually worked. Luckily, Joy was such a good-natured baby that she giggled and played with her toes throughout the whole ordeal.

Breakfast was definitely an adventure. Audy's attempts to feed her somehow led to applesauce and rice cereal coating the single curl on top of Joy's little head. Not to mention the splatter effect all over Audy's freshly starched and ironed shirt. But, per his request, Brooke stood back and let him handle things.

"I'm thinking she's gonna need a bath now?" He glanced at Brooke out of the corner of his eye. "And that means she'll need another diaper, I'm guessing? How many of those things does she go through a day?"

"A lot." Brooke had to smile at the look on Audy's face. "Don't be so hard on yourself, Audy. You actually did well. She ate almost the whole bowl… I mean, what she's not wearing." She paused. "Well, and what you're wearing, too."

"I should've thought to bring a clean shirt." Audy held the shirt away from him, a frown of disgust forming as a particularly large glob of cereal and applesauce rolled down his shirtfront and onto his jeans. "I guess I should have just worn a raincoat."

Brooke couldn't help it, she was laughing. A lot.

"You hear Brooke laughing?" Joy was looking up at him all smiles. "Maybe we should throw applesauce at each other more often."

Joy slammed her hands against her high chair tray, sending the remainder of the rice cereal and applesauce everywhere.

"Why, thank you, Joy. I needed to make sure that my shirt was evenly coated. Now it is. Good job." Audy sighed, but he was still smiling.

The more he smiled, the more off-balance Brooke felt. She didn't like it. Not one bit. "It looks like you're getting your first bath lesson today."

"Now, hold on, I'm thinking I should master one thing at a time." Audy stood and headed to the sink. He ran a dish towel under warm water and started wiping his shirtfront. "I'm still working on diapers. And as you can see—" he held his shirt out "—I'm not exactly dressed for the occasion. She'd get clean and I'd get her covered in this all over again."

"And now you see why people carry diaper bags everywhere. They're prepared in case of an emergency." Brooke moistened a washcloth and set about de-cerealing little Joy. "There is no help for it. You have to have a bath."

"I'm guessing you don't have any men's clothing stashed away somewhere? Something I could change into?"

Brooke shook her head. The last man who had stayed in this house was her father. And that was over ten years ago. Her mother had kept up with him for a year or two but then it was like he dropped off the face of the earth. If he knew that his wife was dead, and his girls were alone, it hadn't mattered enough to bring him home. Tess had only the vaguest memories of the man—and absolutely no expectations. But Brooke had grown up with a father. At least, until Tess was born and he'd taken a job as a "traveling salesman" that allowed him one week a month home. Then it was a few days. Then his visits got more sporadic. He'd call or write a letter now and then but it could be weeks, then months, before he'd show up. And when he did, he was so handsome and funny and charming that, somehow, her mother would magically forget the worry and stress his long absences caused.

Then he was just *gone*. No letters, no phone calls, no nothing. Her mother held on for six months, hoping and waiting that he'd show up. He never did. Her mother's cancer diagnosis came not long after they'd accepted he wasn't coming home. Brooke could remember the doctor telling her mother to hold on to hope and fight as clearly as if it was yesterday. Mostly, she remembered the look in her mother's eyes. Her father had robbed her mother of all hope—she'd been no match for cancer. That was why Brooke had pulled every single piece of his clothing, and anything that reminded her of him, and taken them all to the resale shop in town. She didn't want a single thing in that house to remind her of the man who chose to leave them… The man who forced her to stay home and throw away her hopes and dreams.

As far as the rest of Garrison knew, their father was dead. When her mom had gotten sick people kept questioning where he was and when he'd be coming home. Initially, her mother had told everyone he was working in South America on the oil fields—which was believable as he'd worked as a rough-neck before. But once her mother's health fell into a deep decline people wondered why he didn't return—to help out. It was a constant reminder that there was no help coming. Having her father quote "die in a tragic accident" wasn't too far-fetched. No one had expected a service due to her mother's health and after her mother passed, it wasn't mentioned again. Brooke assumed they didn't want to remind her she'd lost both of her parents. She'd rather live with a lie than have people whisper and gossip about how her father had deserted them. Death wasn't as scandalous as being deserted.

"No. There hasn't been a man living here in years, Audy. And I'm pretty sure you couldn't fit into anything I own." Brooke shrugged, giving him a quick once-over.

"Probably not, but I certainly appreciate the offer." Audy kept wiping at his shirt. Instead of cleaning the mess, he mashed everything in the fibers. "Well, this is working."

"Be thankful she didn't have green beans. Or prunes. Or sweet potatoes. Then you wouldn't just have globs of stuff on your shirt, you'd have stains." Brooke knew there was really only one option. "Want to just go on home now, Audy? You can change, do what you need to do on the ranch and then come back for dinner?"

"And what are you gonna do with Joy? Don't you have to go to work?" Audy gave up trying to clean his shirt, tossed the towel in the sink and turned to face her.

"Are you offering to take her?" But Brooke already knew what his answer would be.

"Oh, no. Definitely not. She'd probably end up with a diaper on her head… I was just curious how you were going to handle cutting hair while juggling a baby?"

She'd been wondering the same thing. "We'll have to figure something out. Neither one of us are in the position to stop working and stay home to take care of Joy. Well, at least I'm not. I have bills to pay." She smiled at Joy and tapped the tip of her little nose. *You're about as precious as they come.* "I'm sure it wouldn't take much for us to find a good nanny or even look into the local day care center. I just feel like leaving her right now is…wrong. I know it's silly, I know she doesn't know what's going on. But *I* know what's going on. And I just can't leave her alone with a whole new set of strangers."

"I get that." Audy nodded, looking at Joy. It was hard to miss the tightening of his jaw.

It was a small thing, but it was enough to make Brooke's lungs and heart ache. She had let herself think about Dara and Kent today. She knew she wasn't strong enough for that. Better to focus on Joy and Audy and what their new life was going to look like. "Unless you're just itching to become a stay-at-home caregiver with her?"

"Me? The guy dripping applesauce and rice cereal all over your kitchen floor?" Audy shook his head. "I think that's a bad idea." He pushed off the countertop. "If you're sure you got it for now? I guess I can head back into town about, what, four? Five? I know dinner is at six."

"Five should do it." She pulled Joy from the high chair, jiggling her until she giggled. "You and I can have fun today, can't we, Joy? Just me and you and no stinky boys."

"I might be a little dirty at the moment, but I am not stinky."

"I hadn't noticed." Brooke shrugged.

"You two have fun, then... As long as

there's no songs about old women eating things." He put his hands on his hips and tried to look like a disciplinarian. "I have strong objections to that. As you know."

"I won't play 'There Was an Old Lady Who Swallowed a Fly' unless Joy needs cheering up. That's the best I can do." Brooke spun Joy around again, loving the sound of her giggles.

"I know you're not keen on the idea, but I do want to let you know that Beau has never said or shown the slightest interest in any young woman in all of Garrison except Tess." His gaze met hers. "I didn't even know who she was until I got here. Your Tess is Beau's Tess. I don't know if it will make you feel better or worse to know that. But I think it's a testament to the man he is. He doesn't take things lightly or play with people's emotions or say things he doesn't mean. Not that you're asking."

Brooke didn't like the slight tug inside her chest. As romantic as it sounded, they were both better off admiring one another from afar. "I wasn't asking. And it doesn't make me feel better. If anything, it means the two of them shouldn't be riding to school together anymore."

Audy's sigh was over-the-top and dramatic. "Whatever. I guess I'll be here at five."

Once Joy had her bath, was in clean clothes and happily playing on the floor, Brooke called the salon. Myrna already knew what was coming. She, Inez and Portia had sat down and divided up her schedule. Not only did Myrna assure her that they had everything under control, she told her to focus one hundred percent of her attention on baby Joy.

"And, yes, you had best expect each of us to show up with food. But only because we want to see that baby girl." Myrna's voice was happy. "I'm so glad that their baby girl is right here, safe and sound and loved with you."

Brooke was too choked up to say a word.

"But is it true about Audy Briscoe? Are the two of you really co-guardians? I understand he and Kent were close but, well, it's just a surprise, is all."

"It is." There was no denying that.

"Of course, this is one of those situations that can change a person. I've often thought Audy, being a Briscoe, had it in him to be a good man. Up until now he just didn't have a reason. I can't think of a better reason than raising his best friend's baby girl. If that's not a reason to step up, I don't know what is." She sighed. "You take these four days and you get as much settled as you can."

"Yes, ma'am. Thank you, Myrna. And please tell Portia and Inez thank you, too."

"Oh, I wasn't kidding about all of us dropping by. We can't wait to meet the little angel, but we'll give it a few days. You take care, now. We'll talk later."

Brooke hung up the phone, mulling over what Myrna had said. There was no arguing Myrna's logic, but Brooke had known Audy an awful long time. Being a *good man* had never been high on his priority list. As much as she wanted to think Myrna was right, bits and pieces of his phone call with Forrest still troubled her—especially the part about how some people aren't meant to be parents. He'd been talking about himself. He tried to deny it when Forrest was here, but she suspected it was how he really felt. If he'd made up his mind that he was one of those people, then all his good intentions didn't mean anything.

"It doesn't matter, Joy." She sat on the play mat beside Joy. "You and me and Tess—" she picked up the patchwork puppet and made it dance "—I'd say we make a pretty nice family, wouldn't you?"

Joy clapped her hands, watching the puppet dance.

"I'm glad you agree." Brooke ran a hand over Joy's curl and took a deep breath. With or without Audy, Joy would grow up in a loving family.

AUDY HAD TAKEN off his button-up and was in the process of pulling off his equally sticky undershirt as he opened Brooke's front door. Just his luck, Miss Ruth and Martha Zeigler were standing on the doorstep, clearly stopping by to drop off a covered casserole dish and a large brown paper bag. Miss Ruth, he could handle, but Miss Martha was in a perpetually bad mood. Uncle Felix said she had more money than any one person should have so she didn't feel beholden to folk about being polite.

"Are you taking off your clothes? Or putting them on?" Martha Zeigler was eyeing him with open disapproval.

Audy proceeded to tug his arm back into the sleeve of his undershirt and smooth it down over his chest and stomach. "Good morning, ladies. I—"

"Hush now, Martha," Miss Ruth interrupted. "You leave poor Audy alone. I'm sure he and Brooke are still…working through things. Not just with the baby, but between the two of them."

Audy nodded his thanks. But one look at the all-too-delighted look on Miss Ruth's face told him there was a whole different meaning to Miss Ruth's statement. He was pretty sure it was the sort of meaning he didn't want attached to him and Brooke. "I was—"

"Humph. Brooke Young is too smart to cast her net for the likes of you, Audy Briscoe." Martha sniffed, as if she'd caught a whiff of something foul.

Over the years, he'd done his fair share to rile Martha Zeigler. Most of it had been good fun, boys being boys and all that, but she didn't see it that way. He might have turned a skunk loose in her garden, set off firecrackers on her porch after she'd pushed to ban fireworks for a holiday, shaved her prize collie's fur and broken out her front window with a baseball—three times—but all of that was years ago. He hadn't done a thing to her since, preferring to avoid the woman altogether. Why she felt the need to hold on to such childish pranks, he didn't know. Probably because she had nothing better to do with her time. Still, he didn't let it get to him. He'd learned humor was the best tool for deflecting insults. "Smart or not, Brooke might not be able to resist all my charm. Guess we'll have to see."

Miss Ruth's eyes all but bugged out of her face.

"You always did have a mouth on you." Martha stood tall, her hands on her hips, and her gaze sharp and clear. "Too bad you never learned to say anything useful. Or do anything, for that matter. You come from a good family, Audy. Respectable. Such a shame." Her sigh was long-suffering. "The food is for *Brooke*, not for *you*. Not one single bite. As far as I'm concerned, she's been saddled with two young'uns to bring up on her own." Her smile was anything but pleasant. "You being one of them, in case you didn't catch my meaning."

"Oh, I did, Miss Martha." He aimed for earnest as he added, "But I appreciate the clarification. Nothing worse than a miscommunication, after all. I wouldn't want to go around thinking you thought well of me all of a sudden. Or, worse, that you'd grown fond of me."

Miss Martha snorted. "No fear of that."

"Now, now, there is no need for things to get…unpleasant." Miss Ruth's attempt to smooth things over was half-hearted at best.

"Who's unpleasant?" Miss Martha snapped. "We're done here." But she gave him another hard look. "I know you live for being the center of attention, but Brooke works hard, she lives a quiet life, and people respect that about her—something you know nothing about. But she is a handsome single woman, living in a small town, and if a fella starts coming and going *and* he's missing clothes?" She was flustered now. "People will talk. I'm wasting my breath on you, I just know it, but this needs to be said. You go on and keep making a mess of your life, but you leave Brooke Young out of it. Or you will answer to me." She shook her finger at him, as if she were disciplining a child. "And keep your clothes on, boy." With that, she whirled and stalked back to her car, Miss Ruth trailing behind.

From his place on the porch, he waved

them off, then put the food inside Brooke's front door before reaching his truck and starting the drive home.

You go on and keep making a mess of your life, but you leave Brooke Young out of it.

He wasn't sure how he was supposed to leave Brooke out of his life now that they were tied together by Joy, but he got what she meant. And, surprisingly, he appreciated the sentiment behind it. He hadn't thought about the repercussions of running out of her house, shirtless, when it was clear no one else was home. People would jump to conclusions. Most likely, none of those conclusions would involve rice cereal and applesauce.

By the time he parked in front of his sprawling family home, his shirtfront was crunchy and dry.

His brother Webb was heading out the front door right as Audy was going in. "I heard you went and got yourself a baby—" Webb broke off, his nose wrinkling as he gave Audy a once-over. "What happened to you?" He poked at Audy's shirt. "What *is* that?"

"Haven't you ever seen rice cereal with applesauce before?" Audy shook his head, his tone dripping disbelief.

"No. And I hope I don't see it again any-time soon." Webb shuddered. "Since you're here, can I get some help replacing the wire? Or are you just gonna change and hightail it out of here?"

"I'm all yours until four thirty. Then I have to clean up and head back over to the Young place." This time, he'd be sure to take extra clothes just in case his on-the-job training led to more messes.

"You're gonna wind up putting a whole lot of miles on your truck." Webb headed down the front steps. "I'll see you out there, then." He yelled back over his shoulder.

Audy headed inside to find Harvey, tail wagging, waiting to greet him. "Morning, boy." He stooped to give his dog a good rub-down. "I guess I'll talk to Brooke tonight, see about taking you along tomorrow. If you promise to behave, that is?"

Harvey yawned.

"Now, don't get too excited on me."

That's when Harvey caught a whiff of Audy. Harvey was a big dog, a big dog that loved to eat. Audy was squatting, so all it took was a nudge for Harvey to knock Audy onto his rear for a closer inspection of Audy's shirt.

"Now, see, this is exactly what I'm talking about." Audy pushed at the massive dog's shoulders and stood. "That's not polite. You can't just go around knocking people over. And you shouldn't try to eat a man's shirt—especially when he's still wearing it. You hear me?" He paused. "You pull that kind of thing over at Brooke's house and you'll never be welcome there again." He sat up, patting Harvey's back. "And just so you know, there's pie there for no particular reason. You play your cards right, I can make sure you'll be the one cleaning out the pie tins."

Harvey was more interested in sniffing Audy's jeans and circling him, looking for an opening, all the while making a low whimper at the back of his throat.

About that time, Uncle Felix came out of the kitchen holding a large cup of coffee. "What's gotten into Harvey? He looks ready to maul you."

"He just loves me, I guess." Audy grinned and stood.

"Uh-huh." Uncle Felix snorted, his eyes fixed on Harvey as the dog made another slow circle around Audy, before shifting to look Audy over. "What's all over you?"

"Applesauce and rice cereal." Audy bobbed his eyebrows. "Apparently, babies like to eat it. I don't get it. I am not all that fond of the smell."

Harvey was still grunting and sniffing.

"Harvey doesn't seem to mind." Uncle Felix sipped his coffee. "Did you forget to feed that dog? I know you've been busy with…everything. Might want to carve out some time to take care of things here, too." Uncle Felix wasn't just talking about Harvey. He was telling Audy he expected a full run-down of what was going on. "I'm thinking Forrest has told me the important stuff?"

"Probably. But I should have told you. About Kent." Audy swallowed the lump in his throat. Not just for missing Kent, but for letting down his uncle. Uncle Felix didn't ask for much, Audy shouldn't be expecting Forrest to play messenger.

"Sad thing, losing Kent." Uncle Felix stared into his coffee. "Good boy. Good man." He shook his head.

Audy agreed, one hundred percent.

Harvey sat, staring up at him and whimpering.

"I fed you and you know it." Audy sighed,

noting the smile Uncle Felix was wearing. "He'd never have let me out of the house otherwise. But he'd eat 24/7 if I let him. Don't let those big brown eyes of his guilt you into giving him more, either." He gave Harvey a stern look.

"No dog's going to guilt me into anything." Uncle Felix gave Audy an odd look. "He's a dog." He took another sip of coffee, his gray-blue eyes settling on Audy's shirtfront once more. "If you were feeding the baby, I'm thinking you might need a little more practice."

"That I do." Audy chuckled. "Not just with the feeding, either."

"You were all mostly walking and talking when I came to care for you, I got to skip all that." He pointed at Audy's shirt. "This little one? Her name is Joy?"

Audy nodded. "Yes, sir." *Or Miss Muffet.* But that one was just for him.

"Forrest says, well…she's a Briscoe now." Uncle Felix waited for Audy to nod before going on. "Might not hurt for you to consider bringing her out here sometime. Be nice to lay eyes on her, get to see who's doing this." He pointed at Audy's shirt.

"I can do that." It made sense to have Brooke here, get her take on things—for Joy. Might be easiest to ask both Brooke and Tess to dinner. *Beau would love that.* Brooke, on the other hand...

"Mabel called last night and she is plumb over the moon about the little girl. She said it's about time there was another woman on the ranch. I guess I'd never thought about it that way. She was set to come home but I told her to finish up her work... It's not like the baby's going anywhere, now, is she?"

"No, sir." His poor sister, Mabel, had grown up in a house full of loud, ornery, overprotective men. As a result, she had the patience of a saint, didn't rattle easily and tended to keep to herself. *Which is probably why she spent so much time with horses growing up.* And why he could see his sister and Joy taking to one another. "I'm sure she and Joy will get on like two peas in a pod."

"About that..." Uncle Felix took another sip of his coffee, peering at Audy over the rim, before he finally said, "She has all sorts of ideas for Joy's room. Mabel kept calling it a nursery."

"She does?" Audy hadn't gotten that far.

Of course Joy would need her own room. Here. Under this roof. "That's good." What did he know about putting together a room for a baby? A baby who would grow into a little girl… The thought knotted his stomach. "I'll let her take charge of that." He'd have to look over the child protective services checklist Mr. Vincent had included in their packet. Whatever Mabel decided to do would have to keep in line with those requirements—or Brooke would eat him alive.

"You know that little one will wind up a horse lover like Mabel, then?" Uncle Felix shook his head.

"I can think of worse things." Audy liked the idea of Joy following in Mabel's footsteps. "But that's a way down the road. Right now, all she does is eat, sleep, cry and mess her diaper. She makes all sorts of nonsense noises, too—though Brooke acts like Joy's carrying on a full-blown conversation. Brooke's got the whole baby thing down." He shrugged, an image of Joy with one of her shy smiles popping into his head. "But she's real cute, I can tell you that much." He grinned at his uncle. *Not that I've spent much time looking at babies…*

Uncle Felix was studying him closely. A little *too* closely. "Brooke? Or Joy?"

"No denying Brooke's a fine-looking woman but I was talking about Joy." Audy chuckled. "I gotta get myself cleaned up or Webb will likely wind up tangled in the new fence line." Which was only partly a joke. His younger brother was as independent as they came. Too many times, he'd dive into something headfirst instead of waiting for help. Too many times, he'd wind up needing help getting out of or fixing the thing he'd dived into without waiting for help. "I'm thinking Webb and razor wire won't make for a good combination so I should be there from the get-go."

"That boy." Uncle Felix sighed. "Not much sense in cleaning up now? Change your shirt and get after him before he winds up in the emergency room again and Forrest has already set off for the south pastures."

"Yes, sir." Audy was tugging off his shirt as he ran down the hall to his room. He tossed it onto the floor, grabbed a work shirt from his drawer and tugged it on as he was headed back down the hall and into the great room where Uncle Felix was now sitting, enjoying his coffee.

"Be careful, now," his uncle called out, making Audy pause.

"Yes, sir." A rush of words clogged up his throat. From "I'm sorry" to "I'll try harder" to "Thank you for putting up with me," he wasn't sure where to start. Audy not sitting down and explaining the whole co-guardianship to him, man-to-man, was plain disrespectful.

Respect… *Something you know nothing about.* Miss Martha's words rang out loud and clear, taunting him. It didn't matter that he was floundering and still adjusting to all the changes while trying to process his grief and newfound guardianship. There was no excuse. Uncle Felix had been there for him, always. He needed to take an example from the man who'd stepped in to raise him and his siblings. *No more excuses.*

CHAPTER EIGHT

FOR FOUR DAYS, Audy showed up on time—with an extra change of clothes—and tried. He helped Brooke with all the babyproofing and fixed the front porch step. Joy still made Audy nervous and he couldn't bear it when she cried, but now he smiled when she smiled and he laughed when she laughed. Sure, it took him four times as long to bathe Joy, he wound up wearing whatever he was feeding her, and diaper changes still triggered his gag reflex, but she thought they were making progress.

Dara and Kent's funeral had been nice, though Brooke didn't remember much of it. She'd been too numb to do much but cuddle Joy and try not to cry.

Two days after that, they'd had their first surprise visitation. Brooke didn't know what to expect but Mrs. Elaine Trenton wasn't it. Audy had compared the old woman to a turtle, all hunched up and wrinkled. Brooke had chastised him for being rude but, in her mind, she saw the resemblance. Mrs. Trenton took a total of ten minutes poking around the house before she asked them five questions, glanced at Joy—saying he was a sweet boy—before leaving. While Brooke wasn't sure what to make of the whole thing, Audy seemed to think they had nothing to worry about.

But now that her time off was over and she had to go in to work the next day, Brooke couldn't help but worry. And, for the first time ever, she dreaded it. Not the work itself, but leaving Joy—even for a half day. "You're sure you're ready for tomorrow?"

Audy opened his mouth wide as he spooned yogurt into Joy's mouth. "I was feeling ready, but now that you've asked me that four times, I'm beginning to think you don't think I'm ready?"

Brooke sank into the chair across from them. "No…no, I do. I'm sorry, Audy."

"He'll do fine," Tess said, looking up from her pre-calculus book long enough to give Brooke a disappointed frown.

"You'll do great," she agreed. Her little sister was right. She had to stop shortchanging

Audy. When it came to Joy, so far, he'd done everything he said he would. That was worth acknowledging. She propped an elbow onto the table and smiled as Joy picked up a piece of cooked carrot, mashing it between her little fingers, then eating it up. "Good stuff, isn't it, Joy?"

"Num-mum." Joy smiled widely.

"Nothing like cold, squishy carrots to make my meal." Audy chuckled, scooping up more yogurt.

Brooke giggled, watching. The closer the spoon of yogurt got to Joy, the wider Audy opened his mouth. It might be her imagination, but Joy seemed to be watching, too. She'd stare at him, grinning, with wide eyes and wait until the very last minute—when Audy's mouth was stretched as wide as it could get—before opening her little mouth for the bite. At times like this, she almost forgot this Audy was the same Audy she held in such contempt.

This Audy was adorably awkward and uncertain.

This Audy panicked at the first sign of Joy's distress.

This Audy now wore a towel like a bib

whenever he was feeding Joy—without batting an eye.

This Audy dozed off while holding Joy in the rocking chair last night...

Joy offered Audy a carrot, her little fingers stretching out as she opened her mouth—just like Audy—in encouragement. Audy's smile wavered and he eyed the mushy vegetable with mounting concern, but Joy wasn't going to give up. And Audy, well...

Tess's indrawn gasp sounded just as shocked as Brooke felt.

He did not... He did. He ate the carrot.

It was a struggle, Brooke could tell, but he managed to swallow it. Those crystal-blue eyes pinched shut and that chiseled jaw clamped down, but he did it. And that's when Brooke's chest felt heavy and there was a sort of...tug... It was so unexpected and alarming that Brooke wasn't sure it had really happened. But if it had?

"Goo ja. Goo ja," Joy said, clapping her little hands and flinging bits of mashed carrots and cereal all over her high chair tray and Audy's towel.

"Good job, huh?" Audy chuckled and took

a long sip of his iced tea. "Thank you, Miss Muffet."

"Daba," Joy babbled.

Tess burst out laughing. "You two."

Audy shuddered. "One thing's certain, Joy, you have reaffirmed my lifelong commitment to avoiding cooked carrots." He made a face and took another sip.

Joy giggled.

"Yeah, you are cute." The corner of his mouth cocked up and a dimple appeared. "No denying that. Why else do you think I ate that carrot?"

Tess started laughing all over again. "I'm not sure I could have done it."

Brooke tore her gaze away. It was all a little too…much. All of it. It seemed like only yesterday she and Audy were driving to Houston and yet, everything was different. Part of her was delighted with how easily Joy had settled into things. The other part of her worried about what happened once real life intruded into the little world she, Audy, Tess and Joy had built in such a short period of time.

"You okay?" Audy asked.

Brooke looked up, startled by the question. "You look…sad." Those blue eyes seemed brighter than normal. No, not brighter. Warmer?

Brooke stared down at her Formica-topped kitchen table, ignoring the undeniably real tug in her chest. Hopefully, he didn't pick up on the waver of her indrawn breath. "I'm only sad I didn't record that."

Tess, however, had not missed it, and her light brown eyes were taking an all-too-thorough inventory.

Audy chuckled. "That was your one chance, too. Cute or not, that's a hard pass for me from here on out." He glanced at Harvey, snoozing in a patch of sunlight by the all-glass back door. "Some help you are."

"Daww." Joy stressed the *w* as she strained to peer around the high chair at Harvey.

"Yep," Audy said. "That's a big, old, good-for-nothing daw, all right." He pronounced *dog* exactly like Joy.

Joy nodded.

The two of them, nodding at each other like they were sharing some sort of deep moment of understanding, was a little too much for Brooke. The sheer adorableness of it all. Both of them. This big, beautiful man, wearing a towel, and this sweet angel of a baby girl… It's good. The two of them were bonding. That was wonderful.

It was only *bad* because it caused another tug in her chest, from a region far too close to her heart. *Nope.* Audy Briscoe wasn't going to have any effect on her heart. *Not now. Not ever.* She pushed out of her chair and headed for the sink and the single pot needing to be washed.

"I think Brooke's worried," Audy said to Joy. It was something he'd started doing, talking to Joy about Brooke—instead of directly addressing Brooke. "I think she thinks I'm going to make a mess of things and she'll come home to me and you crying, surrounded by dirty diapers."

"Now, that's a picture," Tess murmured.

It was safe to smile, her back was to him. Which was good because she *was* smiling. The image he painted was just too—

"Did you know there's a window over the sink, Joy? And that I can see Brooke's reflection? Like now. When she's smiling at something *I* said."

Brooke stared at the window and stuck her tongue out.

Audy hooted with laughter. "Joy, don't you

look now. Brooke's not acting like a very good role model at the moment." But he was still laughing.

Tess didn't quite manage to stifle her laughter, either.

"Don't be too hard on her. It's got to be hard work, being a grown-up all the time." Audy sighed. "I'm tired just thinking about it."

It was enough of a reminder to help Brooke steady herself. Audy was right, it was exhausting being responsible. But that was who she was, it was who she always had been. For Audy, this was all new. It took at least sixty days for a habit to become automatic, or thereabouts, and Audy was on day six… The road ahead of them was long and uncertain. Brooke finished scrubbing the pan, placed it on the drying rack by the sink and wiped her hands on a kitchen towel—turning to find Tess once more poring over her textbook while Audy and Joy were both watching her.

Joy waved.

Brooke waved back.

Audy… Audy was staring at her. He was still smiling, but it was a different sort of smile. One she'd never seen him wear before. And between the blue eyes and the dimples and the rigid jaw and that *look*, he was downright…unsettling.

"I—I think it's bath time," Brooke said, wiping her now-dry hands on the towel again to hide their trembling. What was this feeling? Where had it come from? And why, oh, why, did Audy Briscoe have to be the one to cause it?

AUDY WASN'T ONE to overthink things. He wanted something, he got it. He felt a certain way, he acted on it. That was part of living life to the fullest—doing, engaging, being in the moment. But this moment, right here in Brooke Young's kitchen, was outside his norm. He was wanting and feeling, all right, but there was no way, *no way*, he could act.

For one thing, there was a baby in the room.

For another, Tess was sitting here—being all studious.

Finally, *this* was Brooke. Brooke *Brooke*. The woman who normally scowled and rolled her eyes and generally let him know that, to her, he was about as useless as a person could be. Only now, there was no scowling or eye-rolling or anger or…judgment.

There was a softness to her that triggered every instinct he had. To protect her. To comfort her. To…to what?

He ran a hand over his face. He was a fool, but this was a whole new level of foolishness. "Bath time, it is."

"Oh, can I help?" Tess asked, looking up from her pre-calculus book. "I need a break." She made an extra-goofy face at Joy. "Don't I, Joy?"

Joy squealed with glee.

Audy chuckled. As much progress as he'd made with Joy, he couldn't hold a candle to Tess. Something about that girl made Joy light up.

"Are you sure?" Brooke asked. "I know you have that big mid-semester exam this week—"

"And I've been studying really hard." Tess tapped her book with her pencil.

Audy didn't look at Brooke as he said, "You know, Beau'd be happy to study with you. He's a math whiz and I know he'd—"

"I'm sure Beau has enough to do. Besides, Mr. Hillard offers tutoring—if that's something you're interested in?" Brooke's words came out in a rush.

Tess blinked, set her pencil down and stood. "It's not like I'm failing, Brooke. I have a B average. A high B, too. And, once I ace this test, I'll have an A." She came around and scooped Joy up, rubbing noses with the baby. "Because Tess is the smartest girl in her class, isn't she, Joy?"

Joy grabbed Tess's face in her sticky hands. "Teh…"

"Are you saying my name? Is she saying my name?" Tess asked. "Can you say Tess? Joy, who am I?" She patted herself on the chest. "Tess. You can do it. Say my name. Tess."

"Teh." Joy patted Tess on the chest. "Teh."

"That's me." Tess smiled. "I'm Teh." She hugged Joy. "You're supersmart, too, aren't you? I bet you'll be the first in your class when you grow up. Let's go have a bath. With extra bubbles." She kept up a steady one-sided conversation as she carried Joy from the kitchen and down the hall to the bathroom.

"I'm thinking Joy has a favorite?" Audy untied the towel from around his neck. "Not that I blame her. Tess is a whole lot more fun than we are. Well, you, anyway." His attempt to tease was met with a locked jaw and blazing eyes. "What?"

"Don't you *what* me, Audy Briscoe. You keep…keep trying to shove your little brother onto my sister." Brooke tossed the hand towel onto the counter. "I thought I'd made it clear that I don't feel comfortable with the two of them…you know…getting together."

"Getting together?" he repeated, wishing he understood why she was so dead set against this.

"Why are you choosing to be so thickheaded about this?" she asked. "Tess needs to focus on her studies, and Beau—"

"Has a full ride to the college of his dreams." Audy sat back in his chair, stretching his long legs out in front of him. "I know you said they're too young—" he used air quotes around "too young" in case she missed his sarcasm "—but I get the feeling there's more to this than you're saying."

"My reasoning is none of your business, Audy." She took a deep breath. "We are co-guardians for Joy. Tess is my business and I'd appreciate it if you'd respect my authority instead of trying to undermine me."

"I'm not trying to do a thing to you. I'm trying to give two young kids a chance at a little happiness." Audy saw the red drain from Brooke's cheeks.

"Tess is happy." But she didn't sound so sure.

"I didn't say she wasn't. Beau's happy enough, too, I suppose." *Way to go, Audy.* The last thing he'd wanted to do was make her doubt her sister's happiness. "But I do think they could be happier."

Brooke stared at him, slowly crossing her arms over her chest. "Audy." She took a deep breath. "How about we talk about tomorrow?"

It was a pretty pathetic dodge, but he'd let it be—for now. There was plenty of time to wear her down about Beau and Tess, and while he'd never gone the slow-and-steady way of going about things, he figured this might be the perfect time to give it a try. "I'm showing up at noon. You're going to work until five. Joy will sleep for two hours when I first get here. When she wakes up, I change her diaper and get her a snack." It's not like they hadn't gone over the schedule she'd stuck on the refrigerator about a dozen times.

Brooke nodded.

"After that, we play." He sighed. "And, if she needs it, I change her diaper again. Did I miss anything?"

"No." Her gaze shifted to the refrigerator. "All my numbers—"

"Are taped right there beside the schedule." He stood then, crossing to her. "I get that you've got a bit of a control streak…" Seeing Brooke get her back up made him frown. Every now and then, things were so peaceable between them he'd forget how defensive she could get. *With me, anyway.* "Back up. Forget that, will you? What I mean is I get that leaving Joy with me likely goes against every instinct you've got, but this is what we decided on." He was thankful Brooke had voiced her opinion on waiting to put Joy into day care. It'd happen eventually, but he didn't mind keeping it just them for now. They'd both work half days this week. Monday, Wednesday and Friday he'd do afternoons and stay for dinner and bath. Tuesday and Thursday, he'd be over before the sun was up to get Joy out of bed and ready for the day. "If this doesn't work, we'll figure something else out, okay?"

"It will work." Brooke's gaze met his, the sheer determination in the slight tilt of her head was a challenge. The spark in her big, hazel eyes had Audy leaning in. Her eyes weren't just brown, they were a whole host of shades flecked with gold. "It will."

The sudden pressure in Audy's chest was so great his only option was to nod.

She smelled like the lemon hand soap and lotion she kept by all the sinks in the house. Up until now, he hadn't thought there was anything special about the scent of a lemon. How wrong he'd been. Lemon was his new favorite scent. Warm. Fresh. Light. Clean.

She'd fixed the band holding her hair too many times to count but it had already slid down, barely hanging on to one thick strand. Up close like this, he saw threads of red and copper woven through the waves of her caramel-colored hair. The urge to reach out, to slide his fingers through the softness, made his hands flex. He should not reach around to slide the band from her hair... *This is Brooke*... He definitely shouldn't take another step closer to her.

Her eyes went wider but she didn't step back—she didn't move. Only the slightest hitch of her breath and the waver of her shirt-front assured him she wasn't immune to the current drawing them together. "What are you doing?" It was a whisper.

I'm thinking about kissing you. He tried to imagine saying that out loud but couldn't. Brooke would put him in his place so fast, his head would spin. Even if she was thinking the same thing, she'd never let on. "Nothing." He reached around her for the hair band, but the slide of her hair against his fingertips sent warmth rushing up his arm and down his spine. It so surprised him, he stepped back, unsteady, and knocked the kitchen counter with his hip. The bin full of clean baby bottles fell onto the floor at their feet.

Harvey jerked up, his massive head cocked to one side, as bottles and caps rolled across the tile floor.

"Here." He held out the band but couldn't bring himself to look at her. *Audy Briscoe, you're a fool.* Whatever *that* was, it could never happen again.

She took the band from him but stayed quiet.

Instead of acknowledging the mounting tension in the room, Audy picked up the bin and set about collecting all the bits and pieces he'd spilled. When that was done and the room was still quiet, Audy dared to look in Brooke's direction.

No Brooke.

He was alone.

Well, Harvey was there—his thick plume of a tail thumping against the tile and a pink plastic baby bottle in his mouth.

"Thanks, buddy." Audy retrieved the bottle and carried the whole tub to the kitchen sink. One of the things Brooke had harped on and on about was keeping everything as clean as possible. That went double for things like bottles and pacifiers. "No germs for Joy," he murmured to Harvey, who trotted across the floor to sit at his feet.

He washed everything, twice, using the little bottlebrush to scrub every nook and cranny. When everything was hanging on the bottle rack, he gave Harvey a pat on the head and surveyed the rest of the room. Since Brooke had disappeared and he could hear Tess singing nonsense songs to Joy in the bathroom, he started washing the dinner dishes.

Audy had cleaned and dried and put everything away when Tess walked into the kitchen with Joy.

"She's all ready for bed," Tess said, cuddling Joy close. "She sure loves her bath time." She turned. "Where's Brooke?"

"I'm not sure. I guess something came up." He reached out for Joy, who waved. "But I don't mind putting Miss Muffet to bed."

"Is that your nickname for her?" Tess asked, shifting Joy into his arms. "I think that's sweet. I love that nursery rhyme."

"I don't remember much—except for the Miss Muffet part." He bounced Joy. He was by no means comfortable with something so little in his arms, but he didn't immediately worry about dropping her.

"Little Miss Muffet, sat on her tuffet…" Tess broke off. "I don't know what a tuffet is?"

"You got me," Audy admitted with a shrug.

Tess went on and on, "Along came a spider who sat down bedside her and frightened Miss Muffet away."

Audy frowned. "What is it with these nursery rhymes and songs? Spiders and old women and babies rocking in the treetops." When he'd been young, he'd never pondered the words to the songs and poems read to him from storybooks. Mostly, he liked the pictures and sitting in his mom's lap while she read. They were good memories. "I'm not sure those Mother Goose people liked children all that much." He wrinkled up his nose and puffed out his cheeks.

Joy giggled.

"What?" Tess asked, giggling herself. "Why do you say that?"

"If they did, they'd sing about cupcakes and baby animals or lemonade and sunshine. Not spiders scaring you. Or old women eating a farmyard of animals. Or babies falling out of trees. Who thinks that's the sort of thing that'll ease a child into sleep?" Audy tapped Joy on the nose. "How about we come up with a new version of 'Miss Muffet,' Joy? No tuffets or spiders."

Joy clapped.

"See, that's just what we'll do tomorrow." For the first time, thinking about tomorrow made him nervous. It was silly, he and Joy were getting on just fine. But if Joy fussed or cried, he could hand her off to Tess or Brooke and not be forced to face her lip-flip or big dewdrop tears that twisted his heart into knots.

"I look forward to hearing it." Tess patted Joy on the back, then resumed her place at the kitchen table—textbook open and pencil in hand.

"For now, let's get you to bed, eh, Miss Muffet?" He carried Joy down the hall to her nursery. He turned on the night-light and sat in the rocking chair. "You see all the butterflies?" he asked, pointing at the ceiling. The night-light shade rotated slowly, casting butterfly silhouettes all about the room, while Audy rocked and rocked and little Joy went soft and pliant, sound asleep in his arms. He sat awhile longer, then carefully stood and carried Joy to the crib. Slowly, he bent forward, holding Joy close until he could ease her onto the mattress. He pulled up the pink and white blankets and stood back to make sure he'd done it right. She seemed so still. Too still. He reached over the side of the crib and rested his hand on Joy's chest so he could feel the thump of her heart against his palm.

He nodded, then backed out of the room, pulling the door shut behind him. Since there was no reason for him to linger, he told Tess good-night and led Harvey out the front door. It didn't sit right, leaving without saying goodbye to Brooke, but it might be for the best. The last thing he needed to do was get caught up in all the little details that made Brooke downright…irresistible. *No. No woman was irresistible.* Which was good because, irresistible or not, Brooke Young was the one woman he couldn't have.

CHAPTER NINE

"You can sit up," Brooke said, squeezing out Kelly Schneider's hair before wrapping it in a towel.

"Can you believe it?" Kelly Schneider held the towel in place and moved to the salon chair.

"No." If what Kelly had heard was true, it was a scandal in the making. She couldn't quite wrap her mind around it. Garrison was built around The First Tree, Der erste Baum to the descendants of the original German settlers. It was part of the town's history, the town's logo, and the location of many celebrations and gatherings. There was no way a true Garrisonite would allow the massive tree to be cut down. It didn't make sense. "But, why would Lance Devlin be considering this? He's never been the sharpest tool in the shed, but this? His aunt can't be the least bit happy about this." His aunt, Martha Zeigler—the wealthiest woman in four counties—would never let anything happen to The First Tree. It was the very heart of Garrison.

"I'm certain she hasn't caught word of his scheme yet." Kelly's gaze met Brooke's. "But when she does, boy-howdy things are going to be interesting."

Brooke had to chuckle then. "That's one way of putting it." But Kelly was right. Nothing and no one could get past Martha Zeigler. "She'll put a stop to it."

"I might even feel a little sorry for old Lance," Kelly added.

Brooke met her gaze in the mirror.

"Nah," they said in unison.

"As far as I know, Lance didn't come this morning, not that I'd known any of this then. But he is on the schedule for a shave next Monday morning." Brooke ran a comb through Kelly's shoulder-length black hair. "I'll stop by with Joy to give him an extra donut and see what I can get out of him."

Her mother had started Monday Morning Shave and a Donut. It was the one day a week the shop opened early, had donuts and coffee on hand and offered a good old-fashioned shave. Relaxing the chair back into a comfortable angle. A steaming towel wrap. The first coat of lather. Another steam wrap. Then more lather and, finally, a straight-razor shave. It wasn't just the shave that brought the men in, though. It was the camaraderie. It was the one day a week they could converge for a little pampering, coffee and donuts, and male companionship. She and the other stylists kept talk to a minimum, listening closely but interjecting very little. These were the decision makers, the old-timers, the ones who knew and saw all—Mondays never failed to deliver an inside scoop or a new perspective on some town lore. Granted, as this was her first day away from Joy, she was a little scattered but that wouldn't last.

Next Monday, she'd be ready for Lance Devlin. Once he was hired as the city manager and moved to Garrison, he'd shown up every Monday. Without fail, he arrived a good thirty minutes after most of the other men. It was probably a good thing since the others didn't think too highly of him. To them, he was an outsider. But, to them, you were an outsider if your family hadn't been in Garrison for, oh, several generations. Lance Devlin might have been Martha Zeigler's nephew but, to the menfolk, that didn't count.

No wonder he didn't show up this week. Who knows how the men would have treated him?

"So—" Kelly's tone changed, more hesitant than before "—how's it going?"

Brooke focused on trimming away Kelly's dead ends. "Fine."

"Uh-huh." Kelly tapped her nails on the arms of the chair. "You know you're going to have to give me more than that, don't you?"

"What do you want to know?" Brooke hedged. Thankfully, Kelly was too polite to ask anything too probing.

"How are you getting along with Audy Briscoe?" Kelly kept on tapping. "How is he doing with Joy?"

"We are getting along just fine," she answered, snipping away. "He's learning. He can't feed her without making a mess and it takes him so long to bathe her that I have to turn the heater on so she won't catch a chill, but he's getting there."

Kelly chuckled. "That's good, Brooke."

Brooke nodded. It was good. *He'll be fine. They're fine.* She believed that, for the most part. But she was still checking the time every ten or fifteen minutes and scanning her phone for any texts or messages. *Just in case he needs anything.*

"It's hard," Kelly said.

"What?" Brooke asked, glancing up from her phone.

"Leaving them that first time." Kelly pointed one freshly painted nail at the phone. "You've checked it, oh, at least three times since you finished washing my hair."

"I have?" Brooke frowned, flipped the phone over and focused on finishing Kelly's cut. "They did fine yesterday but…Joy was asleep for most of that. I guess I am a bit anxious. I'm sorry, Kelly."

"Don't be. I get it." Kelly smiled. "The first few times I left Dickie alone with Alice, I was a mess. I'd left him a whole checklist of what to do, things to watch for, when to call me— all that. Poor man was a nervous wreck, and this was on child two. Of course, they both survived—"

"Survived?" Brooke frowned. "That's not exactly reassuring, Kelly."

"They were both fine. More than fine." Kelly laughed. "So much for being a comfort." She paused then, her nails tapping once more. "How is Tess doing with all of this?"

Maybe it was her tone of voice, but something had Brooke looking up. "Why?"

"Oh, it's probably nothing but I wondered if she'd mentioned anything about Beau Briscoe? At all?" Kelly went on. "Alice came home from school talking about how she'd heard Beau was planning on asking Tess to prom. I didn't think much of it until Stephen came home and said the same thing, more or less." She shrugged. "You know boys never say all that much."

Prom? Tess and Beau? "Oh."

"Tess hasn't said anything?" Kelly asked.

Brooke set the scissors down. "Did he already ask her? Or there is a rumor he is going to ask her?" Tess had never kept secrets from her before.

"No, no." Kelly reached up and took Brooke's hand. "He hasn't asked. I just assumed, since Alice and Stephen knew, she might have heard something."

Because Alice and Tess were best friends and best friends tell each other everything. Brooke chewed on the inside of her lip. "If she has, she hasn't told me."

"I'm not saying it's true, either—you know how these things get started." Kelly lowered her voice. "I know how protective you are of Tess, is all."

She was. Of course she was. It was her job. But now she was beginning to wonder if she was being too protective. There was no question about Tess's feelings for Beau. It wasn't Beau that Brooke was worried about so much as Tess. She was so young and sweet—just like their mother had been when their loser of a father had wandered into her life. Tess didn't need any distractions, she needed to focus on her future and the limitless possibilities ahead of her. It was Brooke's job to remind her of that.

She eyed the ends of Kelly's hair, decided it was straight and started blow-drying, but she couldn't let go of the whole Tess-and-Beau thing.

Beau hadn't asked Tess to prom—yet. But if Alice and Stephen had heard similar stories it was only a matter of time before he did ask. And then what? It was prom. Part of the whole high school experience. *I don't want her to miss any of that.*

And yet, she'd seen the whole Tess-staring-at-Beau-staring-back-at-Tess thing and the two of them being all red-faced in her kitchen… That was the problem. Not that Tess was going to prom, but that she'd be going with Beau and Beau was the only boy who had ever made her sister red-faced and frazzled.

She set the blow-dryer aside, sprayed some heat treatment onto Kelly's hair and reached for her straight-iron.

"I didn't mean to worry you." Kelly was watching Brooke's reflection. "She's a teenager, Brooke. She's growing up. And, as far as teenage boys go, Beau is a good kid. I'll go so far as to vouch for him. He and Stephen have been friends for years. I've watched him grow up. Good manners, soft-spoken, smart and favoring Forrest way more than Audy."

Brooke would almost prefer he was more like Audy—then she'd have a viable reason to keep him and Tess apart. "You think I'm being overprotective." It wasn't a question. She wasn't really asking because she already knew the answer. "It's just…"

"She's your little sister," Kelly finished. "And after your mom and dad…" She shrugged, one of the few people who knew the truth about her parents. "I get it, I do. But Tess has a good head on her shoulders, you know that. Which, I might add, is thanks to you. Don't worry."

"I think...I think she really likes him," she whispered. "Tess. And Beau, I mean."

"Oh." Kelly sighed. "That's why you're worried."

"It'd be one thing if they were just going as friends..." But as soon as she'd said the words, she realized that wasn't true. "Okay, fine, I'm being way overprotective."

"You have every right to tell me to mind my own business but—" Kelly lowered her voice so no one could overhear their conversation "—I don't want you to make Tess defensive or for her to stop telling you things because she's scared of the way you'll react. You know how hard it is to be a teenager. She needs you."

Brooke finished smoothing Kelly's hair into a sleek, flipped-under style before saying, "I hear you." No, she wasn't thrilled over the whole crush thing—not at all. But Tess meant everything to her—Tess and Joy. If Tess wanted to go to prom with Beau Briscoe, Brooke would bite her lip, take her dress shopping and take pictures like any parent would do. "If you say he's a good boy, I believe you." She'd try, anyway.

"He's a good boy," Kelly assured her, reaching up to run a hand over her now-silky-smooth locks. "And I look like a million bucks. Dickie will be all tongue-tied when he sees me." Kelly and Dickie had one of those rare marriages that actually seemed to be working. They talked and laughed and flirted and generally seemed to be happy together.

"You two." Brooke shook her head, but she was smiling.

"Are blessed to have one another," Kelly finished for her. "You'll find your fella, one day. I just know it."

That makes one of us. The prospects in Garrison were few and far between. And now, with Tess and Beau and Joy and Audy... The very idea of Audy Briscoe underfoot while she was trying to date? She frowned. Right now, the last thing she needed to worry about was her love life. Or rather, the lack of one. She had too much to deal with already. Why add something else—especially when she could predict the outcome?

AUDY STOOD, SWAYING, with Joy dozing against his chest. "Thank you, Kelly." He watched the woman unload the brown paper grocery sack onto the kitchen table. He'd never heard Joy make that sound before and he never wanted to hear it again.

"I'm glad you called," Kelly said, placing one box of the teething biscuits into the pantry and leaving the other on the kitchen table. "I wasn't sure which one you'd want, so I got a couple."

Audy surveyed the box of biscuits and plastic teething toys. "I guess I'll let her pick."

"I'll give them a good washing first." Kelly pulled off the cardboard labels and carried the teething rings to the sink. "Then we can put them in the refrigerator."

He nodded, continuing to pat and dance-sway with Joy around the kitchen. She'd started fussing within an hour of his arrival and hadn't stopped until he'd picked her up. Even then, she kept reaching for her face. She'd drooled so much, there was a wet spot on his shoulder. Instead of panicking, he'd done some searches online and consulted the baby book they'd brought back with them from Houston.

Teething. Joy was teething. And it was a horrible, miserable thing.

Worse, they didn't seem to have a thing

for teething in all the supplies they'd brought from Houston. He knew this because he'd gone through every drawer and box and bag hoping for some sort of miracle cure. Even though she hadn't outright cried, her consistent sniffs and hiccups were taking a toll on his confidence. To make matters worse, she kept flipping her little lip and staring up at him with her big brown eyes. It'd been enough to send his heart rate into overdrive. Even Harvey had vacated the nursery for the kitchen. Tess's cat, Marzipan, had hidden beneath one of the sofas in the fancy formal rooms that never seemed to be used.

He'd figured out the only way he couldn't see the lip-flip and those tear-filled eyes was by holding her. He'd been holding her for the last two hours and his back was starting to hurt, but putting her down? No, better a sore back than a distraught Joy.

Once he'd figured out what was happening, he'd called Kelly Schneider. She was a mom. Beau thought she was awesome, and she'd always been levelheaded and no-nonsense—both things he was in dire need of. He'd been looking for advice about what things to order to help Joy with her teething. Kelly had gone above and beyond by delivering what she said were surefire teething tools. She'd laughed, saying this was when it helped that she was co-owner of the grocery store in town.

The time between the phone call and Kelly's arrival was the worst. Joy's sniffles had turned into real tears. Not shrieking crying, but like sad little muffled sounds of discomfort that had to be ten times worse than a full-blown tantrum.

"She was doing fine when I got here. Guess I broke her?" Audy stared down at the top of Joy's head, doing his best to find the humor in the situation.

"It looks like you're doing a terrific job to me." Kelly patted his arm and smiled at him. "Look at it this way, you had a situation, and you figured out the problem and the way to fix it. I'd say this morning was a success."

"I'm not sure I would consider this morning a success." He'd found a washcloth folded neatly in the linen closet, soaked it in cold water, and let Joy suck and gnaw on it, hoping it would help. He wasn't sure it had done much more than make his shirt and Joy's pink-and-white-dotted onesie wet but Joy had eventually fussed herself out. Now she dozed, her little cheek resting against Audy's chest.

"I think you need to give yourself a break." Kelly kept washing the teething rings as she glanced over her shoulder at him. "Figuring out what Joy needs without her being able to tell you? It's just part of the parenting thing."

Audy understood that part of it, even if he didn't like it. But he'd reached his limit when Joy had done the lip-flip. Now that he'd seen it, he wasn't sure he'd ever be able to look at a baby the same way. Never in his life had a slight action had such a major impact. But maybe it was just him. It had to be. Otherwise, there wouldn't be as many babies born every day.

"Thank you for this, Kelly. I didn't mean to pull you away from work." Audy sighed.

"You didn't." Kelly waved his thanks aside. "I offered. You and Brooke have been thrown in the deep end on this one."

"She's swimming. I'm sinking." He kept gently bouncing Joy.

"Brooke's good at coming across like she's got it all together." Kelly smiled.

Because she did have it all together. If she'd come home to find him pacing the floor and

Joy screaming, she'd have gone back to giving him judgy looks and sighing all the time. He didn't want that. He wasn't sure how he'd explain the mess he'd made in Joy's nursery, but he'd figure it out. He'd been desperate, so his search for some sort of teething aid hadn't exactly been orderly.

"You two just need to give each other some time and space." Kelly started drying off the teething toys with a clean kitchen towel. "You and Brooke, I mean. Not you and Joy. Believe it or not, I think the two of you are doing pretty well. You and Joy, I mean."

Audy wasn't sure what to say to that. He wanted to believe her—she did have first-hand experience with all of this. Even though she said he needed to give himself a break, that today was a success, and he and Joy's relationship was going pretty well, that didn't match up with how he saw things. Still, he appreciated her vote of confidence. More than that, he appreciated her coming over.

He knew it was going to take time for Joy and him to get to know each other. And until the whole teething thing happened, he'd felt like they were off to a good start. But she'd done more fussing and lip-flipping in one morning than she had the whole time she'd been in their care. Inasmuch as he didn't want to feel responsible for it, he felt wholly responsible for it.

"She really does look like a little doll, doesn't she?" Kelly hung up the kitchen towel and smoothed it into place. "We can only hope she's not half as rowdy a teenager as you were."

"Let's get through teething and walking and talking before we start thinking about her as a teenager, okay?" The idea of Joy being old enough to talk back to him made Audy's stomach hurt.

This was why he'd never wanted to be a parent. He wasn't one to think too far into the future. Since he'd always lived each day to its fullest, he didn't make plans all that far ahead for fear of missing out on unexpected opportunities.

"Mark my words, Audy, time flies once you have kids." Kelly patted Joy's little back. "It still seems like yesterday that I was rocking Stephen through colic. Now he's bigger than his father, barreling down the football field and looking over college applications."

By the time Kelly finished talking, Audy

was feeling more than a little panicked. Not about the here and now, though. More like the next eighteen years.

"Do you need me to get anything else for you?" Kelly asked. "Dickie can handle things for a while, but it's getting late and things pick up around lunch. But I'm happy to drop things back here if you need something?"

"I think we're good. Other than teething, Brooke has most everything covered. Thanks to you, we're okay on that front." He winked at her. "We're rotating half days right now, but I'll tell Brooke about your offer."

"Anytime, Audy. Being a first-time parent isn't easy—even under normal circumstances."

There was nothing normal about any of this.

"You add teething to the mix…" She broke off, shaking her head.

"Yesterday was fine. And this morning was good, we were good." He stared down at the top of Joy's head. "Then little Miss Muffet's teeth decided to shake things up." Audy couldn't remember the last time he'd felt that shaken. "Poor little thing wasn't any happier about it than I was. She was just louder than me. She's got good lungs."

The sound of the front door closing reached him about the same time as Brooke walked into the kitchen. "Kelly? Hi." Brooke's light brown gaze bounced from him to Joy to Kelly, concerned. "What happened?"

"Nothing." He kept patting Joy's back, his tone calm and soft.

"You had to call in reinforcements?" She shot another look at Kelly.

Brooke's instant assumption that he needed help put his back up. "I called Kelly for advice, yes."

Brooke nodded. "It's fine if you needed help. But why didn't you call me?" She didn't sound upset, but the tick in the muscle of her jaw said otherwise.

He tried his hardest to keep the anger from his voice. "You were at work. I had things under control."

Brooke's nod said one thing, but the look on her face said the exact opposite.

"Brooke, hold up." Kelly put her hand on Brooke's arm. "Audy didn't ask—"

"Looks like Brooke's already made up her

mind about what happened today, Kelly." Audy cut in. "No point arguing with her."

Kelly glanced between the two of them. "Well, isn't this a pickle? I didn't mean to cause any trouble."

Audy sighed, shooting Brooke a sidelong look. She could be as snippy as she wanted with him, but Kelly was her friend—and she'd rallied when he needed help. "You didn't."

Brooke ran a hand over her head, tension bracketing her mouth. "I'm sorry, Kelly. I am. It's good to see you and, you know, you're welcome anytime."

Kelly accepted Brooke's hug. "Okay, good, because I am coming back to play with that little angel when she's up for it." She patted Brooke's back. "And I'll bring some pecan brownies for us."

"That sounds wonderful." Brooke smiled. "I can't wait."

He waited until Kelly had closed the door behind her before he said, "How about we back things up and start again. You could ask, 'How was your day, Audy? Did you and Joy get on okay?' Or even, 'Let me tell you all about my second day back at work.'" He paused, still dancing with Joy. "Instead of you acting all prickly and jumping to assumptions—like I couldn't handle things on my own."

"It was a pretty easy assumption to jump to." Brooke hung her purse on the hook on the wall. "If you're not ready for this, then just tell me. It's not bad or anything. Remember, this halfsies thing was your idea."

"I know and I'm ready. We were fine yesterday, weren't we?" Brooke didn't answer, so he glanced down at Joy. "And since you asked…" He paused, leveling Brooke with an unflinching gaze. "Joy, here, had a rough morning. Teething. I gave her a washcloth to chew on but that only worked for so long. I didn't want to take her to the store, get her even more out of sorts, so I called Kelly to ask what to order to help Joy—planning on picking up once you got here and dropping it back here before I headed home. Kelly helped me order and then dropped by with the stuff. I didn't ask her to. She chose to. It was real thoughtful of her. Joy's been hurting something fierce and I didn't want her to keep hurting."

Brooke stared at him, her brows rising slowly. "Teething?"

"Yep. Unless Google and the baby book

and Kelly are all wrong. But the washcloth helped—until it didn't." He shot her another look. "Maybe you would have handled things differently, but I worked with what I had. If you want to get all bent out of shape over it, I know there's nothing I can do to stop you."

For a minute, it looked like she was going to unleash the signature "Brooke Young Glare and Fury" his way. Instead, she drew in a deep breath and said, "I apologize, Audy. You put Joy's best interests first and I came in here, jumping to conclusions about you asking for help... Well, I'm sorry. And I appreciate you and what you did, and Kelly, for getting Joy things that might help with her discomfort."

Had Brooke Young just complimented him? Audy Briscoe? He was pretty sure saying he'd put Joy first was a compliment— something that wasn't easy for her to do. He was...surprised, to say the least. But he'd be lying if he said it didn't mean something. It did. Why? He shied away from answering that question. Something told him he wouldn't like the answer. He cleared his throat and said, "Apology accepted. And you're welcome."

"Good." Brooke looked sincere. She sounded sincere. Still, Audy couldn't help but hold his breath and wait to see what she might say next. But Brooke didn't say anything. Instead, she opened the refrigerator, pulled out the iced tea and poured herself a tall glass. "You want some?"

"I'm good." His back was hurting, but he was good. "How was your day?"

Her eyes widened in surprise but she answered, "You know Garrison. There's always something to talk about." She sat in the kitchen chair, propped her chin in her hand and took a sip of tea.

"Anything worth sharing?" It might be his imagination, but she seemed a little deflated.

She turned her tea glass, considering. "Where do I start? Lance Devlin is looking into selling the property surrounding, and including, The First Tree. You can imagine how that's going over."

"He's a little thickheaded, that one." Audy had to chuckle. "But his dear aunt Martha will put an end to that before it gets too far along."

"Whatever put the fool notion into his head

to begin with? I'll never know." She took another sip of her tea.

"City folk." He shrugged. "The first time I laid eyes on Lance Devlin, I knew he had no idea what he was doing. All slick talk and expensive suits might have worked in a corporate boardroom but they don't impress anyone here. Never did understand why he got hired. I guess, other than the town not wanting to make an enemy of Martha Moneybags Zeigler."

Brooke chuckled. "Moneybags, huh?" Her gaze shifted to Joy. "I can take her, if you want."

Instead of taking her up on her offer, he said, "You take a minute and finish your tea. Miss Muffet, here, is finally sleeping. I'd hate to wake her up."

"Audy..." She trailed off and stared at him with those big brown eyes. Just when he thought she was going to say more, she took a sip of tea.

He waited. And waited. Until he couldn't wait anymore. "Audy...what? I'm pretty sure there was more coming."

"This weekend..." She paused. "Are you

still planning on participating in the Holsum Rodeo?"

"I'll be honest and say it almost slipped my mind." Which was surprising. Unnerving was more like it. How could he have forgotten? Rodeo was what he did, who he was. After today, well, it'd be nice to feel like he knew what he was doing—and spend time with people—women—who appreciated his physical prowess and skill. A few beers, some dancing, a little flirting with the ladies… He broke off, his gaze crashing into Brooke's. He knew she didn't approve, he saw it plain on her face. But he had every right to live his life. "Probably."

"I'll plan to keep her this weekend, then," Brooke said, her voice flat. She stood, finished her tea and closed the distance between them so she could reach for Joy. "I've got it from here."

Audy eased Joy, sleeping soundly, into Brooke's arms but didn't immediately run for the door. "The teething rings are clean and in the refrigerator." He wasn't sure what had happened, but she wasn't looking at him anymore. "And there's some teething biscuits there. And another box in the pantry."

"Thanks." She carried Joy into the nursery, Audy trailing behind her. He almost slammed into her back when she came to a dead stop square in the middle of the doorway. "What…"

He peered over Brooke's shoulder at the mess he'd made. "Let me—"

"I've got it, Audy. I'm sure your brothers need you on the ranch. I can clean this up." She still didn't look at him. "I'll see you tomorrow around one?"

"Are you sure?" He eyed his handiwork. It looked like a tornado had hit, spitting out clothes and fluffy bloomers and ruffled socks and big-bow headbands all over. "I—"

"I'm sure. You have a good evening, Audy." She sat in the rocking chair, cradled Joy close and started humming "There Was an Old Lady Who Swallowed a Fly."

Four hours later, Audy still couldn't get the song out of his head.

CHAPTER TEN

"AT LEAST IT'S a beautiful day," Brooke said, pushing the stroller along the bumpy sand path leading from the parking lot and winding all the way down to the wide-open field surrounding The First Tree, the play equipment and soccer fields visible in the distance.

"It is," Tess agreed, pushing her braid from her shoulder.

Brooke's Saturday had started off with two scheduled appointments. But now, she was free to enjoy the rest of the weekend with Joy and Tess. It was only when she'd come home to find Tess was wearing a dress, something she rarely did, and some lip gloss, something she never did, *and* had taken extra time to braid her hair—Brooke felt a prick of unease. If she acknowledged her little sister's efforts, she'd have to consider Tess's motivation... And, even though she'd made peace with the possibility of Beau Briscoe asking Tess to prom, she didn't want to think Tess's extra efforts had anything to do with that. She didn't want to dwell on Tess or Beau or ruin the glorious weather and the birdsong and Joy's cheerful chatter from beneath the canopy of her stroller.

They were here to take part in the Garrison Ladies Guild picnic. Brooke wasn't a formal member—she didn't have the time for volunteer work the guild required—and Tess was too young. But the guild always invited Brooke, so Brooke always came. Meetings were mostly discussions about the year's events, festivals and farmers markets that would take place up and down Main Street. The Ladies Guild was instrumental to every one of them. Since her salon had a storefront on Main Street, she liked to know what was happening and how it might affect traffic in and out of her shop.

"Can I spend the night with Alice tonight?" Tess asked. "My pre-cal grade is now a ninety-six because I totally aced my quiz, thank you very much. That's my lowest grade, too. So, *I* don't think it'd hurt me to, you know, eat popcorn and paint our nails and listen to bad music and just hang out. Do you?"

"I don't think it would hurt." She smiled at

her sister. "Did she already ask her mom?" If Kelly said no, Brooke would be all too happy to have Alice over for a girls' night. In a way, she hoped Kelly would say no because it sounded like fun. *Hanging out with a couple of sixteen-year-olds on a Saturday night, listening to music, doing their nails and eating popcorn sounds like fun?* Maybe she did need to get out more. Or get a hobby? If she ever had the time…

"I think so." Tess nodded. "But I'm sure she'll be here. Mrs. Schneider, I mean."

Kelly was on the Ladies Guild, so she would definitely be here. As owners of Garrison Family Grocery, Kelly and Dickie Schneider were important to the community. They still gave store credit, stocked the county food pantry and always stepped up when anyone in town needed anything. Dickie was one of those rare men who gave his wife unconditional support, no matter what. Once, Kelly had worn a bright pink wig home from Brooke's salon just to see what Dickie would do. According to Kelly, he'd blinked, told her he'd have to wear sunglasses it was so bright, but he would if pink hair made her happy.

"There she is." Tess waved. "Alice, too."

But it wasn't Kelly or Alice or the twenty or so women gathered around picnic tables beneath the canopy-like branches of The First Tree that snagged Brooke's attention. No, it was the group of teen boys just beyond in the field—tossing around a football. And there, right in the middle of them—taller and broader and altogether more manly looking than every boy out there—stood Beau Briscoe.

Brooke's heart sank. "There they are," she murmured, risking a glance at her little sister.

Tess looked ready to pop from happiness. There it was. *That* look. The light-up-from-the-inside thing that Tess got whenever she saw *him*. The very look that filled Brooke with dread. How could she not panic when her sister was practically glowing because of some…some boy?

Somehow, she managed not to say a thing until Alice and Tess had wandered off—conveniently in the direction of the football game. But once they were out of hearing range, Kelly turned to her, an almost apologetic look on her face.

"Okay. I get it." Kelly nodded. "That was… intense."

Brooke sighed. "I know. You saw?"

"Oh, yeah." Kelly glanced after the two girls. "Worse, I saw *him* see her."

"I don't want to hear it." Brooke held up her hand and went around to unbuckle Joy. "Joy and I don't care a bit about some stinky boy."

But Kelly just laughed.

Brooke stood, Joy in her arms. "I guess I get to keep one eye on you and one eye on Tess."

Kelly tickled Joy. "Oh, Joy, tell your momma to go easy on your big sister. First loves can be overwhelming."

Brooke wasn't sure which part of that statement was more startling. The fact that Kelly had called Brooke Joy's "momma," Tess Joy's "big sister," or that her little sister was in love. "Just so you know, I'm not okay with a single thing you just said."

"What?" Kelly frowned. "Come here, Joy. I miss holding a baby." She held her hands out and since Joy was all smiles, Brooke handed her over. "You're the cutest little thing I've set my eyes on in years. A little angel. And all these ruffles."

Out of nowhere, Brooke heard Audy's voice in her head, calling Joy "Miss Muffet." He said it with such affection it never failed to catch Brooke's interest. But recently, she'd noticed that his sweetness didn't just catch her attention—he sort of…turned her insides all warm and soft. If she were being completely honest with herself, she'd developed several alarming reactions to her co-guardian over the last two weeks of their shared days with Joy… All of which she needed to put a stop to.

No more laughing at his jokes.

No more listening to his stories.

No more getting caught up in him dancing Joy around the kitchen. Or any other time, for that matter.

And definitely no more going warm and soft on the inside over anything Audy Briscoe said or did.

Most important, no more thinking about Audy Briscoe—unless it was absolutely necessary.

Not when he kept going off to do the thing she most objected to. For all the progress he'd made with Joy, he didn't seem to get that his risk-taking ways and rodeo days needed to stop. He was a guardian now. There was no denying he and Joy got along, all anyone had to do was see the two of them together to know that. And yet, he'd still headed down the road to Jasperton for this weekend's rodeo—because it was clear he'd never considered giving up rodeo. *Because, at the end of the day, he was still the same selfish, reckless man he'd always been.*

There was no point in being angry with him. He was doing what she'd known he'd do. But she was disappointed in herself for thinking he'd change. *No more daydreaming about Audy.* Just blue skies and catching up with friends and planning all sorts of good things for Garrison.

Brooke turned to check in on Tess but wound up watching, in horror, as the speeding missile of a football came out of nowhere and slammed straight into Beau Briscoe's head. The impact was so hard his head popped back and he fell back, flat, onto the ground.

Brooke didn't realize she was running until she was on the field. A few of the boys had already gathered around and were staring down at Beau, but none of them seemed to be doing anything.

"Beau?" she asked, as she peered at his face.

Beau lay there, dazed, blood trickling from his nose. He didn't seem to hear her.

Her lungs emptied as she knelt in the grass

beside him. "Beau? Beau Briscoe?" she asked, a little louder.

"Oh, Brooke, is he okay?" Tess dropped to her knees beside her.

Brooke was pretty sure the blood and being this out-of-it was bad. "I think that's a good—"

"Tess?" Beau ran a hand over his face, blinked rapidly and tried to prop himself up on his elbow.

"Whoa, now, hold on." Brooke placed a hand on his shoulder. "You give yourself a minute, Beau."

He blinked again but didn't resist.

"Ice?" she asked. "We need ice." Brooke pointed at the picnic. "Hurry."

"I'll get my mom. She'll know what to do." Stephen Schneider took off—flying across the field to the gathering. Already, half of the women were making their way onto the field. The others stood beneath the shade of The First Tree, watching.

Seconds passed before Beau asked, "What happened?" His hand was steadier when he reached up to press his palm to his forehead.

"You got pegged," one of the boys said. "Hard."

"Here." Brooke pulled the burp rag from her dress pocket and handed it to Beau. "For your nose."

Beau took the pink-heart and rainbow-covered towel, gave it a look, then offered it back. "I don't want to stain it, Miss Young. It's no big deal."

The combination of worry over staining the towel and his impeccable manners took the edge off Brooke's fear. He seemed to be more alert, his gaze focusing—at least, she hoped so.

"But you're bleeding," Tess said, her voice wobbling.

That was the moment Beau seemed to *see* Tess was there. And once he saw her, she was all he saw. "I'm all right, Tess." He pressed the towel to his nose and propped himself up on his elbow, wincing.

"Why are you moving?" Tess glanced at Brooke. "Should he be moving?"

"I bet you've got a concussion," another boy said.

"Might have even broken your nose." This kid leaned down, studying Beau's face. "Maybe."

"Not helping, guys," Beau muttered. But his gaze was glued onto Tess.

"Boys, boys, give me a second." Kelly arrived, all calm efficiency. "Let me get a look at him, please." She had an ice pack in her hand and some wet wipes in the other. "It's times like this, I'm glad I've been a football mom since you boys were all in kindergarten." She gave them a reassuring smile before turning her attention to Beau. "I think it'd be wise for you to drive Beau to Doc Johnston, Stephen." She gave her son a long look. "No side trips. I'll text him and let him know you're coming."

"I'm fine, Mrs. Schneider," Beau argued.

"I think you are, too, Beau, but we would all feel better if you let Doc Johnston give us the all clear." Kelly sat back, glancing at Tess. "Wouldn't we, Tess?"

Brooke saw how close Tess was to tears and took her sister's hand. She may not want Tess to be infatuated with Beau Briscoe, but she couldn't bear to see Tess hurting.

"Yes," Tess managed, but her voice was still wobbly. "Yes. We would."

Beau stared at her for a long time. Tess stared right back.

And Brooke's heart sank deep into her chest. She'd got this all wrong. Her little sister wasn't crushing on Beau. That would have been too easy. A crush was passing—easily recovered from. This wasn't *that*. This was way worse. Tess was in love. Love *love*. With Beau. Brooke swallowed hard.

"Okay," Beau said, taking Stephen's hand.

Two of the other boys helped him up, standing by in case Beau wasn't steady on his feet.

"Joy?" Brooke asked, still reeling from this latest Tess-Beau development.

"She's with Hazel." Kelly patted her arm. "I know she's getting baby-fever."

Knowing Joy was safe was all that mattered to Brooke.

"I can take your truck home," one of the boys offered.

"Don't let him. Have you seen him drive?" Stephen argued.

Tess was staring at her, Brooke could feel it, silently willing her to offer help.

"We'll take care of your truck," Brooke murmured.

"I don't want to be a bother, Miss Young," Beau said.

It would be less of a bother if his gaze

didn't keep landing on Tess—again and again. "You're not. But you will be if you don't move it and head straight to Doc Johnston's." She felt her sister squeeze her hand in thanks. *I'm such a pushover.* But she gave Tess's hand an answering squeeze.

"Yes, ma'am." He nodded, pulling his keys from his pocket and handing them over. "Thank you."

Brooke nodded, shoving the keys into her pocket.

"You want to come?" Stephen asked Alice and Tess.

Alice shrugged. "I guess. Tess?"

Brooke stared up at the sky overhead. If she let Tess go, she'd be a fool. If she made Tess stay, Tess would worry and fret and be miserable. From the corner of her eye, she saw Kelly trying not to laugh. *What was funny?* Nothing.

"Brooke?" Tess asked, all nerves.

Brooke took another deep breath. "Yes. Sure. Just keep me in the loop. We'll get the truck situation sorted out."

Tess nodded. "I'll text you. I will. Thank you."

"Keep that on your nose," Kelly said to

Beau, pointing at the towel-wrapped ice pack in his hand.

"Yes, ma'am," Beau agreed, but he didn't seem to be paying all that much attention. Tess had taken his arm and was helping him, with Stephen, back across the field to the dirt parking lot.

"That boy is feeling no pain," Kelly murmured.

All Brooke could do was sigh again. *What am I doing?* Tess had no reason to go. Beau and Stephen could handle this—Alice, too. Tess didn't *need* to be there. *She wants to be there.* If Joy hadn't started crying, Brooke would probably have talked herself into calling Tess back. But Joy was crying, loudly.

"She and Hazel were all smiles when I left," Kelly explained.

"Poor thing probably saw that whole… mess between Beau and Tess and dissolved into tears." Brooke's pace quickened.

Kelly burst out laughing. "It's not that bad."

"You're telling me you'd be fine if Alice looked at…at Hans Zeigler like that?" Hans was Martha's grandson. He was on the football team with Beau and well-liked by everyone— especially the girls.

Kelly frowned her way.

"Uh-huh." Brooke nodded. "That's what I thought." She located Joy on the lap of Hattie Carmichael—who looked close to tears herself.

"I told Hazel that little one is just too cute not to share," Miss Ruth said, smiling. "And look. We were just telling Hattie how good she looks with a baby in her lap."

Brooke shot Hattie a look of understanding. Being young and female and single in Garrison meant you were a problem that needed to be fixed. It didn't matter that Brooke and Hattie, the county game warden, were both successful and happy as clams. They weren't married with a passel of kids trailing after them and, until they were, the Garrison Ladies Guild wouldn't rest.

"She's teething," Brooke explained, taking Joy from Hattie. Joy quieted instantly and rested her head on Brooke's shoulder. "You're okay," she murmured, pressing a kiss to her forehead. "Let's find your teething ring." She paused, asking Hattie, "I heard something about a big chain store wanting to buy up The First Tree and Garrison Park? Is that true?"

"What?" Barbara Eldridge asked, repeating

the question for those who hadn't heard. All at once, the Garrison Ladies Guild erupted in outrage—earning Brooke and Hattie a reprieve from the guild's misguided, if well-meaning, attention.

AUDY SAW STARS. Not the sort of stars that were there shining brightly in the wide Texas night sky overhead, though. The kind that flashed behind the eyelids after a hard fall or blow to the head. Or, as was the case now, a mix of the two.

He heard the collective "oh" and a few gasps from the audience but knew he had to move.

Dirt Devil wasn't going to stand aside and let Audy be just because he'd had the wind knocked out of him. No, sir, the eighteen-hundred-pound bull would be all too happy to pound Audy into the dirt beneath him. With a quick glance, he rolled over, pushed off the ground and sprinted toward the metal fencing surrounding the arena.

He heard a few panicked cries. One woman screamed. The thunder of hoofbeats coming right up behind him was unmistakable. For a minute, the hot breath of Dirt Devil all but singed the back of Audy's neck. But his feet kept moving, faster and faster—his battered lungs would likely rupture long before he reached the fence.

Closer now.

The crowd was all fired up.

And he was there, grabbing the top bar of the pipe railing and swinging his legs up and over before he dared look back. But before he'd let go, the fence jerked with such force that the muffled popping of his shoulder and the tingle that shot straight down his arm and into his fingertips weren't surprising. He gritted his teeth, pried his fingers from the railing and did his best to land on his feet.

The crowd went wild. Whistles and clapping and a whole lot of screaming. The rodeo emcee blasted "I Wanna Be a Cowboy" in his honor, so Audy sucked in a breath at the pain in his left hand, waved with his right and acted like he had all the time in the world as he made his way toward the holding pens, chutes and the ambulance waiting on the other side.

"Hey, Audy." Mikey Woodard set aside his kettle corn and dusted his hands off on the front of his EMT's uniform pants. "What'd I miss?"

"What makes you think I'm not just stopping by to say hello?" He tried to tease, he did. But he was hurting.

"Well, your lips are gray and your right arm's holding your left arm and you got dirt coming off your back like you recently made an unplanned stop on the ground back-first? Or something along those lines." He pulled an alcohol wipe from a bin mounted on the inside of the open ambulance door, wiped off his hands, then shoved it into a trash bag tied to the fender. "Plus, I can tell your shoulder's out of whack from here. Want me to take a look or are you planning on walking it off?"

Audy wanted to laugh, but moving—like walking and talking and breathing—was more challenging than normal so he said, "I'd appreciate the help."

Mikey nodded. "How's life?" he asked, moving his hands along Audy's arm and shoulder.

"Good," Audy grunted.

Mikey paused, meeting Audy's gaze as he said, "Best relax or you'll bruise worse."

"Relax, huh?" he chuckled and instantly

regretted how the movement rattled around his shoulder socket.

"Yep." Mikey pointed. "Easier if you lie down."

"I can take it," Audy argued.

"Easier on your joint and tendons." Mikey shook his head. "Nothing to do with your ego."

Audy climbed into the ambulance and lay on the paper-covered bed. "Let's get this over with."

Mikey took Audy's left wrist in both hands, taking care to keep Audy's arm straight and level and his forearm facing down. Slowly, he moved Audy's arm up and toward Audy's head. It probably didn't take more than five minutes, but by the time the soft pop rang in his ears, Audy was covered in sweat and shaky.

"I'm guessing you won't take a sling?" Mikey asked.

"Why would I need that?" Audy sat up. "You fixed me, didn't you?"

"I fixed your arm. I didn't fix you. Any man who climbs on the back of an angry killing machine needs a whole lot more than a shoulder pop and a sling, let me tell you."

Mikey handed him a cellophane-wrapped package. "Take it."

"Thanks, Mikey. I'm mighty obliged to you." Audy took the package.

"Just doing my job." Mikey rubbed his hands down with another wipe. "I hear you got yourself a kid?"

"Yeah, I guess I do have a kid." He paused. "I mean, she's not mine. I'm not her biological father or anything—"

He nodded. "Whatever you say."

Audy sighed. "My buddy died. So did his wife. She, Joy, was their little girl. And now… I'm raising her."

"Sorry to hear that, Audy." He paused. "On your own?"

"No." He chuckled, rubbing his shoulder. "Brooke Young and I. You know Brooke?"

"Yes, sir." His smile was a little too bright. "Almost got up the courage to ask her out once, too. Still planning on it. She's something, isn't she?"

Audy wasn't exactly sure what that meant, but he nodded all the same. Mikey and Brooke? He gave the man a looking-over—something that made Mikey's brows raise high.

"Oh. That means you and Brooke…" Mikey let the sentence hang there.

"No." He held up his right hand. "No. No. She and I? Well…no." Did she make things get all scrambled up in his head? Yes. That's why he was here. To clear his mind. No Brooke. No Joy. Just Audy, doing what Audy did. Hanging with RJ. Having a few beers, some laughs and the company of a fine-looking woman. A woman who looked nothing like Brooke Young—and certainly didn't treat him like she did. *Like the good old days.* Not that he remembered the good old days hurting like this.

"That's a lot of nos." Mikey's eyes narrowed.

"There he is. Got your time. Got the score," RJ Malloy called out. "You still alive and kicking?" He had a beer in each hand. "I figured Mikey'd have you patched up by now."

"For now." Mikey shook his head. "You best take more care, Audy. You've got a little one that'll need looking after."

RJ rolled his eyes. "There are plenty of bull riders that got kids."

Audy took the beer RJ offered him. "Yep."

"Audy Briscoe is a bull rider. No changing that," RJ added.

"I'll drink to that." Audy sipped the ice-cold beer.

"Audy Briscoe was third runner-up at last year's world championship. Third." RJ held up three fingers. "How many folk you know that can say that?"

Mikey shook his head. "Most of the folk I see here aren't doing much talking. Mostly moaning. Some bleeding. A few crying."

Audy frowned at Mikey.

"I've never seen Audy cry. You know why?" RJ went on.

"Because he's a bull rider?" Mikey asked. "How many of those have you had?" He eyed the beer. "And how much do you pay him to follow you around making you sound special?"

"You wait now, I'm just getting started." RJ grinned. "But you're right. Audy don't cry because he *is* a bull rider. A real one, too. He's had his collarbone broken, ribs cracked, a hairline fracture in his pelvis…" He broke off. "I'm forgetting something."

"He gets it." Audy cut in, not liking the direction this was going. Mikey probably wouldn't consider his battle scars worthy of respect. He was in the grow-up-and-be-responsible camp, so Audy's scars would be further proof that he needed to be making better choices.

The thing was, people not approving of his choices didn't make those choices wrong. *I take care of Joy.* When he wasn't with her, he was working long hours at the ranch. If he wanted to spend his downtime riding a bull, then that's just what he'd do.

No, RJ was right on this one. He was a bull rider. It was in his blood. It was something he was good at—even if his scores the last few rides hadn't reflected that. Now, just because Joy was in the picture, he was supposed to give all that up? "Thanks for tonight, Mikey."

"Hope I don't see you again anytime soon, Audy." He shook Audy's good hand. "Tell Brooke I said hi, will you?" Mikey said. "Might have to stop in and meet this little one."

"Sure." Audy nodded. *No way, no how.* If Mikey was interested in her, he needed to be man enough to pursue her himself. Was Brooke interested in him?

"You two have infant CPR training?" Mikey asked. "I can get you set up."

"I get your angle." RJ nodded. "Get the girl through the baby. Smart."

Mikey shook his head, giving RJ a disapproving look. "Actually, I think all parents should be CPR certified."

"Parents?" RJ's eyes went round. "Audy? Did you hear that?"

Audy heard it, all right. Co-guardian was hard enough. *Parent?* His stomach clenched tight.

"You? A parent?" RJ kept going. "Now, that'd be a sight."

For some reason, Audy found RJ's teasing on the annoying side. He wasn't Joy's father, he never would be. But he was…something to the little girl. RJ might be having a hard time wrapping his head around the concept of Audy being a caregiver, but Audy was getting pretty good at it. He and Joy…

No. Tonight was a break. *No thinking about Brooke or Joy—*

"I forgot." RJ pulled Audy's phone from his pocket. "You got a few calls."

Audy took the phone. "Probably Forrest…" Forrest always seemed to need him most when he was rodeoing or out. But the messages weren't from Forrest. They were mostly from Beau. One from Brooke. And several from Doc Johnston.

He set the beer down, put the phone to his ear and covered his other ear as he walked down the fairway—away from the booths and vendors and noise.

"Audy?" It was Doc Johnston.

"Yes, sir? Has something happened?"

"Beau took a knock to the head, is all." Doc Johnston paused.

Audy changed direction and headed for the exit. He covered the mouthpiece to yell "I gotta go" RJ's way but didn't bother slowing to hear his response.

"He's got a concussion and a swollen nose and I'd feel better if he was watched for a bit. Miss Young has offered to take him home with her, seeing how the rest of your family is out of town and it might take a spell for you to get home. I needed to get permission."

Forrest, Uncle Felix and Webb had all gone to a livestock auction. Audy hadn't exactly volunteered the fact that he was going to Jasperton, so his family assumed he was looking out for Beau—if something came up. Like now.

His pace quickened. "You said Miss Young?" Why was Brooke there? And why had she volunteered to take Beau home? He had a feeling there was a whole lot more to the story.

"Yes. Brooke Young." Doc Johnston's voice lowered, to almost a whisper. "I feel it is my duty to inform you that your brother is mighty sweet on Tess Young. Reminds me of the days when Pearl and I were young. Time sure does fly, Audy. Mark me on that one." Audy had a hard time imagining Pearl Johnston young. Or in love. Or smiling all that much. "Nothing like young love," Doc chuckled.

Audy couldn't stop himself from smiling. "Yes, sir." As he headed across the gravel-covered parking lot, he could imagine the state Brooke was in. Tess and Beau. She couldn't be happy. Still, she'd volunteered to watch Beau, so maybe things had changed. "Is Brooke there?"

"She is," Doc Johnston said. "Hold on, I'll give her the phone. And I'll send follow-up care paperwork home with her. You've had your fair share of knocks to the head, you know what to watch out for."

"Yes, sir, I do. I appreciate it." He unlocked his truck, slid behind the wheel and connected his phone to Bluetooth. The engine roared to life and he put it in gear, leaving a spray of pebbles in his wake. He flew across the parking lot, took a quick look, and pulled out and onto the highway, his foot on the accelerator.

"Audy?" It was Brooke.

"I'm on my way."

She sighed. "Slow down."

His gaze darted to his speedometer. "How'd you know I was speeding?"

"Your truck. The faster you go, the louder it gets."

"Is that so?" And why did he like that she knew that? He slowed down a hair under the speed limit.

"Getting pulled over for a speeding ticket won't get you here any faster. And…he's fine. I mean, besides the concussion. His nosebleed stopped and he…well, he seems…"

"Do I want to know what happened?"

"I'll tell you later."

His smile grew. "Tess there?"

"Yep."

He could hear the tension in her voice. If this was making her tense, her being there didn't make any sense. "I can call Kelly—Beau practically lives over there anyway—if you'd rather. Don't get me wrong, I'm grateful, it's just…why are you doing this, Brooke?"

"Because—"

"Because?" he pushed. "Last time I mentioned my little brother and your sister in the same sentence you about took my head off and now you're offering to keep an eye on him?"

Silence.

Interesting.

"Brooke—"

"Because Tess is my everything, Audy. Well, Tess and Joy." She muttered something he didn't catch. "And—and I want her to be happy." A deep breath followed. "Yes, I have reservations and worries and doubts and… you know. But her happiness is more important than any of that."

Simple as that. For Brooke, that's the way things were—without hesitation.

It was the tenderness in her voice washing over him, breaking something loose inside and shaking him to the core. Had anyone ever talked about him like that? Had anyone ever wanted his happiness above all else? His parents maybe, but that was so long ago he couldn't say for sure. "Tess and Joy don't know how lucky they are."

There was a long pause. "Why do you say that?"

"You have a fierce capacity for love, Brooke Young. Real and unconditional." He'd caught glimpses of it. The way she'd smooth Tess's hair or smile down at Joy, the tight morning hugs before Tess left and the one she got when Brooke got home from work, how Brooke listened to Tess even when she was drooping with exhaustion or held on to Joy long after she'd fallen asleep.

"You don't think I'm being…foolish?" The hint of fear in her voice surprised him. "This could end terribly—"

"Or not."

"But they could both get hurt." She pushed.

"Or not." He reached up to rub the back of his neck and winced, his left shoulder throbbing. "They're kids. Being kids."

"No, Audy, I think it's more than that." Her whisper was breathless. "Tess is in love with him."

Love? He almost argued but… Kent and

Dara were about Tess and Beau's age when they said they'd known they were meant for each other. *And they'd been so happy.* "Well, now…" As someone who avoided anything that resembled commitment and responsibility, he'd managed to avoid any long-term entanglements. "I can't help you much there, Brooke. I've yet to make the mistake of falling into that trap."

To his surprise, Brooke laughed.

"I miss something?" he asked, turning off the highway onto the farm-to-market road that led to Garrison.

"No. No. It's just… You and I actually agree on something."

Tough luck, Mikey. It was a surprise, though. How had someone like Brooke wound up so jaded? Had something happened? Had she had her heart broken? It wasn't his business but…he wanted to know. She was a good woman, any man would be better off with her beside him. And that was a fact. "I'll be home shortly." He turned onto Main Street. "How about I assess Beau's…emotional state and we go from there?"

"Okay. I've got some leftover chili, if you're hungry?"

"I won't say no." He paused. "Thank you for taking care of Beau."

"You're welcome, Audy." And she hung up.

But her voice saying his name set all the hair on his arms on end—and the back of his neck, too. An odd ache landed in his chest and, for a split second, he almost considered the idea that maybe he was wrong. What if love wasn't a trap, but a gift to give and a treasure to receive?

"Where did that come from?" he asked out loud. He'd never been one for entertaining nonsense, he wasn't going to start now. He shook his head and turned up his music.

CHAPTER ELEVEN

HOME. BROOKE BALANCED Joy on her hip, unlocked the front door and stepped inside. Even though they'd only been gone a little over four hours, it seemed longer—way longer—and she was exhausted. Not that she could relax, not yet. She'd brought the...*enemy* home with her. No, *enemy* wasn't the right word. He was—he *seemed* like a nice kid. All "yes, ma'ams" and "no, ma'ams"—even with a concussion. *But that doesn't mean I want him spending time with Tess.*

It was her fault, really. Tess had texted that they were still at Doc Johnston's office, so Brooke had stopped by after the Ladies Guild meeting had wrapped up. Once she'd learned Beau was stuck there until Audy was reached, she had a moment of weakness and felt sorry for the kid. Somehow, that had turned into offering to watch him until Audy was home again.

Audy, who'd been off doing who-knows-what with… She didn't want to think about it. He'd gone with RJ and RJ was nothing but trouble—meaning Audy was out doing nothing good. *Not that I care.*

Instead of leading Beau to the small living room at the back of the house, where it was comfy and cozy, she turned on the lights in the formal living room. "Let's get you set up in here."

"Ba ba," Joy said, adding a long string of noises before giggling.

"All that, huh?" Brooke asked, looking over her shoulder to see Beau holding the front door open for Tess. *The kid has a concussion and he's holding the door open for her.* Tess beamed up at him and the two of them stood there, all googly-eyed and…and…

"Let's get you set up in here," Brooke repeated a little louder this time, loud enough for the two of them to snap out of it. Thankfully. "Audy said he'd be here soon."

I'll be home shortly. Audy's words. He'd been talking about her house… Not his.

"Ma ma ba," Joy said, patting Brooke on the chest. "Daw."

"No doggie," Brooke said, rubbing noses with Joy. "Harvey isn't here."

"No no no," Joy said.

Unfortunately, *no* was Joy's first official word. Her noises and gurgles were taking on more defined tones, but most of it was still gobbledygook.

"Are you comfortable?" Tess asked once Beau sat.

Brooke watched the two of them and swallowed another sigh. He might be hurting some, but he didn't seem to mind.

"I'm good. Thank you." He nodded up at Tess, a crooked grin on his face.

Apparently, the grin was a Briscoe thing. Brooke suspected her little sister's knees were all rubbery and her chest weighed a thousand pounds… *Where did that come from?* Wherever it came from, she did not like it. Not one bit. Audy grinned all the time and…and she rarely had rubbery knees or… She didn't finish that thought. She couldn't. There was no point in lying to herself.

"Ma ma." Joy patted her chest again, ending Brooke's rather alarming stream of thought. "Ma ma."

"I told you," Tess said, crossing to them

and smiling at Joy. "She calls me Teh. But she doesn't call you Brooke. To her, you're momma."

One second her heart was warm and full, the next, twisted and frozen. "She's just jabbering. Aren't you? Just talking away?" Brooke let Tess take the baby, brushing aside Tess's assertion. "I'll get some chili warmed up. We could all eat, I'm thinking?" Hungry or not, she was making food to occupy herself. Besides, she needed a few minutes to herself.

"You need a hand?" Beau offered.

"Beau, I appreciate the offer but you have a concussion. How about you sit right where you are, don't move, and Tess and Joy can keep you company while I cook?" Brooke didn't wait for an answer.

The kitchen was quiet and dark, two things that suited Brooke's mood. She flipped the switch over the stove, and it gave off all the light she needed. Then she carried the large pot of chili from the refrigerator to the still-warming stovetop and put the lid on so it could come to a slow simmer.

You can't have chili without cornbread. She turned on the oven, then gathered everything she'd need. Her grandmother's cast-iron cornbread muffin pan from the cupboard, the ladle that held the perfect amount for each muffin, and the cornbread mix from the pantry, plus flour and eggs from the refrigerator. She mixed it all up, added a pinch of salt and set the batter aside to rub shortening on the insides of the corncob-shaped muffin pan.

Slowly, her mind settled enough for her to sort through what was bothering her—thread by thread—while slowly filling each mold with the golden batter.

Tess. In love. Real love? *As if I'd know.* Real or not, it made her uneasy.

Beau. In love with Tess. And concussed and too big and manly and adult looking for her little sister…

Breathe. She closed her eyes and took a deep breath before she scooped up more batter. She needed to think about something else or she'd lose it.

The First Tree debacle. How had Martha Zeigler not known about it until today? Martha was a bit of a hermit but that wouldn't have stopped one of her friends from saying something. Then again, who would want to be the one to tell Martha her nephew was the one who had cooked up the idea? All that mattered now was that Martha did know and she was about as all-powerful as a person could be. *But*...could this happen? Could Garrison lose The First Tree? No more proposals and birthday parties, weddings and picnics beneath its sprawling branches? No more Der erste Baum Festival? It couldn't happen. *No, it won't happen.* She'd do her part to make sure of it.

She scooped out more batter and forged ahead.

Joy calling her "momma." Her heart about melted every time Joy said it. *But it's wrong.* Dara was Joy's momma. She always would be. Brooke could never, ever take Dara's place—she didn't want to. Hearing Joy call her momma, liking Joy calling her momma, felt like a betrayal of her and Dara's friendship. *I'd never do that.* Surely Dara knew as much. *I miss you. I wish I could talk to you. I need your advice...* On Tess and Beau and The First Tree and Audy.

Audy. She paused, mid-pour. Where to start? Those blue eyes. The way he danced with Joy and called her Miss Muffet. Audy calling her place home...well...*everything about Audy.* Especially his smile. She sighed. Thinking about him wasn't helping clear things up. And since she'd promised herself she wouldn't think about him unless it was absolutely necessary, she shouldn't be thinking about him now. But she was and there was no stopping it. The more she thought about him, the more twisted up and hollow her insides felt. *Enough. This isn't his home.* So why had hearing him say *I'll be home soon* made her...happy?

No. Nothing about Audy made her... happy...

He was selfish and reckless and clueless. Tonight was a perfect example. What sort of risks had he taken, without giving a single thought about her or Joy?

She frowned. *Why would he think about me?* She didn't want him to think about her. She didn't...did she? "No. I don't. *Definitely* not," she snapped, dumping the rest of the batter from the ladle and drizzling more than half across her clean counter. *That's what I get for thinking about Audy Briscoe.* "Of course."

"Of course, what?" Audy's voice.

She spun around, the ladle in her hand

flinging a streak of cornbread batter in a semicircle around the room—ending on Audy's shirt.

He glanced down at the stripe of batter across his chest. "Guess I should tie on my towel as soon as I walk in the door from now on, huh?"

She smiled. "You scared me." *Stop smiling.*

"I feel like I'm interrupting a conversation?" He glanced around the kitchen. "Not that I can see anything in the dark."

"I wanted it dark. It's quiet and calming…" Not that she was especially calm. She opened the oven, slid the cornbread tray inside and closed it, wiping her hands on the apron she'd tied around her waist.

"Okay," he whispered. "I can be quiet."

"I doubt it." But there was no bite to her words. He was making it very difficult for her not to smile. Especially now, when he was standing there, staring at her, wearing an all-too-disarming grin. She didn't know if it was the standing or the staring or the grin that started it, but there was no stopping the sudden rush of heat rising in her chest. Rolling. Molten. Pressing against her chest from the inside and knocking her so off-balance she had to grip the kitchen counter and lean back against it for support. *This is bad.*

"Who are you talking to?" he asked, whispering.

Her throat was just as tight, but she managed to say, "No one." She rolled her eyes, hoping he wouldn't notice her hands shaking or how uneven her breathing was. *Get a grip.*

"I saw that." He pointed at the stove, and the light she was standing next to, before he crossed the room. He opened the stew pot and took a deep breath. "Smells good." Eyes closed, leaning forward, his thick dark hair windblown and the beginning of stubble lining the rigid angle of his jaw...

Clearly, the getting-a-grip thing wasn't happening. She shook her head. "It's my gramma's recipe." She'd never thought life was fair. But having Audy Briscoe stir up all of these...*feelings* took the whole *unfair* thing to a new level.

"I'm surprised you let those two alone." He leaned against the counter beside her.

He'd said something but she'd gotten caught up in how blue his eyes were beneath the bright white bulb over the stove. "Who? What?"

His head cocked to one side and those blue eyes wandered. Her jaw, her neck, her eyes, her mouth… Real or not, the brush of his gaze had substance. Enough that she could almost feel the brush of his fingers where his eyes touched her.

He stepped forward, too close, but she didn't move.

She couldn't.

She didn't want to.

"Brooke…" His voice was low and gruff, plucking along each and every nerve. His right hand came up, hesitant, hovering beside her cheek.

And even though it was a terrible idea that she'd deeply regret, she leaned into his touch. Once it was done, there was no undoing it. She couldn't breathe or move or think. All that registered was his touch. His calloused fingertips were rough against her temple. His large palm gently cupped the side of her face. The brush of his thumb along her cheek was featherlight. And all together, it felt…right.

Another step and the air between them seemed to wrap around them, drawing them closer, reeling her in until she no longer remembered all the reasons this was wrong.

How could it be wrong when he was looking at her like she was something to cherish. That was why she stopped fighting the pull between them. That was why she leaned into him.

He smoothed the hair from her forehead as his left hand rose, then stopped suddenly. Audy jerked back, his right arm supporting his left arm as a sharp hiss of air slipped between his tight-pressed lips. His features twisted, his jaw locked and he drew in a deep breath. Seeing Audy in such pain was more effective than being doused with ice water.

"Audy… You're hurt?" she asked, taking his left hand in hers.

He winced but didn't pull away. "Not bad."

She turned his hand, eliciting a muffled moan from Audy. "Not bad?" she asked, carefully releasing his hand. "What happened?"

"I fell." He shrugged. Well, his right shoulder shrugged.

Not bad. His left hand and his left shoulder were hurting him so much it hurt to move them. "You fell off of what? Onto what?" she asked, crossing the kitchen. Within seconds, she had the lights on, effectively erasing any and all lingering traces of what had just happened—almost happened. *Nothing had happened.* It didn't matter. Audy was hurt. "Audy?"

He sighed. "Off a bull. Onto the ground."

A bull. Of course. What had she expected? She'd been with his brother while he'd sustained a concussion playing a game of catch. Audy had *willingly* put himself in a situation where a concussion was insignificant to the damage a bull could cause. *Because Audy is Audy.* He would never change. "And?" She waited, crossing her arms over her chest.

"And, I got hung up on the fence bailing out. Wound up dislocating my shoulder." Another one-shouldered shrug. "Mikey popped it back in, all good."

All good?

"He sends his best," Audy added, his eyes narrowing.

She was still picturing Audy hanging off a fence. "Who?"

"Mikey." Audy's gaze shifted to the floor. "Good guy. I got the impression he might be asking you out soon."

Brooke shook her head. "Let's finish the important bit first—"

"We did. I fell. My shoulder popped out.

Mikey popped it back." Audy tried to cross his arms, gritted his teeth and went back to leaning against the counter. "And he said he's going to ask you out. Actually, he told me to give you his best. But he told me he wanted to ask you out."

"Mikey Woodard?" She shook her head.

"Do you know any other Mikeys?" He ran his right hand along the back of his neck.

"He's going to ask me out? I doubt that." Mikey was a friend. A nice guy. Smart and funny and hardworking. If he'd been interested, he would have asked her out by now.

"Fine. Don't believe me." He pushed off the counter. "Just don't be surprised if he calls offering to give you a one-on-one baby CPR class."

"At least one of us should be certified," she murmured. It had been on her list of things to do.

Audy was frowning at her now, the line of his jaw clenched tight.

"You are going to frown at me? No, that's not how this works. I didn't do a thing to deserve you frowning at me, Audy Briscoe. I certainly didn't go off, willy-nilly, and leave my little sister on her own so that a near stranger could sit with her in a clinic after she's been hurt because no one could reach me." She hadn't meant to say a thing. She certainly hadn't meant to get so worked up over it. But now that she'd started, the words just kept coming and she was walking toward him as she kept talking. "You come here after that and act like it's nothing that you were thrown in the dirt by an animal that would be all too happy to kill you. And then you frown because I say one of us should be CPR certified for Joy?" She jabbed her pointer finger into the rock-hard wall of his chest. "You know what? I'm warming up chili and making fresh cornbread so you and Beau and Tess are fed before I feed and bathe Joy and put her to bed. That's what I do. Take care of everyone. All the time. Instead of frowning at me, you should smile and say thank you." She stared at him, waiting, hoping for some sort of acknowledgment or apology.

"No one asked you to do *all* this." He was still frowning as he stared down at her. "You could ask for help. You could voice your opinion instead of saying nothing and then getting your nose out of joint because *someone* goes off and does something they didn't know you didn't want them to do—'cause you never said so."

"You can't be serious." She was quivering with anger. "You know how I feel about bull riding—"

"Knowing you don't like it doesn't mean I'm not supposed to do it. If I find out you don't like broccoli, am I supposed to assume I'm not supposed to eat it?"

She blinked. "Are you serious? You're comparing broccoli to riding a bull? That makes absolutely no sense."

"Um... Brooke? Audy?" Tess leaned in the doorway, waving them over. "I think you want to come see this. Right away. Like now. Quick." She disappeared.

Brooke swallowed down the litany of words she wanted to unload onto Audy and hurried after Tess. But what she saw made her come to a complete stop in the doorway... "Audy," Brooke whispered. "Come here—"

"I'm fine where I am," he snapped.

"Fine. Be a stubborn idiot and miss seeing Joy crawling," Brooke said, too entranced with Joy rocking on her knees, smiling from ear to ear at Beau and Tess, to care what Audy did.

Audy was at her side in an instant. "Look at her go." He was smiling. "She's smart. Like…" He swallowed.

The sudden sting in her eyes and the lump in her throat made it impossible to speak. *I hate that you're missing this, Dara.*

Joy took off, her turbo-powered crawl sending her across the floor into Tess's out-stretched hands. She was so delighted that she squealed and, once Beau had scooped her up high, she clapped her little hands with glee.

"I'm pretty sure Beau shouldn't be doing that," Brooke whispered. "His head. You know? I don't want him to hurt himself."

"I'll take care of it." Audy's hand was warm at the base of her spine before he headed into the room. "Look at you, Miss Muffet. Who knew you had jet engines under those ruffles and bows?" He took her from Beau and tickled her tummy until she was giggling. "You rest that big head of yours," he said to Beau. "Brooke's orders."

Beau looked her way. "Yes'm." He sat back.

Brooke was pretty sure she'd never seen a person more uncomfortable-looking than Beau at that moment. But, even with Beau's swollen nose and general awkwardness, and

Tess being doe-eyed over Beau, and Audy favoring his left arm and shoulder, they were all smiling and laughing when Audy set down Miss Muffet and she sped across the floor—only now Joy was headed straight for her.

Joy's ruffled diaper cover was a pink-and-white blur as she scooted across the floor. "Ma ma ma," she said, reaching up for Brooke.

Brooke crouched and held Joy close. "Good job, Joy. I'm so proud of you." A tangle of emotions crashed into her. Pride, sadness, delight and grief. But when her gaze met Audy's, there was an altogether different emotion struggling to break through. With effort, she shoved it aside. Brooke wasn't naive, her emotions had been put in a blender until all her reactions and feelings made no sense. They certainly weren't reliable—just because she felt it, didn't mean she should believe that it was real. The momentary weakness they'd both succumbed to in the kitchen was a perfect example of that. In what world would she and Audy ever be attracted to one another, let alone have feelings for each other.

There was nothing to worry about—nothing serious or permanent. It wasn't like she'd ever let herself fall for Audy, she was too practical for that. The very idea was…ridiculous.

AUDY WASN'T SURE what to make of things. His shoulder hurt. His arm hurt. But neither of those was the problem. This was something different. Unfamiliar territory.

It was a sort of *pang*. An ache. A hollow sort of…yearning.

This was no heartburn. He'd chewed a couple of antacids to make sure. Not a lick of help.

Whatever was troubling him, he couldn't shake it. He wanted to—it made him all kinds of unsettled. But it had a hold of him and hung on tight. And since the aching-yearning-tugging thing got worse every time he heard or saw a *certain* person—the brown-eyed, on the judgy side, silky-soft-skinned, feisty and beautiful loving person feeding Joy bananas—he was pretty sure he knew the cause of it.

Maybe he'd hit his head harder than he'd realized. Maybe he had a concussion, like Beau. *It'd explain why nothing's making sense.*

"Not hungry? Did you eat at the rodeo?" Tess hadn't stopped smiling since he'd arrived. She was smiling so big, Audy's cheeks hurt just looking at her. "You're missing out. Brooke makes the best chili."

"Just taking my time." He broke open his cornbread, refusing to look at Brooke—since she was the problem here. He took a bite of cornbread.

"Ba mm ga," Joy announced.

"Banana." Brooke used a different tone with Joy—all gentle encouragement. "Yummy, huh?"

Audy chewed diligently on his cornbread, his gaze landing on Joy.

"Mana," Joy repeated, holding up a piece of banana.

Miss Muffet looked so proud of herself, Audy had to smile.

"Yes, banana," Brooke said.

Joy nodded and ate the banana.

"You okay?" Beau whispered. "You seem… awful quiet."

"Good." He scooped up a spoonful of chili. "Great." He reached for the basket of cornbread, instantly regretting it. The snap of pain had him dropping the basket and pulling his arm in to his chest. All eyes were on him, he felt it.

"Ba na na?" Joy asked, holding out her banana for him.

"For me?" Audy asked, eyeing the piece of fruit warily.

"Na na." Joy ate the banana.

"Thank goodness," he chuckled. No one else did. "Sorry 'bout that." He glanced at Beau and Tess—but not Brooke. "Guess I didn't count on how heavy that was."

"It's okay." Tess put the cornbread back into the basket. "Is…is your arm okay?"

"What'd you do?" Beau asked, leaning back in his chair.

"What'd I do?" Audy turned the table, dodging what would likely lead to another argument with Brooke. Right now, the less interaction with her, the better. "How'd you wind up getting hit with a football?"

Beau's face went scarlet. "We were just… having fun. Got the sun in my eyes…"

Audy almost looked at Brooke for confirmation but caught himself. He didn't need confirmation from Brooke to know he was trying to save face. His brother was laser-focused on the field—a truly gifted player. He could read the field, anticipate throws and he was surprisingly light on his feet. The sun in his eyes? He didn't buy it. "Playing up at the school?"

"No." Beau stirred his chili. "Stephen was helping his mom get ready for the Ladies Guild meeting, so a bunch of us helped and hung around to play in the field."

"Ah." Audy nodded, getting a clearer picture. "You a member of the Ladies Guild, Brooke?"

"No." Brooke sighed. "But, after today, I'm thinking of joining."

"What happened after we left?" Tess asked. "Alice and I heard how upset they got over Mr. Devlin's deal selling Der erste Baum and the park."

"Oh, really?" Audy leaned back in his chair. "You mean Martha Zeigler didn't know? I imagine there were all sorts of fireworks."

"That's a nice way of putting it." He could hear the smile in Brooke's voice. "If Miss Ruth, Hattie Carmichael and Dorris Kaye hadn't managed to get her keys away from her, I fear Martha might have done something dreadful to Lance Devlin, regardless of their relation. I have never seen Martha that upset, never."

"She has every right." Audy nodded. "I thought the sale was just talk."

"Hattie said Tyson said there's been some phone calls between Lance and an Elsa Nash, who is the Quik Stop & Shop development officer."

That had Audy looking at her and, once he'd gotten past the fearsome tug in his chest, he asked, "Quik Stop & Shop? As in, the big blue box that price gouges all the small businesses out of business Quik Stop & Shop?"

"The very one." A deep crease formed on Brooke's forehead. "It's…it's unimaginable."

That was one word for it but Audy could come up with a whole list of more aggressive, less appropriate descriptions for the man willing to forever change Garrison for profit over the community's long-standing traditions, heritage and well-being. "If this doesn't get Devlin kicked out of town, I don't know what will." The worry on Brooke's face drew Audy up short. "What's got you so worried, Brooke?" Audy leaned forward, put his right elbow on the table. "You honestly think Garrison would let Devlin get away with something like this?"

"Times have been testing some folk—

financially. I'm not so sure everyone will be as against it as we think." Brooke cut more banana and placed it on Joy's high chair tray.

"But, Brooke, don't they understand?" Tess asked, her smile fading for the first time since Audy had arrived.

"A lot of people see big business coming into town as a way to see the community grow. But people like me—" she looked at Tess "—it's a real danger to our livelihood. Most of those Quik Stop & Shops have in-house salons. I doubt we could compete with their costs."

"So, it's the Garrison Ladies Guild to the rescue? I have to say, I don't think there's a more likely group to bring this whole scheme down. Especially with Martha leading the charge." Audy did his best to give Brooke a reassuring smile. He knew how important her salon was to her. It had been her mother's shop, and her grandmother's before that. It was a sign of her family's resilience, hard work and independence. "I have a feeling Martha will rally the troops. No one will touch a single limb on The First Tree."

"I'll drink to that." Brooke lifted her iced tea. Tess, Beau and Audy followed suit.

"To the Ladies Guild running Lance Devlin out of town," Audy said, winking when Joy held out one of her teething biscuits. He tapped his tea glass to the biscuit, earning him a giggle from Joy. "See, Joy isn't worried. This will all work out just fine."

"I think you're right, Audy," Tess agreed. "I can't imagine anything happening to The First Tree."

Audy saw the look that flashed between Tess and Beau, and for the first time, he saw more than two kids infatuated. Maybe he was reading too much into it. Maybe it was because Brooke was so scared. Or maybe it was because the way they looked at each other reminded him of Kent and Dara… But something told him this wasn't an infatuation at all.

His gaze swiveled around and met Brooke's.

Her brows rose and she wore a see-what-I-mean sort of expression, but he could tell she was concerned. The thing was, he'd always been a little jealous of Kent and Dara. The two of them had had such faith in one another. They never questioned each other, never doubted each other, they just knew. They were each other's best friend and biggest supporter. A part of him, one he didn't pay all that much attention to, wondered what that would be like.

Would that be such a bad thing? For Tess and Beau to have that?

Yes, they were young. There was no denying that. But that just meant they had more time together. Surely that wasn't a bad thing?

Something told him Brooke wouldn't see it the same way. She had big dreams for her sister—and he respected that. But being in love with Beau didn't mean Tess had to give up on any of those dreams. It just meant she would have Beau there to help her reach them.

Then again, Audy didn't know if Brooke and Tess shared the same dreams for Tess's future. But that was a conversation he knew he had no right to be involved in. Considering the way he was feeling right now, the best thing he could do was stay out of it. Things with Joy and Brooke were complicated enough without him sounding off on Tess's future.

"So did the Ladies Guild come up with a plan?" Beau asked. "I might be able to get some of the clubs at the high school involved? For fundraisers or posters or whatever we can do to help."

"That's a great idea, Beau." Tess was all smiles again.

"So far, Mrs. Zeigler suggested storming city hall or chaining ourselves to the bottom of The First Tree. But both ideas were tabled, for now, anyway. Hattie said she'd try to find out exactly what sort of deal Devlin is considering." Brooke offered Joy more banana but the baby shook her head. "The land is public land, so there is a question about whether the city has the rights to sell it."

"It's been quite a day." Audy found himself looking a little too long at Brooke. He knew it wasn't the smartest thing to do, but he didn't seem to have much choice. That was the thing that bothered him most. He didn't seem to have control over the situation, it had control of him. More like she had control of him.

"I'll clean up the kitchen," Tess offered, carrying her bowl to the sink.

"I'll help." Beau stood and started collecting dirty dishes.

"I'm not sure that's a good idea. You know, the whole concussion thing?" Brooke took the pink-and-white wet washcloth Tess offered her for baby cleanup.

"It won't hurt a thing," Audy said, pointing back and forth between Tess and Beau.

"He's not slurring his words or tripping over his feet. I'd say he's on the road to recovery."

"I've got it." Tess took the dirty dishes from Beau. "You should rest. Just to be on the safe side."

Beau just stood there, staring down at Tess. The two of them fell into a trancelike state, completely oblivious to everyone and everything around them. For a minute, it looked like Beau was going in for a kiss but caught himself. Instead, he carefully moved the braid from Tess's shoulder to her back.

"How about we get you set up on the couch again?" Brooke offered, pure panic lining her voice. "Audy?"

"Can do." Audy stood, placed his hand on Beau's shoulder and steered his brother back to the couch in the front room. "You'd best watch yourself around Brooke. She's having a hard time with this whole you-and-Tess thing."

"I don't know what you're talking about." Beau sat down, avoiding Audy's gaze.

"You keep telling yourself that, kid." He sat beside his brother and propped a foot up on the coffee table. "She the reason you got hit in the head?"

Beau didn't say anything.

"You caught sight of her and lost sight of the ball?"

"Yep." Beau shook his head. "I didn't even know it was coming."

Audy had to chuckle at that. "I hear that's the way it happens. Minding your own business, and out of nowhere, it's like a bolt of lightning." He used air quotes for extra emphasis.

"I don't know about lightning… But I definitely saw stars." But Beau was smiling now.

"I know you're my brother—" he gave Beau a stern look "—but you treat that girl right, you hear me?"

"I hear you." Beau wasn't smiling anymore. He looked mad. "I know you have experience with women, but this is different. I'm still figuring this out. I want to be with her. I can't explain… If she's not interested, I won't like it but I'll respect it. Whether or not she cares about me, I—I'd never do anything to hurt Tess. I know she's special."

Audy looked up to see Brooke pause in the doorway. He didn't know how much of their exchange she'd heard, but there was no doubt she'd caught the last of it. Brooke Young wasn't a romantic. She didn't want her young sister to fall in love. She was trying hard not to like his brother. But Beau had just made it impossible for her to not like him. Beau had said exactly what he should, not because Brooke was listening but because that's how he felt.

"That's all I needed to hear." Audy tore his gaze from Brooke and did his best to ignore the growing hollow ache in his chest. As much as he'd like to believe these new Brooke-inspired sensations were caused by tonight's accident, he had a sinking suspicion that it was something far worse. When he woke up tomorrow, he'd still feel this way. And likely, the day after that and, possibly, all the days that followed. Because she, Brooke, was special, too. To him, she would always be special. And there wasn't a thing he could do about it. He was a fool. A fool who was wholly in love with Brooke Young.

CHAPTER TWELVE

HALF DAYS CAME to an end and the renegoti-
ating began.

Audy was nervous about keeping Joy over-
night—at least until his shoulder healed—so
he'd suggested bringing Joy home to sleep
each night and being there first thing in the
morning when Joy woke up on his days.
Brooke hadn't held out much hope that he'd
stick to their schedule but she wasn't about to
send Joy off on overnights when Audy wasn't
ready. So, she'd agreed.

Audy had been as good as his word. It was
one of the few times she'd been happy to be
proven wrong. Audy's arm healed but, since
that was working out so well, they agreed to
stick with it awhile longer.

The new normal was anything but normal. Instead of seeing Audy less and settling
into their long-term plan, things were more
confusing than ever. With Audy, anyway.

He was always around. As a matter of fact, she couldn't remember a day that she hadn't seen him. If it was her day, he'd drop by to see if she needed anything or check in on Joy's crawling or teething—there was always a reason. On his days there was the morning and bedtime routine and the occasional lunch, coffee or tea drop-off he'd make—unannounced. It was all so…thoughtful and disorienting.

She knew there was talk. Audy Briscoe came to town to go drinking at Buck's or to rodeo, but that was about it. And yet, in the last three weeks, Audy had been seen in town daily. These unusual Audy sightings were due to Joy but the good people of Garrison were determined to turn it into something it wasn't. Namely, Audy Briscoe was courting Brooke Young.

"I think it's funny," Brooke said, glancing at the women, busy at their own workstations. The third Saturday of the month meant staying a bit late for inventory, a thorough shop clean and a whole day off to look forward to. She finished counting the bottles of hair color and noted the amount on her inventory sheet.

"Anybody who really knows us knows how ridiculous it sounds."

"Why ridiculous?" Myrna asked, wiping down her stylist's chair with disinfectant wipes.

Because...well, because... Why didn't a mile-long list of reasons immediately spring to mind?

"People change. They do." Portia was folding and stacking the freshly washed towels along the back counter. "Audy Briscoe didn't have a baby girl before. That's enough to change a man. Trust me, if you'd met my husband before we had our kids... You wouldn't recognize him."

"I don't blame you for thinking it's ridiculous." Inez sprayed glass cleaner on the illuminated vanity mirror at her station. "I know Audy is something to look at, but that boy is nothing but trouble. Brooke would be better off with somebody else." She stood back, wiped at one tiny streak, then another, before she seemed satisfied.

"Not that I'm looking," Brooke added, doubtful anyone was listening.

"No? You might want to rethink that and Audy better get ready for a little competition. People are talking about Mikey Woodard being more than a little interested in our Brooke, here." Myrna was far too excited over this information. "Mr. Ellis, over at the feedstore, said something about overhearing a conversation between his son, Tyson, and Mikey. Something about Mikey making sure that Tyson was okay with him asking Brooke out. I think that's very decent of Mikey, since they were friends."

Again with Mikey. He was a sweetie. Always had been. It *did* sound like something he'd do. But she was having a hard time believing it. They'd known each other for years and he'd never once acted like he was interested in anything more than friendship. "Which is all Tyson and I are. Friends. Like me and Mikey." Brooke turned back to her inventory. This conversation had gone completely off the rails. To hear people talk, she had a riveting personal life. *Nothing could be further from the truth.*

"Forget Tyson. Mikey Woodard. Now he's a catch," Portia gushed.

Brooke shot her a look.

"What?" Portia asked, stowing the laundry basket beneath the cabinet. She hopped into her stylist chair and spun to face them. "He's handsome. And funny. A *good* guy. And he's tall."

"We all know how you feel about tall men." Myrna laughed.

"You wouldn't have to train him. Mikey, that is," Inez said. "A definite improvement over Audy Briscoe."

"I still think you are shortchanging Audy." Myrna flipped through the appointment book, made a note, closed it and put it away. "Maybe he just hasn't met the right woman yet. Maybe Brooke *is* the right woman."

"Brooke doesn't want that sort of responsibility. Who would?" Inez shook her head. "I have a hard time believing Audy will ever be fully domesticated."

"He's not a *cat*." Myrna had them all laughing. "From what I've seen, he's already gotten pretty domesticated. He's terrific with Joy."

That had Brooke smiling. It was true. She never expected Audy to become so…so fatherly. But seeing the two of them together left little doubt that he sincerely adored Joy. Audy and Joy's adorableness aside, this conversation had gone on entirely too long. "You do realize that none of you have asked me how I feel about either one of them. It's possible I'm not interested in them, you know?"

"Then you're a fool." Inez threw the used paper towels in the trash can and frowned at Brooke. "You do realize how shallow the pool of single men is in these parts, don't you?"

"Inez, be nice." Portia pulled out a fingernail file and started buffing her nails. "I get where Brooke is coming from. You can't force these things."

"Thank you." Brooke turned back to tallying the boxes of foil, applicator brushes and conditioners. "And then there's the whole thing about *time*?" She wrote down the numbers and closed the cabinet. "Between Joy, Tess, running this place and the Save The First Tree thing the Ladies Guild is kicking off, I don't have…*any*."

"Well, if it's the right guy you make the time." Myrna shrugged. "And I'm just saying, but you should make time for Audy."

The first thing Myrna had said, Brooke agreed with. The second? Audy was getting plenty of time with her as it was. *Too much.* So much so that, even when he wasn't around, she found herself thinking about him. *More time with Audy is the last thing I* need.

"Nah, Mikey. All the way." Inez put her hands on her hips. "He is the only option."

"Are we voting now?" Portia giggled. "You better make it fast because he's here."

Brooke didn't have time to ask who was here because the door opened and Audy came in, with Joy on his hip. He stepped inside and Brooke struggled to keep the air in her lungs. *No man should be this good-looking.* He wore a perfectly starched blue button-up and snug-fit creased jeans. There was a high shine on his boots and his hat sat, just right, on his head. All in all, he was probably the most handsome man Brooke had ever laid eyes on.

"Evening, ladies. You closing up shop for the weekend?" he asked, heading straight for Brooke. "We were hoping you were about done." His gaze swept over her face.

"You were?" Brooke asked, setting the clipboard aside to take Joy—who was leaning forward for her. "Hi, baby."

Joy patted her. "Ha."

Brooke kissed her on the cheek, making a loud smack so Joy would smile. "What are you two up to?"

"We thought we'd invite you to dinner."

Audy leaned against the counter, watching the two of them.

Brooke blinked. "Dinner?" This was a first. And not a good one. What did he mean, dinner? Not a date? Surely not. Like it or not, her heart picked up.

"Mabel's come home so we're having a late family dinner and I thought you and Tess might—should be there." He winked at Joy. "Don't you think?"

Not a date. *What is wrong with me?* Why was she…disappointed? The girls were partly to blame, carrying on about Audy and her as if there was an Audy and her. *There is not.* Which was good.

"When did she get home?" Mabel Briscoe was the only female Briscoe. She was soft-spoken and sweet and had the biggest heart of anyone.

"Today." He chuckled. "Uncle Felix had talked her into staying put when she heard about Joy but he mentioned the whole thing with The First Tree last time they talked and she was on the next flight."

"I'm glad she's home. I can't wait to hear all about the work she's been doing." Brooke gave Joy a bunny-nose rub. "You'll love her,

Joy. She's smart and sweet and pretty and I know she will love you."

"That she will," Audy agreed, his blue eyes meeting hers.

"You go on," Myrna said. "Everything's done, anyway."

"She doesn't have to go if she doesn't want to." Inez gave Audy a look that left no doubt about how she felt about him.

Audy grinned and tipped his hat her way. Inez rolled her eyes.

"Ma ma, ba ma," Joy babbled, animated.

Brooke listened intently as Joy carried on, her little face reflecting so many familiar expressions. A little Tess, a little Brooke and some Audy, too. "You don't say?" Brooke smoothed the curl on her head. "I bet."

Joy smiled, patting Brooke.

"There you go, speaking your secret language. I need a translator." Audy chuckled, walking toward them. "You two."

"Two of the prettiest girls in Colton County, if you ask me," Portia said. "Especially this one." She bopped Joy on the nose. "Oh, when are you going to let me babysit?"

"Soon, I bet. Brooke'll need a babysitter for her date with Mikey." Inez flipped off the lights over her station. "Have a good Sunday, ladies."

If she was going to get a babysitter, it would be for a long soak in a bathtub or to binge-watch some rom-coms, not go on a date with Mikey. It struck her as odd that not five minutes had passed since she'd been all twisted up in the hopes that Audy's dinner invitation was a date... Brooke swallowed, the difference in her reaction was...concerning. *More like alarming.* "'Night, Inez."

"Ba ba." Joy waved, her bright smile impossible to refuse.

"'Night, sugar." Inez waved back, smiling for the first time.

"You made Inez smile, Joy. You're special. She doesn't just smile for anyone." She gave Joy another bunny-nose rub.

Joy clasped Brooke's face between her hands and pressed a kiss to her lips.

"Oh, sweet girl, I needed that." Brooke hugged her close, giving Joy's neck a raspberry that caused Joy to burst into laughter. "You ready?" she asked, reaching for her purse—and she caught sight of Audy's reflection in her mirror. He was frowning, staring at the floor. But it was the way his jaw clenched tight that told her he was angry.

Why? He'd been all dashing smiles and blue eyes when they'd arrived. She scrambled to think of anything that would anger him.

Because of what Inez said? It was unlikely. Everyone knew she had no filter. Ever. She said what she thought, no excuses. Audy *knew* Inez, he knew she was prickly. Besides, Audy was known to speak his mind, so it was hard to believe he'd gotten riled over Inez's picking.

But what else could it be?

Audy chose that moment to look up. Those blue eyes bore into her own—blazing with such force Brooke took a step back.

Just as quickly, he'd turned his attention to Joy. "Want me to take her?" he asked.

Her heart was hammering and her lungs were scrambling to kick in but she managed a "Sure." *What was that?* Brooke wasn't sure what he was thinking but she wasn't going to ask him here. She loved Portia and Myrna but she had no illusions that anything they witnessed or heard wouldn't be repeated elsewhere. Whatever was bothering him would have to wait. "Thank you."

It took another ten minutes to pack up. Myrna and Portia left, Brooke locked the back door, then followed Audy and Joy out the front. She locked up, dropped her keys into her purse and turned to find Audy watching her.

"Audy, I know Inez can be…snippy." She stepped forward, straightening the wide collar of Joy's dress. "It's just the way she is. Don't let it get to you."

"She didn't." He took a long look left, then right, before he asked, "When is this date happening with you and Mikey?"

Brooke blinked. "I—"

"Because we agreed to no dates when we have Joy." His voice was low and gruff. "Remember?"

"I remember." It had been her rule—one she'd put in place to keep Audy on his best behavior around Joy. *He* was the one with the reputation. She was the one with no life.

He nodded, the muscle in his jaw rolling. "Making sure."

She studied him, wishing she could get inside that thick head of his so she knew what this was really about. He wasn't upset over Inez. And there was no reason for him to be upset over Mikey. He'd been the first one to mention Mikey to her. Not that he'd been all that thrilled about it… But he'd had his shoulder dislocated a few hours before that, so she'd chalked up his reaction to discomfort—not Mikey Woodard's supposed interest in her. Was that it? Audy was upset over this date, that wasn't happening, with Mikey? *No*. That made no sense whatsoever.

"I'll see you at the house?" Audy stalked to his truck, carrying Joy with him.

She was at a loss over the cause of his anger. *But, boy, was he angry.* "Mine?"

"Yours." He buckled Joy into her car seat. "If that's all right?"

"Of course it is." Now she was getting irritated. "You're angry but I'm not sure why. Did I do something? What's wrong?"

Audy closed the passenger door. "Nothing, Brooke."

Nothing? "Then why do you sound like that?" *Why was he making this so difficult?*

"Like what?" he growled.

"Like *that*." She stared up at the blue sky overhead. "Angry. You sound angry, Audy." She took a deep, steadying breath. "We have got to get better at this."

"At what?" he snapped.

"At talking." She wrapped her arms around her waist. "We're adults. Adults talk—work things out. We need to learn to do that."

"Fine." He flipped his key ring around his finger. "Sure."

That was it? That was his answer? "Great." *Don't fight. Don't do it.* But she didn't manage to swallow the sound of frustration that slipped out as she walked to her car.

Audy's truck roared to life, backed up, then straightened out and headed down the street.

Brooke took a deep breath. If Mabel wasn't her friend—and Myrna and Portia and Inez didn't know about dinner—she'd have backed out of tonight. The idea of sitting next to a brooding Audy, while Tess and Beau exchanged doe-eyed looks, sounded about as fun as a root canal without sedation. But, if she didn't go, it wouldn't help diffuse Audy's temper tantrum. She took another deep breath. *Mabel is my friend.* And, right now, she could use a friend.

"I KNOW," AUDY SIGHED. "I'm sorry."

"Ma ma?" Joy held on to the straps of her car seat, her big eyes fixed on his face.

"She's coming, Miss Muffet, don't you fret." He'd lost his head and made a fool out of himself. After thinking about her most of the day, he'd been so happy to see Brooke. Watching her with Joy sort of filled him up and made his heart whole. But then Inez had blurted out Brooke was going on a date with— "Mikey?" he asked. "I get it, he's a nice guy, but…"

"Fa gi ma?" Joy's babble was definitely a question.

"You're right. I shouldn't have lost my temper like that." If he could go back, he'd have kept his cool. Well, he'd have tried, anyway. The idea of Brooke, dating… "I don't have a right to get my nose out of joint over this and I know it." He ran a hand along the back of his neck and rolled to a stop at the stop sign. "But it doesn't sit right, Joy."

"No?" Joy shook her head, her little curl bouncing.

"No." He reached over and patted her hand. "Not one bit."

Joy smiled and patted his hand in return. "Dee."

"What's that?" he asked.

"Dee," she said, patting his hand again.

"I don't know that one." But she looked so pleased he added, "But I'm sure it means something. Good job, Miss Muffet."

"Dee." She nodded. "Dee. Ba ba wa la?" Another question.

"I wish I knew what to do here. What do you think, Miss Muffet? Do I tell Brooke I don't want her dating Mikey?" He paused. This wasn't about Mikey. "I'm fooling myself, you know that?"

"No?" Joy asked again.

"No is right." He turned onto Brooke's street. "As in, I have no business telling Brooke she can't date." He swallowed. "If she wants to date him, she should. All I want is… I want her happy, Miss Muffet." It'd be a punch to the throat every time he saw Brooke and Mikey together but… "If it makes her happy, so be it."

"Gee gee Teh." Joy clapped, her little feet bouncing as she spied Brooke's house through the windshield.

"Yep. Going to see Tess." He pulled up in front of the house and parked. "I bet she'll be excited to see you, too." He came around, unbuckled Joy and carried her to the door. "Tess?" he called out while opening the door. "You here?"

"Hey, Audy." Tess came jogging down the hall to meet them. "Hi, Joy."

"Teh." Joy clapped, kicking her legs.

"You look all dressed up." Tess took Joy and pointed at his outfit. "Doesn't he, Joy? Audy is all fancy."

"Dee." Joy waved at him.

"About that. Mabel's coming home." He explained, "I was hoping you and Brooke'd come out and have dinner at the ranch? Welcome her home?"

Tess ran a hand over her curls. "Um... well..."

He'd never been the best at reading people, but he had no problem figuring out what Tess was thinking. Or feeling. "Beau will be there." He didn't see any point in beating around the bush.

Tess froze, staring at him. The sheer horror on her face made him wish he'd never opened his mouth. "I—I mean..."

The door opened and Brooke came inside. She took one look at Tess and turned to him. "What now?"

Now? But he didn't bite. "I might have been a bit forthright about—"

"Nothing." Tess held up her hands. "Nothing at all. Okay? Okay. Please. Like, let's drop it." She nodded, looking at each of them. "I'm going to change. And you are not going to talk about me when I leave this room, right?" She looked at Audy.

"Right." He didn't know what was happening but he was fine not talking about it. More than fine. That's the way he'd preferred it.

"Right?" Tess faced Brooke now.

"Right," Brooke agreed, but she wasn't happy about it.

"Good. Okay." Tess smiled at Joy. "Okay. Let's go get dressed up like Audy."

"Dee." Joy waved at him. "Dee."

Brooke glanced at him. "Joy? Are you saying 'Audy'?" Brooke stepped closer and placed her hand on his shoulder. "Who is this? Is this Audy?"

"Dee." Joy nodded.

Audy's heart thumped, strong and hard. She'd been saying his name? "Me?" He nodded his thanks at Tess as they shifted Joy into his arms. "Is that what you were saying, Miss Muffet?" Who knew hearing this baby girl say his name would make him feel on top of the world?

Joy grinned up at him. "Ma Dee."

Yep. That smile clinched it. *On top of the world.* "Sorry I was slow on the uptake, Joy." He pressed a kiss to her forehead. "I'm your Audy, all right." It was true. She might be little and he might still have a lot to learn, but one thing he knew for certain was that he loved Joy more than he'd ever imagined possible.

She giggled.

He chuckled. "Proud of yourself, aren't you? And you should be." He pressed another kiss to her temple. "You just made my week, Miss Muffet. Month, even."

From the looks of it, Brooke was almost as happy as he was. One of her hands rested on Joy's back while the other had slid from his shoulder to his chest. "Every time I think I'm getting the hang of this, she does something amazing. You're just full of surprises, aren't you, Joy? The best kind, too." Brooke's brown eyes met his…and held.

The tug in his chest wasn't a surprise this time. His heart, called by hers. *Whether she knows it or not.* Between Joy and Brooke, his heart wasn't his own anymore. He was oddly okay with that.

There was a flash, causing all three of them to blink.

"Sorry," Tess laughed. "I was trying to capture the moment." She waved them together. "Y'all smile so I can take a picture. This is the day Audy became Dee."

"Dee," Joy repeated, patting him on the chest. "Ma Dee."

"Yes, ma'am, Miss Muffet. I like the sound of that." He did. So much so that he was grinning like a fool.

"Brooke." Tess waved her in. "Closer."

Brooke shot her sister a look. "If I get any closer, I'll have to climb onto Audy's back."

"Here." Audy lifted his arm, half expecting her to roll her eyes and turn him down. Instead, she stepped in, tight against his side, so he could drape his arm around her shoulders.

"Perfect. Thanks, Dee." Tess held up her phone and took several pics. "I'll send them to you." She scrolled through the pictures, her focus on her phone. "I guess I'll go change? So, we can go to Audy's for dinner?"

Good idea. Had he said that out loud? He wasn't sure. Audy was in no hurry to move. Joy had rested her head against his chest and Brooke... Brooke was staring up at him, which was just about the most beautiful thing he'd ever seen. In her eyes, he saw the promise of things he'd never dared hope for. A family. A partner. Someone he could always count on—no matter what. It wouldn't be easy between them, but it would be worth it. *If...* That word was far too powerful. *If she'd give them a chance?*

"I'm...going to go now," Tess asked. "Okay?" She must have stepped back onto Joy's piano toy because "Old MacDonald" started playing. Joy's head popped up and Brooke jumped.

"Yes." The word sort of erupted from Brooke. "We... Are you... Do you still want us to come to dinner?" Her cheeks flamed red.

He nodded. "If you'd like?" If he hadn't lost his head over Mikey, she wouldn't be asking. She was right. They were adults. It was past time for him to act like one.

"We'd like," Tess answered. "I'll change Joy." She had Joy and was heading down the hall before Brooke said another word.

They were alone, finally. If there was ever a time to speak up, it was now. He should say something. Anything. But his brain wasn't

cooperating. Brooke was still in his arms…
That was a good place to start. But if he didn't
choose his words with care, she wouldn't stay
there for long. Start slow, ease into things,
and if she didn't run, he'd tell her how he felt.

I can do this.

The shrill ring of a phone sliced through
the silence. Once. Again.

Neither one of them moved. That was
good, wasn't it?

The phone rang again, then stopped. A
click and then a voice, "You've reached
Brooke and Tess. Leave a message and we'll
call you back." There was a beep and some
static.

"Brooke, it's Mikey Woodard."

Talk about timing.

"I don't know if Audy mentioned setting
up an infant CPR class but, if you're free, I'm
teaching a class on Wednesday, over at the
community center."

A class, huh? Meaning he could sign up,
too?

"I hope you're well. If you… Well…
Maybe…"

Audy got the distinct impression Mikey
hadn't asked Brooke out, after all—not yet,

anyway. But that might be about to change. *Don't do it, Mikey.* Audy braced himself, waiting. *Don't ask her out on her answering machine.*

"Give me a call, Brooke." He cleared his throat. "Or, hopefully I'll see you Wednesday." And he hung up.

Good call, Mikey. Audy was trying his hardest not to smile.

"What's that look for?" Brooke asked, a hint of a smile hovering.

"I was worried for a minute." Audy shook his head. "Felt like he was on the verge of asking you for that date Inez was talking about. Sorta felt bad for intruding."

Brooke's eyes narrowed. "You'd have felt bad?"

He took a deep breath. "No. Not at all. If a man's going to ask a woman on a date, he needs to do it proper."

"Proper?" She crossed her arms over her chest. "I can't wait to hear this."

"My lips are sealed." He mirrored her posture, crossing his arms over his chest. It was none of his business and, after that call, he felt confident he knew the answer, but he asked, "Out of curiosity, he hasn't asked you out yet?"

"What do you have against Mikey Woodard? You were the one that said he was a good guy."

Which wasn't an answer. "He is."

"Then why does it matter?" She shook her head. "I don't understand why you care about who I do or don't date."

"I don't know, Brooke." He swallowed, hard. "But it matters."

The complete surprise on her face didn't give him much to go on. Was she scared surprised? Happy surprised? Or just surprised surprised?

"Because of Joy?" Her voice wavered. She was angry surprised. *Great.* "You think I'd date someone who—who's *inappropriate*? Audy—"

"Brooke, something tells me you've never dated anyone remotely inappropriate in your life." He sighed. Was he saying it wrong? She was sure taking it wrong. *How did we get here?*

"Oh, Audy." She pinched the bridge of her nose. "You've lost me. Again." She shook her head. "I need to change so we're not late."

She smoothed her bleach-stained T-shirt and walked from the room.

Audy stood there, dumbfounded. How had she so completely misunderstood what he was trying to say? Did she not want to understand him? Was that it? Or was he really just that bad at expressing himself? Considering he'd never had anything to *express* to anyone before, it had to be him. He'd just have to throw it out there. Short and to the point. *Just say it.*

"Right." He stared up at the ceiling, then shook his head. "No." He couldn't do it that way. He'd seen enough movies to know a woman didn't want a man to walk up to them and say it. There was buildup. Flowers, even. Maybe a nice dinner. Or a moonlit stroll. Mabel's favorite movie had one of those—and it always made her cry. Audy didn't get it but… he'd try.

"Blurting out 'I love you' isn't going to cut it," he murmured, taking off his hat and smoothing his hair.

"Um…you should totally say that."

He spun around to find Tess, holding Joy, staring wide-eyed at him. "What?" How did she get here without him hearing a thing?

"You should. Say that." She paused. "Well, only if you're going to say it to…"

His brows rose but he kept his mouth shut. He wasn't saying another word.

"Audy…" Tess sighed, glancing back over her shoulder. "Are you, you know, in love with…my sister?"

Audy laughed. But it was forced laughter—and they both knew it. Up until now, he'd never considered himself a private person. It wasn't that he didn't want anyone to know how he felt about Brooke, he'd be fine with the whole world knowing. But Brooke should know first.

CHAPTER THIRTEEN

BROOKE COULDN'T REMEMBER the last time she'd enjoyed a meal more. Not so much the food, which was good, but the company. Growing up, she and Mabel had been friends but, due to the lack of "reliable" adult supervision on the ranch, her mother had rarely let her visit. As it turned out, Felix Briscoe was a delight. He was a storyteller, sharing anecdotes about "the boys" and having no problem calling them out when they "put a spin on the truth" to make their story more entertaining.

Forrest remained, as always, somber and quiet. The Mondays that Forrest showed up at the salon, he tended to listen more than talk. When he did speak up, he was careful with his words—which Brooke respected. Webb was a mess. He wasn't as serious as Forrest and he wasn't as smooth as Audy or as charming as Felix. But he was funny. Like laugh-out-loud funny. While poor Beau didn't say more than five words through dinner. He was polite and quiet and more awkward than ever with Tess.

Now that the meal was over, they'd moved into the massive great room. Brooke sat in an oversize rocking chair with Joy sleeping soundly in her lap.

"She is the sweetest little angel." Mabel sat on one of the large leather couches, Audy on one side and Webb on the other.

"She is," Audy agreed. "She's smart, too. Knows my name."

"She calls him Dee," Tess offered.

"Dee, huh?" Webb chuckled. "Is that what we should call you, too?"

"Only if you don't want my help fixing the well." Audy shot his brother a narrow-eyed look. Even Brooke picked up the challenge.

"Ah, yes, I missed this." Mabel patted them both on one knee. "All the brotherly love."

Brooke laughed, patting Joy's little back when she stirred.

"Of course you did." Audy hugged her.

He was teasing, but the love between the siblings was sincere. She and Tess were close but they weren't traditional siblings. Tess had been so young when their mother got sick, Brooke had no choice but to step in.

Her gaze shifted to Tess, who was staring around her with wide eyes. Briscoe Ranch was impressive. From the massive log cabin ranch house to the acres and acres of prime Hill Country real estate, the wealth and history of their family was evident. Brooke followed Tess's gaze up, to the thick raw timbers crossing the vaulted ceiling and the massive deer-antler chandelier they supported.

Not exactly her thing, but it fit.

Tess wandered around the room, stopping long enough to study the framed photos or artwork about the room. When she circled round to the far wall, she paused. On either side of a massive fireplace, dead center of the room, were floor-to-ceiling windows that gave an impressive view of the undeveloped land. Cows, goats, some horses and fences as far as the eye could see.

"Wow," Tess said, turning back to smile at her.

Brooke nodded. *"Wow" is right.* Cattle and oil were big business and the Briscoes had plenty of both.

"Wow, huh?" Audy grinned.

"Um, yeah." Tess nodded. "First, I've never been in a log cabin before." She shrugged, blushing when she realized all eyes were on her. "It's gorgeous, really. And huge."

"We Briscoes tend to have big families. Lots and lots of babies." Mabel made a face.

"In no hurry for one of your own, though." Uncle Felix peered at Mabel over his readers, his crossword puzzle book resting on his lap. "Or did you meet someone while you were off rescuing those mustangs?"

"Nope." Mabel shook her head. "Just horses."

"You know Mabel, Uncle Felix—no man can compete with a horse." Webb chuckled.

Mabel shrugged. "I have yet to meet the man to prove otherwise."

Brooke laughed at that, maybe a little too hard. Enough that Audy was studying her in that way he did.

"What's new?" Mabel asked. "What have I missed out on?"

Audy pointed at Joy.

"Are you pointing at Joy? Or Brooke?" Webb asked.

Audy reached around behind Mabel and flicked Webb's ear.

"Hey!" Webb rubbed his ear. "Making sure I didn't miss something. With you, you never know."

Don't I know it. Brooke was still puzzling over their earlier conversation. She wasn't sure if he'd been intentionally vague or if it was just one more exasperating thing about Audy.

"What about you, Beau?" Mabel asked. "You found yourself a girlfriend yet? I know you and Alice Schneider have always been close."

All eyes turned to Beau, including Tess, all waiting for his answer.

Poor kid. He looked about ready to hyperventilate.

"Alice is a friend." He shook his head, glancing at Tess. His face went red and he ran his hands along the tops of his thighs, oozing nervousness. "Nothing new. School mostly." He nodded, leaned back against the couch, crossed and uncrossed his legs. "Same stuff."

"So, Joy and The First Tree?" Mabel asked.

"Pretty much," Felix said, nodding. "It's Garrison, Mabel. No one's in a hurry, there's no need."

"You heard about Casey Crawley? She

died." Webb shook his head. "Her heart. Turns out she had some sort of…" He looked at Audy.

"Arrhythmia," Brooke said. Her death had rocked the community. The Crawley family was just as big and well-to-do as the Briscoes, so when the eldest son married an out-of-towner, people weren't all that welcoming. But Casey was sweet and down-to-earth and people took to her—even more so after she and Jensen had a little girl.

"But she was so young." Mabel frowned, in shock. "She seemed so healthy. Poor Jensen. And Samantha."

"Who's Samantha?" Felix asked.

"Their little girl, Uncle Felix. I know you're not a fan of the Crawleys, but you can't be hard-hearted over this. That little girl lost her mother…" Mabel broke off.

Brooke and Tess knew just how hard that was. Then again, so did Mabel. *And Joy, too.* Her arms tightened around the baby, taking comfort in the solid weight of her sleeping form. Brooke would make sure Joy grew up knowing who her real mother was even if, in her heart, Joy was partly hers.

"Any updates on Der erste Baum?" Audy

asked, his not-so-subtle change of conversation lightening the mood.

"I'm surprised Mrs. Zeigler hasn't disowned her nephew and thrown him out of town." Mabel shook her head.

"Give it time." Audy rubbed his hands together.

"It's all very...suspect." Brooke frowned. "Pearl Johnston, you know she was a county clerk? Doc Johnston's wife? Well, she did some digging and found the property was owned by a Hermann Richter. He died back in 1910 with no heir. He'd bought the land to keep it safe, for town use—at least, that's what the newspaper clippings and letters and such Pearl has unearthed all say. Martha's been talking with the lawyer, Henry Gonzales? He seems to think that a petition signed by the majority of Garrison's citizens *and* Mr. Richter's statements about protecting the tree would stop any commercial-use sales from going through." She shrugged. "Martha has offered to buy the land, since it's technically been abandoned, and form a land trust that would preserve The First Tree and surrounding property indefinitely."

"I'm guessing they need help getting the signatures?" Mabel asked.

Brooke nodded. "The Ladies Guild is putting together a few ideas to draw people to them. A community picnic or a movie night—something along those lines."

"Easier than going door-to-door, I guess. But it still sounds like a lot of work." Audy didn't sound convinced.

"That's why we're looking for volunteers." Brooke waited.

"I'll get the football team to help out." Beau shrugged. "Varsity and JV."

"That would be amazing, Beau." Brooke meant it. "Really."

Beau smiled.

"It's not like I said no," Audy jumped in. "Webb and I'll drag Forrest and Uncle Felix along, too, if we have to."

Uncle Felix chuckled. "Like to see you try it."

They spent an hour sharing memories made under the branches of The First Tree before Uncle Felix started to nod off and Brooke knew it was time to say good-night.

"Audy gave me the thumbs-up to put together a nursery. Once that's done, you two won't have to cart Joy back and forth every day." Mabel shook her head. "I don't know how you two are managing it."

Brooke should be grateful, not disappointed. But disappointment won out.

"I'll see you at the guild meeting later this week." Mabel hugged her, careful of Joy. "It's so good to be home."

"You can't hold on to her and get the car seat moved over," Audy said, holding the front door open.

"Tess can do it." Brooke turned. "Where is Tess?"

"She'll be along shortly." Audy seemed to be fighting laughter as he walked down the front steps and down the path to their parked vehicles. "I think she was helping Beau carry the last of the dishes into the kitchen."

"I'm glad you think it's funny." Brooke followed, standing aside while he moved the car seat over, her gaze returning to the open front door every few seconds. "I can't help but wonder…"

"If Beau will ever make a move?" Audy was laughing now.

"No." Brooke swatted his shoulder. "Stop. No." She swatted him again. "About Lance

Devlin. If he'd heard our stories tonight would it help him understand how important the tree is to all of us?"

Audy shook his head. "Something tells me…no."

"I can see you're going to take some time to consider your answer." She leaned into the car, carefully put Joy into the car seat and buckled her in. She tucked a blanket around Joy and her favorite stuffed bunny before closing the door and facing Audy.

Audy was staring down at her, the corner of his mouth kicked up.

"What?" It was quiet. The lights from the front porch barely reached them. And they were alone. The longer he stared down at her, the more tightly wound her stomach became. Her heart was racing. Her lungs ached—but breathing meant inhaling the layers of cedar, leather and mint that rolled off of Audy.

"Brooke." His voice was pitched low and soft. "There's what I want to say and what comes out of my mouth. Somewhere between the two, I mess up and wind up tripping over my own tongue." He ran a hand along the back of his neck. "This thing with Mikey."

"Audy, there is no thing with Mikey." For

the second time tonight, she was swimming in disappointment. "There never has been. I'm taking his class Wednesday because of Joy. Not because of Mikey."

He nodded. "I'm glad."

"Really, we should both take the class—"

"No, not the class." He stepped forward. "I've got no right to say this, but…I got to thinking about you and Mikey dating and I… It got to me. Not just Mikey, either. You. Dating. It got to me in a way I wasn't expecting." He shook his head. "That's why I was angry. I was, I am, angry at myself because I don't want you dating anyone, Brooke."

Was he serious? Audy Briscoe was trying to dictate her dating life. *Why does everyone keep thinking I have a dating life?* More important, did he honestly think this was okay? "You don't have to be angry with yourself, Audy. I'm plenty angry for the both of us now." She swallowed. "I… You… Who do you think you are? *You* don't want *me* dating anyone?"

"Not unless it's me." His breath hitched.

"What?" She hadn't heard that last bit correctly.

"You and me." He shook his head. "I know

up until now the two of us haven't exactly seen eye to eye on things but… Now… I can't help but think we'd be good together."

"We?" she whispered. "Me…and you?" This was really happening?

"Me and you. If you'll give us a chance." His fingertips traced the line of her jaw before his hands came up to cradle her face. "I'm hoping you will."

Brooke knew their chances were slim. The two of them were night and day. Giving Audy a chance meant giving him a chance to hurt her. But, as scary as that was, her heart was all too willing. When it came to the way she felt about Audy, it was a done deal. She could deny it until she was blue in the face, try to box it up inside or pretend he didn't matter one bit—but none of that would change the truth. She loved Audy Briscoe and she wanted to give them a chance. No, more than that, she wanted to give him her heart.

AUDY WAS TEETERING between hope and defeat. She wasn't laughing or pushing him away but she wasn't exactly hugging him close. She was perfectly still. Staring at him. Absolutely silent. Her eyes gave so much away but here, in the dark, there was no way to know what she was thinking—or feeling—or wanting. And the not knowing was brutal.

Maybe he'd done this all wrong. *Maybe?* More like probably.

He'd rushed it. Flubbed the whole thing. There was nothing romantic about this. *Romance, man.* What was he thinking? That standing between two cars—no flowers, no pretty words, no nothing—would win her over? Just him acting like a fool, and asking her to give him a chance.

And how had she responded?

Silence.

He was pretty sure that was answer enough.

Best course of action? Retreat with whatever dignity he could salvage. *Too little, too late.*

"Brooke." He cleared his throat but the boulder blocking his windpipe didn't budge. It took effort, but he forced his hands to his sides and took a step back. "I'm sorry for this—"

"Brooke?" Tess called out. "Brooke. You will not believe it. You won't." She ran down the steps. "I'm so excited."

Audy wasn't about to rain on Tess's parade.

He smiled, hoping he sounded curious and eager instead of heartbroken. "About what?"

"Guess," Tess said, grabbing Brooke's hand. "You won't believe it."

Brooke held Tess's hands in hers. "Ummm…" There was the slightest waver to her voice. "Let's see. Does it have anything to do with—"

"Beau? Yes. Yes, it does." Tess bounced on the balls of her feet. "He asked me to prom. Can you believe it? He did. We carried the dishes into the kitchen and he turned around all of a sudden and said he wanted to go to prom with me. And I asked him if he was asking me to prom and he said yes. He totally asked me to prom."

"Did you let him down easy?" Audy asked.

"Audy." Tess sounded devastated. "Of course not. No. I said yes. Actually, I think I said, 'I would like to go to prom with you, Beau.' Or something like that."

"And then what?" Audy asked.

"Then…he sort of looked at me and I sort of looked at him and now I'm here." Tess took a deep breath. "I can't believe he asked me."

"Why not?" Audy laughed. "You've taken care of him when he had a concussion and studied pre-calculus together. I'd say you've seen him at his worst and stuck around. A man notices those things."

Brooke laughed. "Audy has a point. Besides, you're pretty awesome, Tess."

"Says my big sister." Tess hugged her. "You're not the most objective person in the world."

"I think you're pretty awesome, too." Audy shrugged. "And I am the most objective person in the world."

Tess laughed. "I'm so happy."

"I can tell." Brooke patted her cheek.

"I guess we should go?" Tess glanced back at the front door.

"I guess we should." Brooke peered around Tess at the open door. "Are you expecting something?"

"I don't know… I guess I just realized I didn't really say goodbye or anything to Beau." Tess shrugged. "I was so excited."

Brooke glanced his way so chances were she saw him smiling. "Do…do you need to say goodbye?"

"Only if you don't mind. Do you?" Tess let go of Brooke's hand. "I'll hurry. I know we need to go."

"Okay." Brooke waved her away. "But… just hurry."

The two of them watched Tess run back up the steps.

"Is this okay? I know she's excited, but I don't want her to come off as desperate." Brooke shook her head. "I'm actually impressed. I didn't think Beau had it in him."

"I guess when you want something bad enough you go for it." Which is exactly what Audy had tried to do. Only, unlike Beau, he hadn't been successful. "I don't know how long my brother has been pining for your sister, but I get the feeling this has been a long time coming." Beau had ended up with his dream date. Audy had wound up feeling like he'd been punched in the gut—not to mention the lump still blocking his throat.

"I guess." Brooke turned to face him. "Audy, you have the unique ability to completely throw me off guard. I feel like you're going to say one thing, and you say the exact opposite." She took a step toward him. "And even though you do trip over your words…I like your words. And even though you make me angrier than anyone, there's a part of me that wants to give us a chance."

"You do?" He shook his head. The ache in his stomach melted away. So did the lump in his throat. But he had to be certain. "I was pretty sure that long silence back there was the only answer I was going to get."

"Like I said, you caught me by surprise." Her voice was soft, even a little hesitant. "Even now I think this is doomed to fail. I mean, really, Audy, what are we thinking?"

"Maybe you've got a little bit of risk-taker in you, after all." And he'd never been more relieved.

"Is that what you are? A risk?" She covered her face with her hands. "What am I saying—of course you are."

"Hey, hey, now." Audy reached out and took her hands in his. "You can't throw in the towel before things even get started."

"Maybe we shouldn't get started." Brooke stared up at him. "None of this makes any sense. You realize that?"

"I know you're all about being practical and making sense… I get the feeling this is one of those situations where that doesn't apply." He squeezed her hands. "Don't listen to that practical side. Listen to the side that wants to give us a chance. The fun side."

Brooke started giggling. Nervous giggling.

He understood. She was scared. She wasn't the only one. Inasmuch as he wanted to kiss her, he wanted to make her feel good about giving them a chance. He put her arms around his waist. "Let's start with this." He slid his arms around her waist and, gently, pulled her into him. His hand slipped up between her shoulder blades, smoothing over the length of her braid. He savored each detail. The slight hitch in her breath. The press of her hands against his back. The warmth of her breath through his shirtfront as she rested her cheek against his shoulder. She went soft in his arms. He'd spent a fair bit of time imagining this, but nothing he'd imagined could come close to this. How could he have imagined how right she would feel in his arms? "How's this?" he whispered.

She nodded.

"Good?" Another whisper.

She nodded again.

Good.

"What about Tess?" She turned into his chest, her words muffled. "Should I go get her?"

He ran his hand over her braid again. "Still worried?"

"My…parents met in high school. To hear my mom talk about him, they were so in love. But it didn't last… And…I don't want that for Tess."

It all made sense. "I'm sorry about your folks."

She nodded. "Me, too."

He was sorry that whatever had happened, had made her so skeptical of love. Maybe, in time, he'd be able to change her mind. "I'll go get her, if that's what you want."

"That's the problem, Audy. I don't know what I want." Her arms tightened around his waist.

She wasn't talking about Tess. Well, she wasn't *only* talking about Tess. He buried his nose in her silky soft hair. Why had it taken him this long to figure things out? Probably because falling in love was part of a life he'd made up his mind he didn't want. Falling in love meant being tied down. It meant owning responsibilities. It meant commitment… After a lifetime of being told he was no good at any of those things, of course he wasn't going to search it out. It was only Brooke who had changed his mind.

He'd made up his mind. But he couldn't make up Brooke's for her. If she was this uncertain, he wasn't going to pressure her. It wasn't easy, but he let her go... Slowly.

"Don't get me wrong, Brooke." He smoothed the hair from her shoulder. "But I don't want to leap if you're not ready. I get that you're torn. We haven't exactly had the easiest relationship. And this? This is a lot. I get it. There's no rushing this." He set her away from him, a sharp hiss of breath exhaling when he released her hands. "When you do know what you want, you let me know."

Brooke wrapped her arms around her waist. "Why are you being so...so cautious? I was expecting you to grab me and kiss me and change my mind for me."

"And as tempting as that sounds, and it sounds mighty tempting, you've got to make up your own mind."

Luckily, they could hear Tess. As much as he wanted to do what he said—he'd thought about kissing her for so long that it was almost painful not to do so now—he didn't want to do something that he'd regret. And he sure didn't want her to have any regrets. When they took the next step...if they took the next step, regret would not be part of the relationship.

"And there you go, doing it all over again." Brooke leaned against the hood of her car.

"Doing what?" It took everything he had not to reach for her. "Being a gentleman? Yeah, it's sort of new to me. I've got you to blame for that."

Brooke laughed. "No, you. Throwing me for a loop all over again."

Tess came barreling down the front steps, more excited than ever. She practically bounced down the path to the waiting cars. "Okay, we're good to go. Thank you. I know we should have gone already. Joy didn't wake up, did she?" Tess peered in the back seat window. "No, good, she's still asleep. Whew." She turned, glancing back and forth between the two of them. "Are we ready to go? Or should I go back inside? Like, I can totally go back inside?"

"No, Tess." Brooke pulled the car keys from her pocket. "It's time to go home." She pushed off the hood of the car. "'Night, Audy. Thanks... For everything."

"I'm glad you came." He stood there, watching as Brooke went around the front of the car and climbed inside.

"Audy, did you tell her?" Tess whispered.

"There's nothing to tell, Tess. But I am glad things went so well with Beau. I get the feeling you two are going to have a great time at prom." He waited for Tess to climb into the car, and closed the door for her. He stepped back and waved, watching the car drive away...until there was no sign of the red taillights.

Audy took his time going back inside. Mabel had always been good at picking up on things. And there had been plenty to pick up on tonight. Still, he couldn't hang out outside forever. Inside, after almost tripping over Harvey, he headed back into the great room with Harvey at his heels.

"That was interesting." Mabel sat with her legs tucked underneath her in the corner of the couch. "How long has that been going on?"

"Not too long." Audy flopped down on the couch beside her. "Still trying to make sense of it, if we're being honest."

"Why are you having such a hard time

with it?" Mabel patted the couch until Harvey jumped up between the two of them. "It's pretty obvious that there's some intense feelings there."

"That may be. But I'm not sure she feels the same." He ran a hand along the back of his neck. "It's not the sort of thing you can force, you know?"

"I do." Mabel was giving Harvey a good neck scratch. "But she seemed pretty excited. Especially after she and Beau talked in the kitchen. Or rather, she talked. Beau seems to get a little shell-shocked when she's around."

Audy propped his elbows on his knees and leaned forward to cover his face. "Right. Tess. Beau. I'd say that's been going on for some time."

"Who did you think we were talking about?"

"You know exactly who I was talking about." He peeked at her from between his fingers. "You need me to say it?"

"Nope." Mabel patted Harvey on the back. "I'm guessing you didn't get as lucky as Beau did?"

"You could say that." He rubbed his hands

over his face and flopped back against the couch. "She's still on the fence. About…us."

"But you're not?" Mabel stopped patting Harvey, focusing solely on him.

Audy stared up at the ceiling overhead. "I should be. She and I… We don't make a lick of sense. But when we're together, with Joy, or without, it's just… It's better. I'm better." He turned his head to look at her. "So, no, I'm not on the fence. I'm giving her space so she can sort out how she feels, but I'm not going to stand by and do nothing. I'm not looking forward to making a fool of myself or giving the people of Garrison something to talk about, but she needs to know."

"She needs to know what?" Mabel rested her head on the back of the couch, her blue eyes searching his.

Audy took a long, slow breath. "That I love her."

CHAPTER FOURTEEN

BROOKE WAS ATTACHING blank petition sheets to the stacks of clipboards, but her gaze kept wandering to Tess and Joy on the blanket she'd spread beneath The First Tree. All around her, people were working toward one goal. The air was buzzing with energy and determination. Martha Zeigler, with her megaphone in hand, had rallied the troops.

The Garrison Ladies Guild was there in full force, along with their relatives. A few people like the Schneiders had brought their relatives' relatives. There was no shortage of worker bees.

"What next?" Beau asked.

"Can you pass these out?" She handed Beau a stack of clipboards. "If they're wearing a red apron, they signed up to collect signatures."

"Can do." He waved over some of the JV football team and repeated her instructions.

Beau was an entirely different person with his football buddies. He was calm, in charge and focused. And his manners were impeccable. But once he caught sight of Tess, he was a ball of nerves. If she needed further proof that the boy was head over heels for her sister, she had it. Not that she needed further proof.

Tess waved at Beau. Her smile lit up her whole face.

Beau smiled back, and tripped over a folding chair in his path.

Brooke was trying not to laugh when she spied Audy headed her way. He'd seen the whole thing and was shaking his head, not bothering to hold back his laughter.

"Don't be mean," Brooke scolded him. "He has been working since the crack of dawn."

"I'm not being mean. I'm being a brother. We laugh at each other. It's what we do." He shrugged. "You look beautiful."

Brooke turned so fast her elbow knocked a stack of clipboards onto the ground. She knelt, feeling her face flush, and collected the clipboards.

Audy crouched beside her, helping her stack the clipboards and putting them back onto the table. "You'd think you'd never heard that before." He shook his head. "That can't be true since I know you look beautiful most days."

"What are you doing?" She glanced around her, knowing full well the eyes and ears of the Garrison Ladies Guild were everywhere. "Are you trying to start a rumor?"

"A rumor that I said you were beautiful?" Audy pretended to think about it. "Sure. It's true." He winked at her. "That I said it. And that you're beautiful."

"What's going on over here?" Miss Ruth asked, leaning closer to the two of them. "Looks like you've got Brooke all flustered, Audy. You behave now."

"Now, what fun would that be, Miss Ruth?" He stepped back, giving Miss Ruth a head-to-toe sweep. "Your hair is looking mighty fine and red today, Miss Ruth."

Ruth Monahan giggled like a schoolgirl. "Audy Briscoe, you silver-tongued devil."

"You see, that's how you take a compliment." Audy pointed at Miss Ruth. "I was just telling Brooke, here, how—"

"Audy." Brooke stared at him in horror. "I think Beau could use your help."

"I think Beau has a team of minions. He's

doing just fine." He took a stack of petition sign-up sheets. "I'd rather stay here and help you."

Miss Ruth's drawn-on eyebrows arched high and her deep red lips curved in a delighted smile. "Isn't that just the sweetest thing."

"That's me." Audy winked at Brooke. "At least, that's what I'm trying to convince her, Miss Ruth."

"Are you, now? Why, Audy Briscoe, you act as if you're sweet on Brooke." Miss Ruth waited, holding her breath with excitement.

Brooke wasn't sure what Audy was up to, but it was nothing good. "Well, that would be just—"

"The truth. That would be just about the truth." Audy's grin was beautiful and mischievous all at the same time.

Brooke wasn't sure whether she should laugh or cry. Not only was Miss Ruth staring at her as if she'd grown a second head, Pearl Johnston had caught that last bit and was already hurrying across the clearing to the rest of the gathered Garrison Ladies Guild. "Audy, stop being a tease. You know better than to take him seriously, Miss Ruth."

Audy shrugged.

"Well, dear, he does seem awfully sincere." Miss Ruth patted Brooke on the arm. "Aren't you just the lucky one?" Miss Ruth pinched Audy on the cheek, smiled at both of them, and hurried to join Pearl and the rest of the guild.

"Audy." Brooke grabbed his arm and tugged him away from the tree.

"You really think pulling me away like this is a good idea?" Audy had the audacity to turn his hand over, linking their fingers. "I mean, I'm fine with it. But you seemed a little upset by my public declaration."

Brooke kept walking, taking him along after her, until they reached the cedar break on the far side of the field. "What are you doing? Really, Audy?"

"Making my intentions clear." Audy reached up and smoothed her hair from her shoulder. "I like it when you wear your hair down, Brooke. You have the softest hair." He lifted one thick strand of hair and twirled it around his fingers.

"You said I needed to make up my own mind." She tugged her hair from his fingers.

"Don't you think you're making that a little difficult?"

"Did I say I was going to make it easy?" Audy grinned. "I want you to make up your own mind. But I figure having me around shows you what you'd be missing out on if you decide not to give us a chance." He shrugged. "Also, I kinda like looking at you."

"Stop." She wanted to be angry with him. She wanted him to stop making a spectacle of the two of them. And she really, really wanted him to stop looking at her like that. "Please stop, Audy."

"Stop what?" He stepped closer, those blue eyes blazing.

"Stop looking at me like that. Stop moving closer…" She shook her head.

"Okay." He let go of her hand and stepped away but he was still focused on her.

"Still doing it." And she liked the way he was looking at her. He'd said she was beautiful. And when he looked at her like that, she felt beautiful.

"I can't help it." He shoved his hands in his pockets. "But I'll try. I know you've got things to do here. I'm here to help, so put me to work."

Brooke gave him a long look. "Okay." After all, the more hands the better.

The two of them headed back across the field, toward The First Tree. She tried to pretend like all eyes weren't tracking every move she and Audy made, but the complete silence that greeted them on their return was hard to ignore.

Kelly Schneider and Mabel had taken over putting clipboards together. They didn't acknowledge her and Audy's arrival, and Brooke was thankful for that.

"Here." She shoved a stack of clipboards into Audy's hands. "Take these to the people wearing red aprons. And see if they need help. I've got things covered here."

Audy grinned, taking a long, leisurely look at her before he nodded. "Yes, ma'am." With a touch of his cowboy hat, he carried the clipboards to the waiting red-apron wearers.

"So…" Kelly said.

"Yeah. That was something." Mabel was smiling. "I can honestly say I've never seen Audy act that way."

"Did he really say he was sweet on you?" Kelly kept assembling clipboards.

"He's just…being Audy." And even though

she was mortified over the scene he'd caused, there was no denying seeing him had made the morning brighter. He'd noticed she'd worn her hair down.

"It seems to me that boy is staking his claim." Kelly straightened the stack of papers. "And how do you feel about this?"

"Um." Brooke shrugged, even though she knew exactly how she felt about this. "I feel like we need to concentrate on our work."

The rest of the morning sped by. After all the clipboards had been distributed, the signature collectors departed, and Brooke started making posters. The city council was meeting next Tuesday and Martha was planning an anti Quik Stop & Shop parade. Hundreds of poster boards, poster paint and glitter were put to good use. The JV football team was surprisingly good at lettering. At noon, when supplies were running low, most of the volunteers went off to find food.

"There's enough, right?" Tess asked, opening the cooler she and Brooke had packed that morning.

"Yes." Brooke knew that Tess had checked their cooler at least four times before she put it in the back of the car. Not only had she checked it, she'd repacked it at least twice. "But if he has other plans…"

But Beau Briscoe was headed across the field, straight for them… Straight for Tess. "Hi."

"Hi." Tess's voice wavered.

Brooke waited, looking back and forth between the two of them, but neither one of them said another word. "Beau, would you like to join us? We have plenty."

Beau looked legitimately surprised. "Are you sure?"

"Absolutely." Even though there was plenty of room on the picnic blanket, Tess moved over for him.

Once the food and drinks had been distributed, Brooke pulled out the lunch she'd packed for Joy.

"Are you hungry?" She smiled as Joy nodded. "Good. I brought carrots and some yogurt and some teething biscuits."

"And don't forget the roast chicken." Tess hobbled across the blanket on her knees, rifled through the cooler and pulled out the small Tupperware container. "Here."

"What are we having?" Audy dropped down on the blanket beside them.

"There are peanut butter and jelly sandwiches. Turkey and cheese. Some sliced apples, pretzels, grapes and some granola." Tess sat back on her heels. "What would you like?"

"To have enough?" Brooke knew they had more than enough, but she couldn't resist teasing Audy.

"I'll have what she's having." Audy nodded at Joy. "That chopped-up chicken looks delicious. But only if I get some of that sweet potato baby food, too."

Brooke laughed. "If you're sure that's what you want."

"I'm sure." But Audy's voice wasn't teasing anymore. His tone was deep and rich and just enough to catch Brooke's attention. "I know exactly what I want."

"Are you sure?" Tess made a face and handed Audy the sweet potato baby food.

But Audy wasn't looking at Tess, he was looking at Brooke. She was vaguely aware of Tess holding out the jar of baby food for Audy before she put it on the blanket and scooted back to Beau's side.

"Dee?" Joy said, patting Audy's arm.

"You want me to feed you? You got it." Audy lifted Joy into his lap. "Afterward, maybe we can get Brooke to take a walk over to the playground with us?" He flashed Brooke a smile.

And Brooke gave up the fight. She didn't want to fight him. She didn't want to fight this. Maybe Audy was right, maybe she did have a little risk-taker in her, after all.

AUDY PARKED IN front of the community center. He was ten minutes late but it couldn't be helped. Somehow, Webb had gotten stuck on the windmill platform. How the ladder had fallen was a mystery, but that was the way most things went with Webb. Now that his brother was safe on the ground, there was nothing stopping Audy from attending the infant CPR class with Mikey and Brooke.

"What are you doing here?" Martha Zeigler, a gym bag over her arm, stopped on the sidewalk to glare.

"Evenin', Mrs. Zeigler. I'm here for the infant CPR." Audy tipped his hat. "Want to make sure I can do right by Joy."

Martha Zeigler put a hand on her hip. "Are you really?"

"Yes, ma'am." He nodded. "I'd do just about anything for that one." Which was the truth. He held the door open for the woman but she stopped in the middle of the doorway.

"And you and Brooke Young? I'm hearing things, Audy."

"Yes, ma'am, that tends to happen. Especially when I make sure Miss Ruth hears what I want people to talk about." He couldn't help but grin at the sly smile spreading on Martha Zeigler's face.

"You are a clever one." Martha shook her head. "Well, now that you let the whole town know that you've set your cap on Miss Young, you'll have to make good on that. You know that, don't you?"

"Yes, ma'am. I certainly do." And now that he'd shown his cards to Mrs. Zeigler, anyone who hadn't known his intentions toward Brooke would now.

"I've said it once, and I'll say it again. You'd best do right by that girl." But the bite wasn't there anymore. And Martha Zeigler was smiling at him. "I guess we'll see how this plays out."

"I'm hoping for the best, ma'am." He chuckled, following her inside the building.

Mrs. Zeigler headed to the door with the Jazzercise sign and he followed the trail of printer paper with arrows and "CPR" written on them. He reached the end of the hall and turned, entering the open classroom. He'd wondered if this was some orchestrated effort on Mikey's part—just he and Brooke and nobody else. But, Audy was wrong. There were at least seven other people in the classroom.

Then again, Mikey is a good guy.

"Sorry I'm late." He slipped into the room and sat at the table right beside Brooke.

"You came." Brooke sounded happy to see him. She looked happy to see him.

"You said it would be best if we both took the class." He shrugged. "Here I am." He glanced Mikey's way and gave him a little salute.

Mikey's smile was pinched but, Mikey being the decent guy that he was, he said, "Glad you came. Better if you're both certified."

"The class is bigger than I expected," Audy said, looking around the room.

During class, Mikey was all business. Audy took notes and alternated between the terror of Joy needing the Heimlich maneuver to the assurance that he'd be able to help her, should the need ever arise. When it was all done, Mikey congratulated them and gave them signed certificates and cards to put in their wallets.

Brooke said her goodbyes, packed up her notes and waited for him at the door. "It meant a lot to me that you came tonight, Audy."

"I get that it's something I need to know. Just in case." Though he hoped he'd never have to use it.

"That's it? That's the whole reason you came?" She was studying him closely.

"Yes." He wasn't sure what she was looking for so he said, "I'm not lying to you, Brooke. I haven't lied to you. I won't. This is important to you, which makes it important to me." He loved it when she smiled like that.

"Do you want to see Joy?" She adjusted her purse strap on her shoulder. "Maybe, have some dinner? We could talk?"

"If you're asking, I'm not saying no." His fingers itched to smooth the braid from her shoulder. "Tess keeping an eye on her?"

"Yes. And Alice. And Stephen. And… Beau." Her shrug was almost apologetic—and more adorable than he could put into words. "Just call me Cupid."

Audy burst out laughing, holding the door open for Brooke.

"Audy! Audy Briscoe." Across the street, RJ Malloy stood outside the Buttermilk Pie Café. He waved his arms and yelled out again, "Audy. Hey, you see me?"

Audy shook his head. "I see you. Flapping your arms and yelling like that? Kinda hard to miss, RJ." RJ was his drinking buddy, no doubt about it. But out and about, when there wasn't any beer involved, he was a little hard to take. And right now, Audy wanted to spend time with Brooke and Joy.

"Hold up." RJ came jogging across the street. He stopped just short of Brooke. "I swear, Brooke Young. You get better looking every time I see you."

Brooke's smile was tight. "Thanks, RJ. I should get going. Joy. And all that." She glanced at Audy.

"RJ, I've got plans tonight—"

"I am starving, Audy. Plumb starving. I was gonna have a bite to eat but there's a forty-five-minute wait. A man could starve waiting that long." He rubbed his stomach to emphasize his point.

"You could go on down to Buck's," Audy

suggested. "It's early yet, they won't be too crowded."

"Come on, now. You know I don't like to eat alone." RJ glanced at Brooke. "Oh. I see. Your…plans, huh?" RJ bobbed his eyebrows. "I won't get in the way of that."

Brooke looked dumbfounded by RJ's dramatics. "We're having dinner. That's all."

"Sounds good." RJ smiled. "I won't eat much. But it's been a while since I enjoyed a home-cooked meal."

"RJ, I know you're short on manners, but you can't just invite yourself to someone's place for dinner." Audy had never been so embarrassed.

"If all you're doing is eating, I don't see why feeding one more is such a big deal?" RJ looked at Brooke and asked, "Am I right?"

Brooke frowned. "You're right. I'll see you two at home." She didn't look back.

"Now, that right there—" RJ shook his head "—that is what you call a real woman. I can see why you'd think about playing house." He winked and ran across the street to his truck.

Five minutes later, Audy was parking in front of Brooke's. RJ pulled up behind him, his truck's diesel engine roaring and kicking up black smoke as he choked it off.

"Sweet little place." RJ nodded at the house. "Her mama died, right?"

"Yeah." Audy gave RJ a long, hard look. "Might be best not to bring that up over dinner. Anything else you want to know before we go inside?"

"Oh, I've got a long list of things I want to know about Brooke." He elbowed Audy in the ribs.

Audy shook his head and led RJ up the steps. He knocked, already dreading the evening ahead of him. And when Tess opened the door, things only got worse.

"Who's this?" RJ turned on the charm.

"Brooke's sixteen-year-old little sister. Can you stop making a fool of yourself?" Audy shook his head. "Tess, this is RJ. Brooke took pity on him and is feeding him dinner."

"Hi." Tess stood back to let them in as Beau came up behind her.

But what was more interesting was Beau's reaction. He stood, half shielding Tess, to glower down at RJ.

"Look at you, boy." RJ clapped Beau on the

shoulders. "All grown-up. Rough and tough, too, I'll bet."

"Dinner is ready." Brooke leaned around the kitchen door, her expression mostly blank. "Hope you like spaghetti."

Audy wasn't sure how this all had happened. While he appreciated her generosity, he resented that RJ had put him in this position. He'd never intended for his two worlds to meet. Especially not like this.

"Spaghetti." RJ shrugged. "That'll do."

Conversation was stilted, but Brooke managed to steer them into neutral territory. RJ had been a couple of years older than them in high school but they still shared quite a few memories. RJ even got a little choked up talking about Kent, and for a brief moment, RJ was human.

"You know Austin is coming up." RJ spun his fork, winding up the last of his spaghetti noodles. "Tad Heffron? He dropped out. That means the number two spot's open." He picked up his garlic bread and pointed it at Audy. "Means the odds are good, Audy. The odds are good."

Audy knew exactly what it meant. Sterling Dunn would be there. Audy didn't normally let smack talk bother him. But Sterling was a different story. It might be wrong, but Audy really wanted to put that kid in his place. And now he'd have that chance. *Earn some points. Put Sterling in his place. And win some money, too.* It was kinda hard to say no to that. Even though he was a Briscoe and money wasn't an issue, he preferred earning it on his own. And this was the only way he could do that.

"When is it?" Brooke asked.

"Friday." RJ stared into his bowl. "Any more? I'd be mighty appreciative."

Brooke stood and carried the pot of spaghetti back to the table. She used tongs to refill RJ's bowl but her gaze wandered to Audy. "The community picnic is Saturday."

"Community picnic?" RJ laughed. "Is that what it's come to? Audy Briscoe, hanging up his spurs for diapers, community picnics and the like—just so you can play house?" RJ turned to Audy, looking confused. "Are you telling me you gonna pass up the chance to go toe to toe with Sterling? If he ever found out, you'd never live it down."

Audy had to grit his teeth on that one. His pride mattered to him. And Sterling had done a good job dinging that. He had to admit, he'd love to see the look on Sterling's face when he showed up to ride.

"Even if you did go, you could probably get back here." RJ shrugged. "If this community picnic is as important as you boosting your standings, that is?"

That was the question.

He wanted to be here. Not just because it was important to Brooke, but because it was important to Garrison. He wanted Joy to grow up in the shade of The First Tree. He wanted to make memories with her there. But he'd made himself a promise years ago, one he'd kept. If you're going to regret not doing it, then do it. And as much as he hated to admit it, he'd regret not riding against Sterling Dunn. It wasn't just about the standings. It wasn't just about the money. It was about showing that kid what real riding looked like.

"I might." Audy leaned back in his chair, avoiding Brooke's gaze. He knew how she felt about bull riding. He knew she was probably shooting daggers at him, right then and there. But he could make it up to her—later.

"Boy-howdy. I knew you'd see it that way."

RJ nodded. "Aren't you glad I came over for dinner now?"

Audy chuckled in spite of himself. If RJ hadn't bulldozed his weight in here, he wouldn't know that Tad was out and he had a chance to ride against Sterling. "I guess so."

RJ stood. "That was good eats. Thank you, Brooke." He patted his stomach. "I'm probably going to head on over to Buck's now, if you wanna come?" He grinned. "Unless the *missus* will pitch a fit over it?"

Audy heard Brooke's exasperated mumble and risked looking at her.

"Oh, no, I insist." She smiled at RJ. "You two go on and have fun. It sounds to me like you have a lot of catching up to do. Since poor Audy's been stuck here with diapers and playing house and all." She wouldn't look at Audy. "Now, if you'll excuse me, I need to give Joy her bath. Y'all have fun."

Audy stood, hating the tension between them. "You need any help?"

"No, Audy, I don't need help." Her tone was razor-sharp but she still didn't look up. "I am perfectly capable of taking care of Joy on my own. You go take care of whatever it is that you feel you need to take care of." It was the first time in a long time she'd used that tone with him. The judgy tone. Like he was letting her down—as expected.

"Yeah, she's not pitchin' a fit, all right," RJ muttered. "I think I'll head on out now. This has been just the sort of reminder I needed as to why domestic bliss isn't for me." He stood, tipped his hat at Brooke, gave Audy a "let's go" look and headed for the door.

Still, Audy lingered. "Brooke—"

"Can't you understand why I'm upset? You made a commitment to Martha. To me. And now? Now you're going to Austin? For what? What are you trying to prove? You have people here that need you. People that love you. Doesn't that matter? Why isn't it enough?"

"Why are you making this into such a big deal?" It was hard to meet her gaze when she was looking at him like he was a disappointment. The more she looked at him like that the more he wanted to go. "Beau can cover for me, setting things up, at the picnic. I won't leave Martha in the lurch." And he resented that she thought he would.

"But you'll leave me in the lurch? And Joy? You told us we'd go together."

"And you just told me you could take care

of Joy on your own. Why do you suddenly need me to be at the community picnic with you?" He shook his head. "You can't have it both ways, Brooke. You either need me or you don't."

She didn't need him, she made that perfectly clear. And love him? She'd never said so. Even now she said *people*, not *I* love you.

"Audy, I don't think you understand. I want you to go. I'm asking you to leave." She turned on her heel and disappeared into the TV room, where Tess and Beau and their friends were watching a movie.

He stood, shaking with anger. She wanted him to leave. He didn't know if it was because he was doing something she didn't want him to or if she was mad he hadn't asked her permission. But he wasn't going to feel guilty for wanting to do something for himself. No, not wanting—needing. She might not understand or see eye to eye with him on this, but he hadn't expected her to shut him out. Worse, to kick him out. *Maybe it's for the best.* And even though it turned the tug on his heart into something sharp and painful, he left.

CHAPTER FIFTEEN

THE MORNING OF the community Der erste
Baum picnic was bright and cloudless. Martha
Zeigler had made sure the plight of The First
Tree was in all the surrounding towns' local
newspapers—determined to shine a light on
what she called a "dirty, underhanded scheme
that would destroy the very foundation of Garrison." It was a quote that had been used over
and over again. Brooke had read it and smiled,
imagining the indignation in Martha's voice.
It had worked because people had come from
all over and The First Tree Park was crowded
with picnickers and a colorful variety of picnic
blankets, quilts and folding chairs. Brooke was
glad she'd insisted they leave early or they'd
never have found a spot.

She shielded her eyes, watching as a big
band from Holsum started setting up a mobile
stage for some afternoon tunes and dancing.

"It's like one big party." Tess pulled one of

Joy's ruffled socks back into place. "It's nice to see so many people turn out."

"Is there any word on the petitions? Did it work?" Beau rifled through the cooler and pulled out Joy's juice bottle. "Here it is."

"Thanks, Beau." Tess laughed when Joy took the bottle and hugged it close. "I think that's a thank-you from Joy, too."

Beau smiled, giving Joy a pat on the head.

"It sounds like the petition did the trick. According to Miss Ruth, almost everyone in town signed it." Brooke shrugged. "The next city council meeting is in a couple of weeks and by then Martha and her lawyer should have a solid plan in place. They'll present the petitions and the preservation land trust." She leaned forward to whisper, "I have it on good authority that there's nothing to worry about. The city council is on board with Martha's plan—but they have to do things the right way." She'd been extra quiet last Monday. As a good portion of Monday morning's customers served on the city council, it would be their voices that determined the fate of The First Tree. "I kind of feel sorry for Lance Devlin." Something else she'd learned, the man would be looking for a new job soon.

Who knew if he'd ever manage to regain his aunt's good favor?

"Nah." Tess wrinkled up her nose and made a silly face at Joy. "We don't need to feel sorry for that meanie-weenie old man. That would be silly, wouldn't it, Joy? Since he was the baddy-waddy who wanted to cut down The First Tree, he doesn't deserve any sympathy."

"I agree." Beau nodded. "Maybe not with the meanie-weenie or the baddy-waddy part, but the rest of it."

Tess started laughing, her hand propped against the blanket as she leaned forward to get a Coke out of the cooler.

Brooke wasn't sure who was more surprised when Beau took Tess's hand. Tess, whose smile was ridiculously big, or Beau— since he went red in the face and sort of stared at her hand in wonder. Brooke still worried about them, both of them, but it was out of her hands. She knew that love wasn't a choice, it just was. Fighting against it was pointless, so... Who was she to stand in their way? Sure, they were young but that didn't mean it wasn't real. Maybe they would make it, like

Kent and Dara. Maybe not. But, for now, they were happy.

Joy drank her juice and watched, giggling, as Tess and Beau tried to toss marshmallows into one another's mouth. After her juice was gone, Joy started crawling, so Brooke stood and let Joy pull herself up and hold on to her fingers.

"Let's get some practice, little miss." Joy was now successfully pulling up and cruising around the house using furniture. It was only a matter of time before Joy took off.

"She's getting so big." Kelly joined their group and knelt on the blanket beside her. "How's it going?" Her gaze darted around the blanket.

"He's not here." Brooke answered her unasked question.

"I see that. Are you okay?" Kelly leaned out of the way to dodge one of Tess's wayward marshmallows.

"I'm fine. Why wouldn't I be?" Brooke smiled, hoping to prove her point.

"Well, you look like you haven't slept in a week." Kelly shrugged and added, "I mean, you're gorgeous, because you're always gorgeous, but you look exhausted. Between Joy and the shop and the hours you've been helping out with this… It's a lot. You should be tired."

"Thanks?" Brooke took a few steps, smiling as Joy jumped up and down, clinging tightly to Brooke's fingers. "I know it's so exciting. You will be running before I know it."

"That's when things start getting fine." Kelly laughed. "I know they're bringing in an ice-cream truck soon. I happen to know it'll be parked over by the playground—but don't tell anybody else or they might sell out before we get some."

"Nice." Brooke shook her head. "Good to know I can come to you for all of my ice-cream intel needs."

"I've got you covered." Kelly stood and waved at Joy. "I guess I gotta get back to my own blanket."

Joy decided to follow Kelly, so Brooke let Joy lead—toddling slowly away from their blanket to explore the ones nearby. Joy made friends wherever she went. *And why wouldn't she?* She was irresistible.

Try as she might, Brooke's gaze kept wandering to the parking lot. *He won't come.* There was no way he would've been able to ride the night before, get any sleep and still make it back in time. And even though she wished he was here, she wished she knew he was okay even more. He'd made light of his shoulder injury but he'd been hurting. What if he had another fall? What if he was hurt? That was why she hadn't slept. It was the not knowing...

She and Joy circled back to their picnic blanket for water.

"Aren't you adorable?" Miss Ruth wore a massive purple hat decked out with feathers and ribbons and a button that said Save The First Tree. She had been selling the buttons in the Garrison Ladies Guild booth—but they were all sold out now.

"You look lovely." Brooke stood and lifted Joy into her arms.

"Thank you for saying so, dear." Miss Ruth's not-so-subtle scan of the surrounding area ended with a look of dismay. "Wherever is Audy?"

Brooke wasn't sure what to say. As angry as she'd been that he'd left, she couldn't bring herself to admit he'd picked the rodeo over the commitments he'd made here today. Whether he realized it, Audy had made strides within the community. People knew he was a charmer but he'd shown up, worked hard and become part of the community. She wasn't going to undo that. "I think he's running a little late." She shrugged, acting like it was no big deal. "Something about a windmill?"

Miss Ruth's painted-on eyebrows rose high. "Oh, dear, I hope it's nothing serious."

"I don't know. I'm afraid windmills are outside my area of expertise." Brooke bounced Joy, doing her best to keep her smile in place.

"Well, I'm sure you'll learn, dear. In time." Miss Ruth tapped Joy on the tip of her nose. "I'll circle back around later, then."

In time. Or had she and Audy run out of time? "Sounds good." Brooke kept on dancing with Joy.

"I thought he wasn't coming." Beau wasn't happy about it. More than that, he was disappointed. "He can't make it. It's not like Austin is right down the road."

"Knowing Audy, he'll try." Tess refused to give up on Audy.

Brooke didn't answer. She had no guarantee he was coming—that he'd even try.

Unfortunately, she suspected Tess and Beau and Alice and Stephen had overheard parts of her and Audy's argument. Brooke was grateful that Tess hadn't asked for specifics, but they all knew something had changed. It had been three days since the argument and Audy hadn't stopped by once. After seeing him every day for over a month, she'd felt his absence—and missed him.

"I think I'm going to take Joy over to the flowers." The Garrison Ladies Guild's flower beds were flush with vibrant marigolds and jewel-tone pansies. She was restless, and now that Pearl Johnston's light green minivan and the rest of the Ladies Guild had arrived, she'd like to avoid the onslaught of questions about Audy that were likely to follow.

"Beau is going to win me something." Tess stood, pulling Beau to his feet. "Have fun."

Not only was the community picnic a final time to sign the anti Quik Stop & Shop petitions, but several local businesses had set up booths selling food and drinks, kites, bottles of bubbles and balloons. There were also carnival-type games that the church and school groups had put together. All the proceeds would go into the legal fund that would be used to develop the land preservation trust.

"Ma ma?" Joy pointed at the brightly colored group of balloons tied to the side of the booth.

"Those are balloons." She reached forward and tapped the surface of a bright red balloon.

Joy giggled as the balloon bounced back.

"It is funny, isn't it?" Brooke pressed a kiss against Joy's forehead.

"Here you go, Brooke." Tyson Ellis offered her the balloon.

"Thank you." She smiled. "Look, Joy. Just for you. Can you say thank you?"

Joy nodded. "Tan too."

Tyson chuckled. "You're welcome."

Brooke made a slipknot and put the balloon on her wrist. "Now it can't get away." She moved her arm, making the balloon move, too.

Joy clapped, staring up at the balloon. "Ba ma gg." She nodded her head and rested her cheek against Brooke's shoulder. "Ma ma."

Brooke dropped another kiss on the top of her head. "Sweet baby Joy." She hugged her close, easing the ache in her heart. "Let's go see those flowers." When they got close to the flower bed, she set Joy on her feet and let the baby girl hold on to her fingers again. Slowly, step-by-step, and with lots of giggles and bounces and squeals, she and Joy made their way to the flowers.

Brooke knelt beside Joy. "Aren't they pretty? Flowers."

Joy nodded, reaching one finger out and carefully touching the petals of one bright pink pansy.

At first, Brooke didn't immediately hear the truck. The park was crowded and between the tuning instruments of the band, the loud voices all around, and more, there was a lot going on. She'd also convinced herself he wouldn't be here—even if she did keep looking for him. But Joy peered over her shoulder, alerted by a sound she recognized, and said, "Dee. Ma Dee."

With her heart in her throat, Brooke turned. "You're right, Joy." She swallowed, watching as Audy climbed out of his truck. "There is your Audy. And my Audy, too." Even now, her heart was so happy to see him.

"Dee, Dee," Joy cried. She clapped her hands. "Go, Dee, Ma ma."

"Okay." Brooke agreed, her insides a tangle of knots. She bent forward again so Joy could walk. "Let's show him how strong you are." Joy was so excited that she wobbled and swayed more than usual, slowing their progress. But Brooke was thankful she had that time to pull herself together. The last thing she wanted to do was look at Audy and burst into tears. It had been three days. Three horrible days of wondering how she and Audy would ever mend what they'd broken. Now he was here—where he shouldn't be—and just like Joy, Brooke couldn't wait to get to him.

Audy reached them first. "I thought I'd have a hard time finding you two. But it was easy. I just looked for the two prettiest girls out here." He reached down and scooped up Joy, giving her a spin.

That was when Brooke caught sight of him. "When did you sleep last?"

"I can't say for certain." He kept bouncing Joy on his hip, but his gaze locked with hers. "I just had to get here."

"You did?" She hated how tight her throat got. And her heart seemed ready to beat its way out of her chest. "I'm glad you're here, Audy."

"I wasn't sure you would be." His gaze was searching.

His eyes were bloodshot, with dark smudges beneath, and the start of what looked like a couple of days of stubble lining his jaw. But even rumpled and worn, she'd never been so happy to see anyone—ever. "I'm sorry." She swallowed. "I don't understand what you do but I should try, since it's important to you—"

"Brooke." He cut in, shaking his head. "All the way here, I've been working through how to say this and I need to say it?"

She nodded, but the flare of unease in the pit of her stomach had her bracing. For three days, she'd wanted to tell him how much she loved him and that she'd do whatever she needed to for them to work this out. But she could say and feel whatever she wanted, there was no guarantee he'd want the same things.

"I GOT THERE, all fired up—so angry." He shook his head, his gaze traveling over her face. "Sterling Dunn, some kid on the fast track, was there and pushing my buttons. I registered, got my number, got my order… Then I was standing there, peering through the fence slats at the bull that I was supposed to ride, and I knew." All he could think about was getting back to Brooke and Joy.

A deep V settled between her brows and

she wrapped her arms around her waist, waiting.

"My whole life I've been chasing after something. It was like something was missing on the inside?" He pressed his hand over his heart. "But I didn't know what. I didn't think on it too much. I always stayed busy, acting like a fool, taking risks... Every time I ride, I think, this'll be it. This'll be the thing that takes it away and I'll feel right." He paused, his eyes closing briefly as he rested his cheek on the top of Joy's head. "But standing there, eye to eye with that bull... There was nothing right about it, Brooke. Nothing. I didn't need to prove anything to Sterling Dunn or RJ or myself. I don't need to be someone special to them."

"You're special to Joy." Brooke smiled when Joy reached for her. "That makes you pretty special."

Audy handed Joy to Brooke. "I get it if we're back to where we started. What I did... I did what you said I'd do. I bailed because I'm an idiot. But if I hadn't gone, would I have figured out that this, right here—me, you and Joy—was the thing I was missing? Standing there last night made everything fall into place. I realize losing *this* isn't a risk I'm willing to take."

"You…you might resent giving that up. One day. You might regret it, Audy."

"You're right, I don't want regret gnawing at me—that's why I'm here. I've been swimming in it since the night I drove away from your place, Brooke."

"Me, too." She blinked rapidly.

He reached forward to smooth the curl on top of Joy's head. "I know I'm stubborn and hot-tempered and I say the wrong things, but I'll try to do better." His eyes met hers. "Just tell me I'm not too late."

"You are not too late," she whispered, shaking her head. "You make me angrier than anyone I've ever known, Audy Briscoe—"

He frowned, shaking his head. "I know. Believe me, I know, but—"

"But I want *more* than…*this*." She paused, swallowing. "We need to be up-front from the start, Audy. I don't want to keep fighting or have any question about where we stand on things, going forward. I don't want to *play* house anymore."

Audy's heart skipped a beat. Playing? What was she saying?

"We may not want the same things, but I know, without a shadow of a doubt, that I am the happiest I have ever been when I'm with *you*. And that scares me, Audy, because I love you." She swallowed hard. "I hope—"

He pulled her close, brushing a soft kiss against her lips. He didn't think about anything else. She loved him. Another kiss, just as light. He could breathe again—think. And there was nothing that would stop him from doing what he'd been aching to do for weeks now. Her arm slid around his neck and she stood on tiptoe, her soft lips heaven against his.

"You have no idea how long I've been wanting to do that." He rested his forehead against hers. He'd driven all night fully prepared to grovel, stupid, stubborn fool that he was. She deserved so much better. But somehow, she loved him anyway. "I promise you, Brooke, now that I know what's worth holding on to, there's no way I'll ever let you go."

She smiled, pressing her hand to his cheek.

Someone cleared their throat. And there was a laugh.

It was more than likely that most of Garrison had turned out for the day. And it was more than likely that most of Garrison was watching him kiss her. "I probably should have thought this through a little better," he murmured. "Taken you someplace more private."

"It's not like this would have stayed a secret for long anyway." She stared up at him. "I'm okay with everyone knowing I love you, Audy."

Hearing her say that eased all the worry and stress and fatigue away. She did that for him—made the world better. "That's all I ever need to know. As long as I have that, as long as I have you, I have everything."

Joy had wedged herself between them. "Ma Dee." She patted his chest.

Another throat clearing. "Um…" Tess stepped forward. "So, I'm going to take Joy now. And…" She leaned forward to whisper, "People are totally watching, like, everyone." She leaned back. "So, you two keep on doing…whatever it is you two are doing." Her laugh was nervous.

"Thank you." Audy dropped a kiss on Joy's cheek and handed her to Tess.

"Okay. So, hi, Audy. Just so you know, I totally knew you were going to be here." She leaned forward again and whispered, "I totally knew you were in love with Brooke." With a triumphant smile and a little wave, she and Joy headed back to where Beau waited on a picnic blanket beneath The First Tree.

"Beau's keeping you two company?" Audy asked, knowing this was a struggle for Brooke. "How are you doing with that?"

"I just want them to be happy. Safe. Careful. And happy." Brooke shrugged, staring up at him. "It's not like I have a choice. Love isn't a choice...it picks you."

"It's a gift." He loved the smile she gave him. "You are a gift." He cradled Brooke's face in his hands. "You're braver than I am, Brooke. You gave me a chance to prove myself—to me and you. Not just once, either. Over and over, you gave and gave and I never once told you how much I love you. Mostly because it scares me."

"That scares you?" Her laugh was soft. "You? The risk-taker?"

"Yeah, well, this is the biggest risk I've ever taken. If I mess up, I lose you. And nothing, *nothing* scares me the way thinking about that does."

"Then don't think about it." Her smile

warmed him through. "We're both too stubborn to give up on us."

"That's true. I feel better already." He smoothed the hair from her shoulder, running the strands between his thumb and forefinger. He pulled her in tight, holding on until all the stress and worry and insecurities he'd been battling the whole ride home no longer existed.

Audy would have been content to stay as they were, but the music started and they were blocking the way, so he caught her hand and led her back toward Tess, Joy and Beau under The First Tree.

"It took you long enough." Beau was holding Tess's hand. "Tess and I were wondering if you were ever gonna come clean with Brooke."

"Everything is okay? No pressure or anything but, well…I really like this… Our family." Tess held Joy close, her gaze bouncing between Audy and Brooke.

"Everything is okay." Brooke sat on the blanket, a sweet smile on her face. "More than okay."

Audy sat, too, close enough that he could touch Brooke. "I like this, too." Audy brushed his fingers along Brooke's cheek. "Our family."

Brooke nodded, leaning into his hand.

"Ma Dee." Joy clapped. "Ma ma." She pointed. "Teh. Boo."

"That's right. You know who's important, don't you, Joy?" He laughed when she nodded, her little curl bouncing. "And don't you ever forget it. Make sure they know how much they matter to you, Miss Muffet, and hold on tight." Brooke took his hand, threading their fingers together. "And never let go."

He turned to find Brooke watching him, so beautiful she near took his breath away. He shook his head. "Never in my wildest dreams did I imagine Brooke Young looking at me like that."

"Like what?" Brooke asked.

"Like you love me." He shook his head, his heart full to bursting.

"Well, I never, ever expected for Audy Briscoe to fall head over heels in love with me." She sighed, shaking her head. "Talk about a surprise. A good surprise."

"Good surprises are the best kind." He was right, love was a gift. "I look forward to surprising you for years to come."

* * * * *

Get 4 FREE REWARDS!

We'll send you 2 FREE Books plus 2 FREE Mystery Gifts.

Love Inspired Suspense books showcase how courage and optimism unite in stories of faith and love in the face of danger.

FREE Value Over **$20**

HARLEQUIN SELECTS COLLECTION

19 FREE BOOKS IN ALL!

From Robyn Carr to RaeAnne Thayne to Linda Lael Miller and Sherryl Woods we promise (actually, GUARANTEE!) each author in the Harlequin Selects collection has seen their name on the *New York Times* or *USA TODAY* bestseller lists!

Get 4 FREE REWARDS!

We'll send you 2 FREE Books plus 2 FREE Mystery Gifts.

FREE
Value Over
$20

Both the **Romance** and **Suspense** collections feature compelling novels written by many of today's bestselling authors.

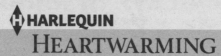
#391 A COWGIRL'S SECRET
The Mountain Monroes • by Melinda Curtis
Horse trainer Cassie Diaz is at a crossroads. Ranch life is her
first love...until Bentley Monroe passes through her Idaho town
and helps with the family business. Will this cowgirl turn in her
boots for him?

#392 THE SINGLE DAD'S HOLIDAY MATCH
Smoky Mountain First Responders
by Tanya Agler
Can a widowed cop and single father find love again? When
a case leads Jonathan Maxwell to single mom Brooke Novak,
sparks fly. But with their focus on kids and work, romance isn't
so easy...is it?

#393 A COWBOY'S HOPE
Eclipse Ridge Ranch • by Mary Anne Wilson
When lawyer Anna Watters agreed to help a local ranch, she
wasn't supposed to fall for handsome Ben Arias! He's only in
town temporarily—but soon she wants Ben and the peace she
finds at his ranch permanently.

#394 I'LL BE HOME FOR CHRISTMAS
Return to Christmas Island • by Amie Denman
Rebecca Browne will do anything for her finance career. Even
spend the summer on Christmas Island. But she didn't expect
to have to keep secrets...especially from the local ferryboat
captain she's starting to fall for.

HWCNM0921

Visit ReaderService.com Today!

As a valued member of the Harlequin Reader Service, you'll find these benefits and more at ReaderService.com:

- Try 2 free books from any series
- Access risk-free special offers
- View your account history & manage payments
- Browse the latest Bonus Bucks catalog

Don't miss out!

If you want to stay up-to-date on the latest at the Harlequin Reader Service and enjoy more content, make sure you've signed up for our monthly News & Notes email newsletter. Sign up online at ReaderService.com or by calling Customer Service at 1-800-873-8635.